Time, Again

Carolyn Lewis

Watermark
Press

For my family for their love and support
and, as ever, for Brian.

Published in UK by Watermark Press 2024

A CIP catalogue record for this book is available from the British Library

ISBN: 978-1-8380043-5-4

Typeset in Book Antigua

Cover design by nb-design.com

Printed by Imprint Digital

Watermark Press
Unit 77 Penn Street, Duo Tower, London, England, N1 5FF
www.watermarkpress.co.uk

CHAPTER 1

Elizabeth glanced at her shoes and pulled a face, wishing she'd remembered to change them. She was wearing driving shoes, flat, comfortable, worn. She kept them in her car and, in her rush to be on time, had forgotten to change into her heels. These were old ladies' shoes, they were frumpy, she didn't feel at her best.

Elizabeth dressed well, she had style, confidence, she walked with a purpose. She was a woman who had places to go. Her hair was sleek, all signs of grey or white, expensively hidden. She knew she intimidated people but this was rarely intentional, just a combination of her personality, the way she spoke and, conversely, the way she listened. It didn't bother her: she had no intention of changing anything about her for other people's concerns.

She shook her head. There wasn't time to go back to her car to change her shoes, besides the new client was a man so there was a good chance he wouldn't look at her feet.

His name was David Armstrong, the marketing manager of Ellis and James, a company specialising in building retirement villages. The new complex, Rosemount, was almost complete but Elizabeth had mixed feelings about the meeting and, for that matter, about David Armstrong.

Shifting, she looked at her watch. He was late. She glanced around. The walls of the reception area had been painted in a muted shade of apricot and the air was perfumed with a cloying smell of a plug-in air freshener. Elizabeth hated it. Wherever she went, it was always the same: a headache inducing perfume of lavender or oriental spices. She tried breathing through her mouth, understanding that she must look odd but there was no-one around to see her behaving like a goldfish. Anyway, it didn't work, she could taste the smell which was even worse.

She put a hand out to touch a chair, there were ten of them, all the same shade, the colour of mushroom soup and they were grouped around a coffee table, brochures fanned out, the pages opened on images of groups of older people, their clothes colourful, faces fixed with determined smiles. Elizabeth raised an eyebrow.

Standing there, her gaze on the brochures, Elizabeth thought of her grandmother, Ruby. She'd not thought about her for a long time. She remembered the Home where Ruby had lived until her death, the row of the chairs, all covered in dark green vinyl, each one facing the tv, each chair holding a resident, each resident still and quiet, eyes unaware of the tv screen and seemingly unaware of their surroundings. Elizabeth thought of how each time she visited, her own voice would always rise higher, forcibly bright and cheerful, talking of events in the family, a minor catastrophe, hoping to get some kind of reaction from Ruby. She wanted to somehow *tether* her grandmother, to make her aware of life outside the Home, although at the time, part of her knew that Ruby was beyond that. Whenever she left, Elizabeth felt a crippling sense of guilt, as if she'd failed her grandmother, abandoned her. She knew too, mixed in with that guilt, was relief that she could go home. She hated herself for that relief.

"Can I help you?"

Her thoughts still in the Home, Elizabeth turned. A woman in her mid forties stood in front of her.

Elizabeth opened her mouth, she felt wrong-footed. She was

about to say that she was waiting for someone, that she had a meeting but the younger woman spoke again, "Are you here on your own?"

Resisting the impulse to turn, to check that there was no-one near her, Elizabeth nodded, "Yes, I am. I'm waiting…"

The woman smiled and held out her hand, "Hello, I'm Rebecca Morris. I'm the general manager." She spoke carefully, enunciating every word. "And you are?" Her face was heavily made up, lashes sticky with mascara and Elizabeth saw the way her eyebrows had been shaped and outlined, like caterpillars marching across her forehead.

"I'm Elizabeth Nicholls and I'm here because…"

"Would you like me to show you around? I've got time, my next appointment isn't for another hour. Everyone is always keen to see our homes." Her tone was bright, her words rehearsed. "We've found that, once the decision has been made, it's a simple matter of choosing which one you'd like."

"Which one…?" Elizabeth frowned, "I'm not sure I understand. As I said, I'm waiting for someone." She kept her tone level, "I'm meeting someone to discuss a business arrangement."

"Oh," Rebecca's smile faltered. She looked at Elizabeth and, with her head to one side, said, "I'd assumed you were here to look at our properties. I meant for you, I thought…"

"*No!* No, I'm not. I have a house, I don't need or want another one. My company works with house builders, we present homes to prospective buyers."

Elizabeth stopped, she wanted to say that she *owned* the company, had a workforce of twenty-two people, had contracts with major builders – but she didn't say any of those things. She knew *why* she wanted to tell Rebecca what she did: she wanted to take the look from the younger woman's face, the look that assumed that Elizabeth was thinking of moving to a retirement property, that she couldn't look after herself. *Bloody cheek. Nowhere near ready for that, doubt I'll ever be ready!* Was Rebecca embarrassed by her mistake? If she was, that was her problem.

Elizabeth blinked. Was that how this woman, Rebecca *saw* her? A resident? An *old* person? Within a moment, Elizabeth knew she'd never tell anyone about what had happened. Not even as a joke, not even in a "guess what happened to me today," sort of way. Elizabeth knew that once it had been said, she'd lose…what would she lose? Something indefinable, something she couldn't put a name to. Respect? Control? Better to keep quiet. She simply wasn't prepared to take the risk.

Rebecca mumbled something indeterminate then asked if Elizabeth would like a cup of tea, coffee whilst she was waiting. Elizabeth shook her head; she wanted the woman to leave and take her wrong assumptions with her. *Where the bloody hell was David Armstrong?*

Finally, the woman backed away like one of the courtiers in Queen Victoria's reign, keeping their front to the monarch before leaving her presence.

"Mrs. Nicholls?"

Elizabeth turned. The man standing in front of her was tall, balding, a fuzz of grey beard covering his chin. He held his hand out and, after a brief pause, Elizabeth took it, it was warm.

"I'm sorry I'm late. I could blame the traffic but, the truth is, I simply didn't allow myself enough time. I do hope you can forgive me."

Elizabeth recognised the mildly flirtatious smile for what it was and raised an eyebrow. "Of course, it happens to us all." Her tone was neutral. "Shall we make a start?" Thankfully Rebecca Morris had disappeared.

Responding to her tone, David Armstrong nodded, moving to open the door and shepherding Elizabeth out of the reception area.

When Elizabeth had spoken to him earlier in the week, he'd talked of offering her a contract, one he said that would benefit both their companies. "I'm positive that a combination of your artistic flair and our reputation for solidly build homes for the retired, will mean that our customers will fall in love with their new homes very quickly."

His voice held a trace of a Welsh accent and, listening to him, Elizabeth felt as though he was reading from a script. His pomposity irritated her and she had to close her eyes. "Send the details over to me so I can see the internal layout of the homes. That way I'll have an idea of what you do and I'll get back to you."

David Armstrong sounded amused, "Mrs. Nicholls, we are a reputable company."

"And so are we." Elizabeth spoke crisply. "As I said, I'll give it some thought."

Elizabeth had started her company in the cramped back bedroom of her home. She'd started before her three children were born, picking up again when they were small. She had what her friends called, "an eye for colour" and after she and her husband, Chris, moved into their first home, she had stripped the wooden floors, polishing them until they gleamed with the soft colour of honey, checked to see where the sun filtered through, brightened up dark corners, rejuvenating the run-down two-bedroomed terraced house.

She scoured junk shops, often walking home with a small table or a chair in her arms, itching to begin stripping down the old varnish, restoring it. Chris grew used to the sight of his wife, crouched over a chair, the house reeking of fumes.

When they moved, following the birth of Kate, their second daughter, Elizabeth felt a sense of grief as she walked from room to room, thinking of the changes she'd made to the house. Holding

Kate in her arms, Elizabeth whispered, unsure of whether she was talking to herself or the house, "Look at you now." When people asked how her business had started, she always told them, "I scavenged for junk. It's the truth." Elizabeth shrugged, she always shrugged as if, she too couldn't quite believe how it happened. "Of course, I did this before it became fashionable."

She knew people struggled to connect her tales of her humble beginnings with the woman in front of them. Elizabeth often embroidered her story, emphasising the horrors of wading through dodgy scrap yards, visiting junk shops with mouldering carpets and armies of beetles, sifting through battered furniture, everything covered in decades of grime. What she could never make anyone understand, was the thrill, the understanding that, once she'd rescued a piece of furniture, it became beautiful again.

Elizabeth remembered the days she'd driven around the country in an old Ford van, its floor rusted, a hole near the accelerator pedal, as the happiest days of her life. Each time she went over a puddle, she had to lift her right food to avoid getting her shoe soaked. How could she explain that it was all part of what she loved doing? Just like the wiping away of filth, of neglect, of seeing a door which only needed its paint stripped away to bring it to life again. She thought about the bentwood chairs she'd found, how she'd repaired the wicker seats, driving home, listening to *Get Back* by the Beatles or, her favourite, *Metal Guru* by T Rex. The sensation – of being cocooned in her van, the music loud, overpowering – was hard to let go. When she switched the radio off, the silence was shocking, sudden. It was hard to leave her van and step into her other life. Before leaving the van, she patted the dashboard, "See you tomorrow, Metal Guru." She kept this to herself.

She remembered the delight she'd felt whenever she found the right shade of paint to apply to a chair, a table, the look of utter bemusement on Chris's face when she'd shown him a can of paint. "Love, it's blue, that's all it is. Call it by a posh name if you must, but it's blue." She didn't blame him, how could she? Finding the right shade, that feeling, that *joy* never left her. She brought things back to life, allowing them to be admired again, and she'd done it on her own. She alone could see beyond the rubbish that everyone else saw, she saw the potential.

Charlotte, Elizabeth's eldest daughter, called the business, "tarting up houses for the gullible." Elizabeth didn't like the words but there was some truth behind them. Once new houses were built, her company furnished them, made them ready for sale by filling them with artfully designed pieces: understated greys, rich creams and a colour Elizabeth always thought of as pale mouse, found in expensive crockery. They peddled an image, a dream. By contrast her own home was filled with soft, pastel colours, quiet and unassuming. Since Chris's death she lived on her own and her house was full of the furniture and colours that she alone had chosen. It reflected her, her taste. Houses for other people were different. Sometimes, if she was working alone in a house, walking from room to room, Elizabeth's eyes narrowed as she held a curtain to the light or moved a Scandinavian rug to the middle of the floor and she felt a pang of, not exactly guilt, but awareness. The rooms she designed were not made for real families, those with kids, with dogs, with bikes and the detritus of modern life. Instead, Elizabeth's company inspired a dream: *Look, you can live like this*.

If a buyer asked whether they could keep the sofa and matching chairs, the elegant curtains and its matching cushions, they generally backed away when the price was mentioned, and spoke of cheaper alternatives – Ikea, perhaps? Instead, when the houses were sold, Elizabeth's company took out the contents and displayed them all over again. She employed over twenty people.

7

Her reputation was solid. At Charlotte's suggestion the company had recently entered the private housing market, advising homeowners about the best way to display their homes, suggesting they paint over pine kitchens and get rid of avocado bathroom suites. The company was ticking over nicely, so what the hell was she doing talking to David Armstrong?

Standing outside the reception area, Elizabeth took a deep breath, needing to be rid of the manufactured smell of air freshener. She felt rather than saw David Armstrong hovering near her, sensed his anxiety, his concern about what she was looking at. He lifted an arm, as if to point her in one direction, waiting to be her guide.

She didn't tell him, wanting to wait for the right moment but her first impressions were good. Although he'd emailed her with the details of the completed sites, it was only when she saw it for the first time, she could see it was a blank slate. She liked those.

The buildings were creamy, "Bath stone," according to the brochure, there were pathways meandering through lush, green lawns with wooden benches placed on every street corner. She pulled a face, *what, do people need to sit down before they get home?* Flower beds were in full bloom and petals from salmon pink geraniums and white roses were scattered on the rich soil. She and David Armstrong were the only two people around. Where was everyone? Normally on a site like this, workmen would be wandering around, high viz jackets and helmets all clearly visible but on this site, there was an eerie stillness. Had Armstrong cleared the site just for her? As she opened her mouth to ask how far off completion was, he touched her elbow, "Shall we? I thought we'd start with one of the three-bedroomed houses."

Elizabeth stepped onto the path and they made their way to a house.

As Armstrong pushed the door open, Elizabeth recognised the

smell of newness, a combination of wood, paint, the adhesive used on the flooring and, mixed in with that was the smell of cigarettes furtively smoked, of stale food, of work clothes worn too many times. She half expected a roll of drums, a "ta da". Armstrong's eagerness, his obvious pride in the house was palpable. Keeping a smile at bay, Elizabeth took her time.

She didn't want him to know, not yet, but she thought the house had been built with great attention to detail. The rooms were spacious, the windows let in a lot of light and all the bedrooms held floor to ceiling wardrobes, gleaming en-suites with impressive walk-in showers. The kitchen was state of the art: an expensive dishwasher, large range cooker with gleaming hobs and a built in fridge-freezer. She recognised that the units had been well thought out and would involve no bending or stretching. A wide window gave her a view of the gardens and they too had been designed with older occupants in mind. Flower beds were raised, the lawn small, contained. *This is nice, the garden is south facing, clematis would grow well on that wall.* She surprised herself with her thoughts.

She turned, aware of David Armstrong's eyes on her face. Ignoring him and his unspoken question, she looked again at the kitchen layout, the size of the windows, the way the sun streamed in. It was then, just then, that Elizabeth understood just how she'd dress the house, starting with the kitchen. She moved to the centre of the room and put her hand out, almost as if she could touch the table she had pictured there. She saw four pale oak chairs, two white mugs and a copper-topped cafetiere on the table. She turned and looked at the window ledge. There, she'd put a distressed wooden box for pots of herbs, their fragrance filling the kitchen. The pots would be terracotta, she knew exactly where to find them. The window itself should have a pale lemon Roman blind, and the walls should be lemon too. Somehow, despite her misgivings, simply seeing what these rooms would look like, had made all the difference. She knew too that her unease about whether her company could cope with an extra contract had gone. She'd changed her mind, she *wanted* to do this.

She looked at David Armstrong, saw the question in his eyes and, for a second thought about prolonging his discomfort, making him wait. Hadn't he turned up late? Hadn't that Morris woman humiliated her?

But she didn't.

After the deal was done, he'd urged her to call him "David" and Elizabeth had promised to be in touch, to work out a date for a proper discussion, to talk over timescales. As she made her way to her car, Rebecca was walking towards her, an elderly couple by her side.

Rebecca's eyes slid across Elizabeth's face and Elizabeth gave her a brief nod. She saw the way the elderly woman gripped her husband's arm, her fingers digging into the fabric of his jacket and Elizabeth increased her pace, wanting to leave, to get away from Rebecca and a feeling she didn't want to name.

Inside her car, she looked at the shoes she'd left on the passenger seat. "Sod it," she said. She swung her legs back out of the car and swapped shoes. She eased her feet into the leather heels, throwing the flat shoes over her shoulder, hearing a soft *thud* as they landed on the back seat. Then she switched on the engine, the radio, grinning as *Dancing Queen* filled the car.

How should she present the new contract to her employees? She'd not told anyone of either her meeting or the discussions she'd had with David; something had stopped her telling her daughters. Both were employed by the company. Charlotte worked in Marketing and Sales and Kate had the role of Administrator. Officially she was the Company Secretary, a title she disliked, telling her mother the title intimidated her. They'd been with Elizabeth for some time. Kate first and then, albeit grudgingly, Charlotte joined the company. Gareth, her youngest child, had shown little interest in joining his sisters. Both girls had gone to university and both had worked for other organisations before joining Elizabeth. They'd worked hard, the company had grown and both girls thought their mother should be CEO. Elizabeth had argued, "I don't need a title," but she'd given in. She understood the girls' passion, their determination to build the company, to turn it into something *bigger*. Privately, Elizabeth thought the girls were *too* passionate. Some of their schemes, Charlotte's in particular, were often overpowering for what was primarily a small, family-run business. Too big, too fast, too much. Elizabeth shook her head, had she now fallen into the same trap?

'As she drove, she felt her shoulders drop. Part of the reason for not telling Charlotte and Kate was because she wanted to do it on her own. She wanted to prove that she could still bring business in, that she still held the reins. True, the girls were keen to promote the company, keen to find new business, but their idea of new business was all about image, marketing. They spoke about attracting new customers, about the *right* customers. In the past, Elizabeth had relied on word of mouth, never worrying about where the next project would come from. Something would always turn up. She shook her head, she hadn't exactly been a failure so far, had she?

She thought about the way her daughters talked in the office, spread sheets splayed out on desks in front of them, *strategizing*. Strategizing? Elizabeth had never had *strategies*. One job came in and when that job was done, one came along behind it. She relied on goodwill, her reputation and word of mouth but Charlotte was ambitious; Kate was the more balanced of her daughters but, between them, they'd orchestrated changes that Elizabeth didn't always agree with or even like. Sometimes, in meetings, she sat bemused, aware that the girls talked around her, as if she was just *there*, not necessarily in the way but something to be manoeuvred past. At times, and she found it hard to admit, she didn't recognise the company the girls talked about. On those occasions, Elizabeth spoke loudly, wanting, needing to assert herself, to remind her staff and her daughters that she was still in charge. Then, after her speech, she was aware of the uncomfortable silence. Charlotte and Kate often sharing glances.

Sometimes, Elizabeth admitted, her attention wandered; an idea for a room came into her mind or an elusive colour and, on those occasions, as the conversation rose and fell, she thought about her childhood. She'd been the only child of largely unconcerned parents and had spent hours staring out of her bedroom window, watching people walk by, seeing dogs straining at the leash, prams being pushed, hearing the cries of younger children playing on the waste ground at the bottom of the road. She rarely joined them, her mother not wanting the bother of calling her in for her tea.

From her bedroom window, she heard the shout of "Any old iron, any old iron," the cry coming before the sound of the horse clopping its way down the road. Sometimes the horse and cart would stop outside her window and Elizabeth watched as the rag and bone man haggled with his customers, his fingers stained yellow by nicotine and his nails rimed with black. She watched in fascination as the junk: the rusted iron bedsteads, flattened mattresses, kettles red with rust, the boxes of old tools that rattled as he lifted up the junk, before hurtling it onto the back of the cart. Then she'd hear the whistle as he urged the horse on and then the cry would go out again.

Elizabeth had told her daughters about the rag and bone man, about her fascination with the whole process, the getting rid of junk, the exchange of coins, trying, she thought to find where her interest in old furniture had started. She'd end her tale by saying that even now, she only had to hear the sound of horses' hooves to take her back to being that lonely child, staring out of a window. More than once she'd tried to talk to her daughters about her early memories. She thought it was something to do with reclaiming *something*, to rein the girls in, to remind them of her honest beginning, a spark of an idea from something commonplace from her childhood.

Did it hurt to remind the girls that she'd started with nothing? What was wrong with that? But whenever she began her tale, wanting to anchor herself and them, the girls rolled their eyes and she saw impatience on their faces.

Elizabeth drove without seeing a high rise block of flats, a newsagents, its windows covered in lurid posters, offering discounts for chocolate, cans of drinks. She drove past an industrial site, high walls topped with barbed wire. She felt her shoe slip, the leather on the sole sliding off the accelerator pedal. Instinctively she flexed her foot, trying to get a grip. The heel of her shoe stabbed at the car mat. Elizabeth looked down, trying to see, trying to ease her foot, her shoe away from the mat, back onto the pedal. Her grip on the steering wheel relaxed and the car moved to the centre of the road. Head down, she didn't see the other car coming towards her. She heard the screech of metal on metal and Elizabeth heard a scream. She didn't know who was making the noise.

CHAPTER 2

The hospital said it was nothing serious. "Whiplash. Your mother has sustained bruising to her face and chest. Force of the airbag inflating."

I don't know who'd phoned me. She must have told me her name but I can't remember. All I heard was, "Your mother's been involved in a car accident."

I asked about her injuries and the woman, it was definitely a woman, said, "She's going to be fine. She's shaken up obviously."

I left the office straightaway. I told Kate what had happened and that I'd phone when I knew more, when I'd seen Mum and I drove to the hospital.

I must have stopped at traffic lights, must have turned left, turned right but all I could think about was Mum. She's 73, she's remarkable, "for her age." Of course I don't say those words. I don't ever say those words. It's almost impossible to think of Mum with the numbers 7 and 3 next to her name, impossible.

Someone waved at me, a man, he was mouthing something. I frowned and put my window down. "I'm leaving, love," he said. I smiled my thanks and parked my car in the spot he'd just vacated. A part of me wanted that to be an omen, that it meant there was nothing much wrong with Mum, that it was a minor bump, that she'd be all right.

I sat for a moment thinking of Mum, about how she'd feel being in hospital. She'd hate it, I knew that. She'd be impatient and insist on getting back to the office as soon as possible. I didn't think that would be a good idea. I also didn't think she'd listen to me. She'd had a shock, she was injured. She should rest. I took a deep breath. I had to move, I needed to see Mum. I needed to see her to make sure she was all ok. I got out of my car.

The doors of the hospital swung open as I approached. A paramedic was wheeling an elderly man in a hospital issue wheelchair and I heard the paramedic say, "Now, George, behave yourself, leave the nurses alone."

The elderly man's voice was weak, breathy, "Chance'd be a fine thing."

The paramedic glanced at me, smiled and patted the man's shoulder.

The walls of the corridor were a pale, shiny green and I wondered whether anyone had ever thought of another colour. That shade should be called *Institutional Green*. It must be on every wall of every hospital I'd ever been in. I wondered if Mum had thought the same thing.

I reached A&E and I stopped to ask where Mum was. "My mother, Elizabeth Nicholls. She was brought in following a car accident."

The nurse pointed to a small area just off the main corridor. There were cubicles, each one with a curtain drawn across the entrance. Even before the nurse told me which one Mum was in, I heard Mum's voice. It sounded strong, positive, "My daughter will be here soon."

I took another deep breath and pulled the curtain back. Before I could open my mouth, she said, "Do you know what's happened to my car?"

Her car. I might have known that would be her main concern. She drives a tomato red BMW. I've never said anything about it but somehow, she's always on the defensive where her car is concerned. If I'm honest, I'd always thought it was inappropriate, age inappropriate but I kept that to myself.

I ignored her question and, instead, grabbed her hand. It felt icy and I asked if she was ok. I hoped my facial expression didn't convey the shock I felt at her appearance.

She was dressed in a hospital gown, one of those blue patterned ones, just like patients wear in *Casualty*, her hair sticking up around her head in untidy chunks. I could see white strands near her scalp, something I'd never seen before. Mum always wore makeup, *always*, but now her face seemed waxy, shiny under the harsh overhead lighting. Flecks of black mascara were smudged under her eyes, her skin pallid.

She pulled away from my hand, her head turned as if she was looking for something. "My bag, where's my bag? I can't see it."

It had been placed on the locker next to the bed. "It's there, Mum. Look, there it is." I heard the tone in my voice, low, gentle, soothing. "How do you feel?"

She frowned and put a hand to her head, raking her fingers through her hair. "Bloody awful." There was a purply bruise near her left temple.

A nurse, dark-haired, pretty, stepped forward. "Your Mum has been badly bruised. She's ok to leave but she'll feel sore for a few days."

As if she hadn't heard what the nurse had said, Mum lifted her head and looked at me. "I'm fine, I want to get back to the office."

I saw the nurse shake her head and I took a deep breath. "Maybe that's not such a good idea, Mum. Maybe it would be best if I took you home and then we'll see how you feel after today." I used the same tone: calming, placatory.

Mum bristled, "I'm not ill. Don't treat me like an invalid. I want to go back to work."

I had no intention of having a row, any sort of disagreement with Mum whilst she was in the state she was in. I thought if I could just get her out of the hospital, in her own clothes, in my car, then I could sort the matter out properly. I also didn't want the nurse to hear this, to witness Mum's stubbornness, her bloody-mindedness. I felt a need to protect my Mum but there was no way I was going to say that to her; instead I wanted the nurse to know that my Mum was a businesswoman, intelligent, successful. She wasn't the dishevelled, querulous, impatient person sitting on the edge of a hospital bed wearing a gown that might have fitted the Jolly Green Giant.

I smiled, "Let's get you out of that gown and into your own clothes. Let's make a start that way." My tone was bright this time.

Mum tugged unhappily at the front of the gown, "I don't know where my clothes are."

The nurse picked up a plastic bag, the same vomit green of the hospital walls. She held the bag out towards Mum. "Your clothes are in here." She took a step back, murmuring that she'd leave Mum to get dressed.

I dithered, don't mind admitting that. It's one thing to be in a hospital cubicle with your 73 year old mother and quite another to be standing near her when she takes off a voluminous hospital gown, revealing her underwear. I thought I should do something, *anything* but with a sense of unease, I turned but not before I'd seen the vicious bruise that covered her chest. I looked as if she'd been punched and, I suppose that's what an airbag does, it punches you whilst keeping you safe. The bruise filtered its way across the top of both arms, almost reaching her elbows. The top part of her body was black. The severity of the bruising startled me, how long does it take for a bruise to appear? Maybe it had something to do with Mum's skin, her age. I didn't know but the bruising was severe.

I must have made a noise, an involuntary gasp because Mum

muttered, "Don't make a fuss, I'm all right."

I fought back tears, there was something so painfully vulnerable about her, the damage to her body coupled with her fierce determination not to let her accident stop her doing what she wanted to do.

I heard the *rasp* of a zip, the rustle of a shirt, the intake of breath as Mum eased her arms through the sleeves. As I listened, I dug my nails into the palms of my hands, willing the tears to disappear.

"Right," her voice was controlled. "All I need are my shoes and then we can be off."

I swear the nurse must have been outside listening because, no sooner had Mum spoken than she re-appeared holding a paper bag. She held it out to Mum, "These are painkillers, Mrs. Nicholls. And there's a card in the bag with a date for a follow-up appointment."

Mum took the bag and, when she opened her mouth, I knew what she was going to say: that there was no need for another appointment. I spoke quickly before Mum could get a word in. "Thank you. Thank you too for taking care of my Mum."

As if she'd been prodded, Mum spoke too, "Yes, thank you. You've been very kind."

Mum's feet were splayed out on the hospital floor. I saw where her shoes had been shoved under the bed and I bent to retrieve them. There was a large scratch on one heel and, as I held the shoes out to her, Mum's fingers traced the mark. For a moment, her face was still then, bending, she slipped her feet into the shoes. "Come on, I want to get out of here."

We walked side by side down the corridor, walking past the green walls, neither of us saying a word. I *wanted* to, I wanted to know what had happened, what had caused Mum's car crash but there was something about the way she walked; head high, handbag clamped firmly under her elbow, eyes straight ahead, that kept me quiet. She held the paper bag of painkillers at a distance, as if it was contaminated.

The doors swung open as we approached and, without thinking about it, I put a hand underneath Mum's elbow. She stopped. My arm jerked. She looked at me, "What are you doing?"

"I just thought you might feel a bit wobbly, that you might feel unsteady…" I shut up. Her eyes were fixed on my face. She didn't blink.

"Well, I don't." She looked away, "Where's your car?"

It was as if she'd put up a neon sign: *I'm not talking about it.* All sorts of questions hammered inside my head: what had caused the crash? Where had she *been*? She'd disappeared, without telling anyone where she was going. What on earth had happened?

We reached my car and I opened the passenger door, watching as she manoeuvred herself into the seat. She grimaced but she made no sound. I felt utterly helpless when I saw how she closed her eyes when she tugged at the seat belt, clicking it into place.

I got into the car and told Mum that I needed to tell Kate that she was all right.

"Oh, don't, don't make a fuss. We'll be there soon. She can see for herself that nothing's broken."

I didn't reply, simply pressed the keypad for the office number and waited to hear Kate's voice.

I had it on speaker phone and, as soon as Kate answered, Mum spoke. "It's me, Kate. I'm all right, Charlotte is bringing me to the office."

"Mum! What happened? Are you hurt?"

Mum glanced at me before she spoke, "Oh, it's nothing. Took my eyes off the road for a second. Could have happened to anyone."

"But are you all right? Should you be out of hospital?"

"Yes! I'm fine. Just some bruising, that's all."

I knew Mum was lying but I kept my gaze straight ahead, hoping she wouldn't notice that I wasn't going to the office but driving towards her home.

Kate's voice was concerned. "You were out for some time this morning."

"I'll tell you all about it when I get there."

There was more chit chat, but Mum managed to avoid answering any direct questions and she said goodbye. It was only then she realised we weren't going back to the office. "Charlotte," she said. Her voice was loud, "I want to go back to work."

I pointed to the clock on the dashboard. "It's almost 5. I'm taking you home."

There was a moment when I thought she'd argue but she didn't. She sighed ostentatiously but I kept my voice level, "You need to rest, you're hurt, you're in pain."

My eyes were on the road but she sat back as if knowing she'd lost that particular battle. Then she leant forward and pulled the visor down and checked her appearance in the mirror. "Oh, God," she muttered, "I look bloody awful."

I kept quiet until Mum spoke again. "You're right, I'm shattered. I would like to go home."

She was sitting with her hands clasped around her handbag and her eyes were closed.

"It's for the best, Mum." I took one hand off the wheel and touched her arm.

Neither of us spoke until I stopped outside Mum's house. The silence was neither oppressive nor uncomfortable but we sat there for a few seconds after I'd turned off the engine. When she moved to undo her seat belt, she let out a small cry. "Christ, that hurt." She sounded surprised.

"Oh, Mum, you've taken a battering. It will take time to

recover." I felt an odd mixture of sympathy, impatience and sadness. I knew she must be furious at finding herself in that situation: barely able to get out of the car, in pain, vulnerable."Stay there, I'll help you." I didn't pause to listen to anything she might say but got out the driver's side and opened the passenger door. I held out my hand and, after a second, Mum took it and eased herself out. She looked at me and said quietly, "Thank you, I'm sorry."

"Don't, you've got nothing to apologise for."

She shook her head. "No, I'm sorry for being so rude. It's just…" She shook her head again, "It's thrown me a bit. I hadn't expected to feel like this."

"Oh, Mum." Again, I felt the threat of tears and I knew that was the last thing Mum wanted or needed. Instead, I smiled, "Come on, let's get you inside and we can both have a cup of tea."

"Bugger tea, I need a drink." She was still holding my hand and I felt the squeeze of her fingers.

We walked slowly towards the front door and, this time Mum made no objection to the fact that I held her elbow. I kept up a meandering stream of chat about her garden, about whether the roses were doing well, that sort of thing. If I needed any proof that Mum was feeling unwell, I had it then. I can't remember ever having that sort of conversation with Mum before. She rarely did small talk.

Inside the house, I steered her into the living room, standing over her whilst she lowered herself into an armchair. "Are you hungry? Would you like something to eat?"

She shook her head and sank into the chair. "No, I don't want anything to eat, thank you." She closed her eyes and leant back. Without makeup I could see the lines on her face, her neck. Looking at her, seeing her like that felt wrong, almost voyeuristic. It felt as if I'd glimpsed her coming out of the shower, powerless, defenceless, her guard down.

I kept my voice bright. "I need a cup of tea. I'll put the kettle on." I left her and went into the kitchen. Every time I go to see Mum, I'm always struck by how lovely her home is. At work, Mum is known for her eye for colour, for detail. She just has this unerring understanding of what will work, which colours will blend or contrast. Yet here, in her home, it's all understated. She had opted for pale, muted colours, ones which reflect light, open up small spaces. It's a joy to be inside her kitchen with its pale lemon walls and high ceilings, the shelves and window ledges filled with dark green leaved plants, glossy and healthy. There are prints of Provence, the Dordogne and the Loire Valley on the walls. She and Dad went to France many times. When she put the prints up, she said she was bringing the memories with her. The whole room seemed to be filled with vibrancy. I once remembered saying to Mum that, each time I went into her kitchen, I felt as if I could out-cook Nigella Lawson. She'd laughed and I'd said that here, nothing seemed impossible. "I could even make meringues." She'd smiled but I knew it was much more than that. Wherever Mum was – her home, her office, anywhere – she was able to turn any environment into a place where people felt at home, rejuvenated. Or is that what I mean? Over the years I've watched Mum look at a room, a space, just standing there, head to one side and I know she's seeing that space with different colours, lighting, wondering whether one chair will make all the difference. I've heard people say to her, "I could move in right now." She has that knack, it's a gift. Since she moved here, not long after Dad died, she's re-decorated every room and it's a wonderful home. Of course, I never told her this but sometimes, after visiting Mum, I'd want to go home and throw everything out of my house and start again. It's true! Looking around, feeling the calm, the peace, seeing the colours in Mum's house, made me upset sometimes, dissatisfied with what I've got.

I filled the kettle and found mugs and tea-bags. I listened to the kettle bubbling and opened the fridge. Telling myself that I was checking to see if there was any milk, I knew what I was actually doing, was checking to see that Mum had food in her fridge. She had, of course, she had. I don't know whether I was expecting to find a hard crust of Cheddar cheese, an out-of-date yogurt on otherwise empty shelves, but I was wrong. Her fridge was stacked neatly with cooked ham, cheese, a small chicken, pots of low-fat yogurt. A wave of guilt swept over me. My Mum wouldn't let things slide. So why was I doing this secretive checking up on her? Was it because of what happened to her? *Was* it an accident? Because that's what had happened; at least that's what she'd said.

The kettle switched itself off and I made tea for us both and carried the mugs into the living room. Mum's eyes were still closed and I wondered if she'd fallen asleep. I put a mug on the table near her and sat down. At that moment, she opened her eyes. Her body stiffened and she seemed startled, as if she wasn't sure where she was. I saw her eyes dart around the room. Then, as if she'd been reassured by what she'd seen, the tension abruptly left her body.

I'd brought the bag of painkillers in from the car and I thought she should take them. I thought too that, I should stand over her whilst she took them. I left the room again and brought back a glass of water.

"Here, take these." I held the water and tablets out to her and, as I knew she would, she shook her head.

"No, I don't want them."

"Look, you've been hurt, the hospital has prescribed these. Are you even listening? I don't know why you're being a hero."

She glared at me but I held her gaze. "Oh, for God's sake..." she took the glass of water and tablets and swallowed two.

We sat there for a while, drinking tea and skirting around the issue of what had caused the accident, instead talking about my family, my daughters, my husband, all things that Mum wanted to ask me.

She yawned and I stood. "You should go to bed. Let me…" I wanted to say, "let me help you, let me get you undressed and into bed," but didn't dare.

Mum nodded and, holding the arms of the chair, she slowly levered herself upright. As I watched her, I dithered, aware that she didn't want my help and then, God help me, I lost it and out of nowhere, came a towering rage. "Oh, for Christ's sake. Look at you! You can barely stand, you must be in appalling pain and yet you think it's perfectly ok to be some sort of bloody martyr!"

"Charlotte?"

Her face was slick with the effort it had taken her to stand. "I'm not, I'm not being a martyr. I don't want to be…" she stopped and breathing heavily, looked at me angrily. "I don't *want* to be a nuisance, I don't *want* to be the cause of you leaving work to pick me up like a child to be taken home." She almost spat the words at me. "I'm sorry if I've upset you."

She turned and, putting a hand on the back of her chair to steady herself, lifted her head and left the room.

Oh Christ. I thought of following her, apologising, grovelling, telling her I hadn't meant to shout, to distress her but I didn't. I simply stood where I was, listening to the sounds of my injured mother making her slow, obviously painful way up the stairs.

To ease my conscience, I waited until I heard the creak of the bed. I imagined her pulling the duvet up, slowly turning, trying to find a comfortable position to lie in.

Then I left. I closed the door quietly behind me and got into my car. It was almost six. There were calls I had to make. I needed to let Jon, my husband know where I was, what had happened. It was his turn to collect the girls from school and they'd be expecting me home. I needed to tell Kate about Mum. Did I also need to tell my sister about the row I'd just had?

I sat for a while looking at the street. Plane trees flanked either side of the road and, in places, their enormous roots had run along the pavements, forcing them up, the fissures like small ravines. Why was no-one looking after them? What if somebody tripped and fell? Still thinking about the roots growing under the road, I picked up the phone and called Jon.

CHAPTER 3

Elizabeth heard the soft *clunk* of Charlotte's car door. She thought she'd keep her eyes closed, didn't want to see, or be aware of anything. She lay still, waiting for the sound of Charlotte's car to pull away. But there was no noise. All she heard was the sound of her own breathing. It *hurt*, the rise and fall of her chest. It hurt like hell. *Bugger, bugger*. It felt as if she'd been run over by a truck. Muscles ached, joints ached, her *skull* ached. "Go," she willed Charlotte to leave. "Please, just go."

The engine started up and Elizabeth held her breath, counting the seconds. *One, two, three, four…*"What are you waiting for? Go home."

The engine accelerated, gears shifted and then, silence.

Elizabeth turned her head, her eyes still closed, waiting for the painkillers to work, thinking about what had happened. Stupid, a stupid accident, a momentary lapse, that's all it was. But now, here she was, lying in bed, frightened to move, aching all over after shouting at Charlotte. What had happened?

It wasn't Charlotte's fault, none of it was.

Without wanting to, Elizabeth replayed the accident, the *thwack* as the two cars collided, the other driver's anger turning to concern, calling for an ambulance, the paramedics insisting on taking her to hospital, ignoring her protestations that she was ok, nothing was broken. As soon as she'd told them her age, there'd been an almost imperceptible shift in their manner, their voices softening, "Best not to take any chances." It infuriated her.

Lying there, easing herself into a more comfortable position, Elizabeth heard the sounds of activity outside her home. People were arriving home from work. Cars drew up outside houses or on the drives. Doors opened, a woman laughed, a dog barked. She heard the sound of a lawnmower.

The painkillers were working and the pain was easing, almost as if it was being smothered. Elizabeth felt pleasantly woozy. The sounds outside continued and she thought of the times when, as a child, she'd lain in bed listening to her parents, hearing their scattered conversation from the room below her bedroom, the lighter tones of her mother, the deeper rumble of her father's voice, the *clinking* sound of glasses. Sometimes it took a long time to fall asleep, her parents' voices growing louder and lounder. A word would reach her, a voice, usually her father's, sometimes in anger or sometimes simply making a point. It hadn't taken long for Elizabeth to understand that the more her parents drank, the louder their conversation became. Her mothers voice grew animated, as if drinking altered her personality, making her girlish, frivolous. Elizabeth thought it was something all parents did: getting the children off to bed so they could drink in peace. Peace was something her mother asked for a lot, "Can't you give me some peace?" For a long time, Elizabeth thought she lacked something because she couldn't give her mother "peace". She didn't know what it meant. What she *did* know was that her parents wanted her in bed, out of their way. Even as a child, Elizabeth had known a sense of *apartness*, with her parents as one unit, and she, their daughter, as another.

Now that feeling came back to her, lying in bed listening to the sounds outside, understanding that she was yet again somehow apart from what was going on outside her bedroom. Hating that feeling, the feeling of being on her own once more. Turning her head, she waited for sleep. Her eyes felt gritty, her limbs heavy. Telling herself a short nap would make all the difference, Elizabeth slept.

When she awoke, the room was in darkness. Gingerly lifting her head, Elizabeth looked at the clock radio. It was 9.45. "Oh, God." Her bladder was uncomfortably full, there was no way she could lie there any longer. Without thinking, she pushed the duvet away, the movement sending shock waves of pain through her body.

"Shit."

Breathing heavily, Elizabeth manoeuvred her way to an upright position and eased her legs out of bed.

For a moment she sat still, her eyes fixed on the ghostly pale skin of her calves and ankles. She had a sense of waiting, building up the courage to move again, knowing that, when she did, it would hurt and hurt like hell. Her bladder was sending even more urgent messages. Elizabeth sighed, "Oh, do I have to?" There was only one correct answer to that. Either she somehow got to the bathroom or she wet the bed. And that, she knew, wasn't an option, at least not one she could contemplate.

Gritting her teeth, she pulled herself upright, her hands scrabbling to hold onto the bedside unit. Closing her eyes, trying to block out the pain, Elizabeth inched her way towards the bathroom. Everything hurt: her arms, her neck, the muscles in her legs. She felt pathetic and miserable.

Lowering herself down, Elizabeth emptied her bladder, groaning with relief. One thought kept coming back. She'd be in work tomorrow, come hell or high water.

But overnight it worsened. She realised that the second she opened her eyes. It felt as if someone had poured cement over her during the night. The ridiculously young registrar at the hospital had said, "Muscles will stiffen, happens to us all but as we age, it takes longer to recover."

He was right. Her body was heavy, leaden with pain. She wanted a shower, wanted to feel human and that meant getting out of bed. Groaning, swearing, she eased herself into an upright position. Her nightdress had slipped, exposing a shoulder and the sight frightened her. The bruising had grown, spread and her skin looked engorged, blackened. Putting a tentative finger on her shoulder, Elizabeth felt its puffiness. With sickening clarity, she knew that it would be impossible to get into work. The knowledge distressed and angered her. There were calls she could make from home but it was about being in the office, being seen there, that was important – at least to her.

Sheer stubbornness propelled her into the bathroom. Letting her nightgown fall to the floor, she deliberately turned away from the mirror. Seeing more of the bruising wasn't going to help.

The warmth of the shower was soothing and Elizabeth let the water cascade down her face, running over her shoulders, her bruises. Shampooing her hair was laborious. The pain meant she could only lift one arm but, keeping her eyes closed, and with fierce determination, she did it.

The painkillers were in the kitchen. Charlotte must have left them there and Elizabeth took two from the blister pack and swallowed them.

It had taken her almost twenty minutes to get down the stairs. By the time she'd reached the bottom, sweat was running down her shoulder blades and she was breathing heavily. She wanted to tell someone, to hear praise, but there was no-one here to tell. The girls had been fobbed off and no-one knew how much pain she was in. The thought only added to her frustration.

There were calls to make, she had to find out what had

happened to her car, she must ring the office, see what needs to be done and she must talk to David Armstrong. When she thought about him, about yesterday, Elizabeth frowned. Beginning a new contract, one with a major builder, when she was incapacitated, was not a good start. Elizabeth knew, better than anyone, the importance of first impressions. David Armstrong had seen her as business-like, a woman in charge. Oh, if he could see her now, with damp hair, tracksuit bottoms covered by an over-sized shirt which skimmed her shoulders, face free of makeup. Without her usual armour of clothes and makeup, Elizabeth felt vulnerable, weary.

After the kettle had boiled and she'd made her first mug of coffee, the phone rang.

It was Charlotte, her voice subdued. "How are you feeling?"

They'd had arguments before, big ones and small, inconsequential ones and each time, Elizabeth knew that Charlotte would take a while to come round, to regain the normal relationship they'd always had. She was not fond of admitting it, but Elizabeth knew she too could be stubborn, intractable. Chris had said more than once, that she could "sulk for Europe."

Elizabeth carefully pitched her voice, wanting Charlotte to hear the warmth in her tone, "Well, the truth is, I feel as if I've been run over by a bus. *Everything* hurts, so that's why I'm staying home today."

"Oh, Mum, I am sorry but I'm glad you're staying home. Rest is what you need."

Elizabeth closed her eyes and, opening them, spoke softly. "Thank you for yesterday. I was so grateful for your help." She stopped, searching for the right words to use, not wanting to rock the boat. "I hope I wasn't rude, it was just that the whole thing seemed, I don't know, trivial, out of all proportion."

There was yet another pause before Charlotte spoke and

Elizabeth knew her daughter was also searching for the right words, the right intonation. "Mum, a car crash isn't trivial, it would have floored most of us."

What's the matter with me? All I can hear are the words she's not saying.

"I'm sure I'll be fine tomorrow. I'll work from home today, there are calls I need to make..." she stopped. "I need to talk to you about yesterday, about where I was but I'll wait until I'm back in the office."

Charlotte's laugh was soft, "Sounds mysterious, anything I should worry about?"

"No, not at all. But I'd rather talk it through with you and Kate. It can wait."

Another pause and Elizabeth thought of saying, "Let's start again, let's go over this, what we're not talking about, what you're not saying." Instead, she asked if Charlotte had spoken to Gareth. "I don't want him to know, not really. There's nothing to worry about but you know what he's like if he feels left out."

Charlotte groaned, "Yeah, I do know. I phoned him last night. He said he'd call you or might pop round. He said something about a new job."

Elizabeth's stomach lurched. "What's wrong with the one he's got?"

"God knows. He talked about not fulfilling his potential, you know, the usual crap."

Knowing she was immediately on the defensive where Gareth was concerned, Elizabeth spoke softly, "He's not a single-minded as you, you know that."

"*Muum!* It's not a question of being single-minded. Gareth still thinks and acts like a teenager – you know, one who thinks the world owes him a living."

"Let it go, Charlotte. I'll be in touch during the day, but if there's

31

anything you think I should know, ring me."

Charlotte's tone was softer, "Do you need anything, shopping or, well, anything?"

"No, thank you."

"Oh, ok. Would you like me to call in after work, just in case you need anything?"

She thinks I'll bark at her again. Elizabeth smiled, hoping the smile would somehow reach her daughter. "That's kind, but I'm ok, I promise, I really am. A day at home is all I need."

"All right, if you're sure." A pause before Charlotte spoke again. "Actually, there is something I want to talk to you about, an idea I've had. I think it's a good one but it too can wait."

"Now it's my turn to be intrigued."

Elizabeth knew the argument had been smoothed over and they talked about a contract, about sourcing garden furniture and then Elizabeth said goodbye and replaced the receiver.

The silence in the kitchen seemed oppressive. She turned the radio on and heard Nick Robinson's aggressive question, "So, what do *you* think the Government should do?"

Sitting in the big, winged armchair, Elizabeth sank back, feeling its soft cushion against her skull. It was almost four o'clock and she had a sense of winding down, as if she'd been on a treadmill. The stillness, once it stopped, gave her a feeling of relief.

A list she'd written in the morning was on the small table and, gingerly leaning forward, Elizabeth picked it up. There, at the top, in her bold handwriting, was the word car. It had taken a few calls to find out what had happened to it. The other driver, Martin Harris, had arranged for the BMW to be collected by a dealership. It would need repair but the damage was solely to the driver's door and the voice on the phone told Elizabeth she could book a courtesy car. It gave her huge pleasure, putting a solid, satisfying *tick* when she'd found her car. It was something she couldn't admit, wasn't even sure she understood, but her car meant a lot to her. Status symbol? No, it wasn't that. Nor did she think of it as her reward, something she had earned. God knows she'd driven enough rubbish in her time. No, it was something private, hidden, her passion for her car. She knew the girls, Charlotte in particular, thought the car was over the top, unsuitable but Elizabeth didn't care. She loved driving it, the opulence, the power it had. And it was red. People saw her coming and so what?

Once she'd established where her car was, her laptop in front of her, Elizabeth worked her way through other calls, other messages. The pain ebbed and flowed and she was aware of feeling weak and hating that feeling. During the day she'd taken more painkillers and, knowing it was something Charlotte would ask, Elizabeth had prepared lunch: a ham sandwich, a piece of cheese. Both tasted like cardboard.

Kate had phoned, her voice soothing, gentle. "How are you feeling, Mum? It must have been an awful shock."

"The only shock was going to hospital. I couldn't believe it. Seemed such a fuss."

"Charlotte says you're badly bruised."

"Did she? It looks worse than it is. " Elizabeth had no intention of telling either of her daughters just how much pain she was feeling. "Nothing broken, bruising won't kill me."

"Do you need anything? I can come around after work..." Kate's voice was high with eagerness.

Elizabeth spoke firmly, "No, I don't need a thing, thank you. I'll be back in tomorrow." She didn't want Kate to see her or her vulnerability.

"Ok, if you're sure." Kate sounded hesitant, "It's just that Charlotte said..."

"I'm *fine*. Please don't make a fuss."

Elizabeth knew that Kate was easier to manipulate than Charlotte. Like her father, she was eager to please, desperate to maintain the status quo. Momentarily Elizabeth felt ashamed of the way she she'd spoken. She tried again, softening her words, "Sweetheart, I'm fine, I promise. I'm taking it easy and I'll be in tomorrow." She knew it was more than that. Kate would feel slighted, aware that Charlotte had gone to her mother's rescue. She'd feel, if not jealous, then left out.

"Mum, I wondered about, maybe, well perhaps you should have a short holiday? A few days, a break from work, somewhere sunny."

No. "I'll give it some thought." The doorbell rang, "Kate, love, there's someone at the door. Got to go, see you tomorrow."

Still holding the phone, Elizabeth made slow progress to the door. Her first instinct had been to ignore it but, after using it as an excuse to end Kate's call, she had an odd sense of obligation, deciding to see who was there.

It was Gareth, head to one side, frowning at her. "God, Mum, you look awful."

Resisting the urge to smooth a hand over her hair, Elizabeth pulled a face, "Thanks for that. Why aren't you in work?"

He shrugged, "They can do without me for an hour. Thought I'd come and see you, check you're ok." He put a hand on the door frame. "Aren't you going to ask me in? Or shall we talk here?"

Stepping back, Elizabeth moved to one side as Gareth walked into the house. He held a brown, leather satchel and, as usual, he needed a haircut.

Walking behind him, Elizabeth was grateful for the fact that he couldn't see her slow progress.

When she reached the kitchen, Gareth was opening cupboards, his voice muffled, "Got any biscuits? Didn't have time for lunch."

Telling herself she didn't need to put food on a plate in front of him, Elizabeth nodded, "Try the cupboard near the fridge."

Watching as he found a packet of Hobnobs, wincing as he tore at the wrapper with his teeth, Elizabeth stayed quiet. Gareth sat, his mouth full of biscuit. "So how are you?" Biscuit crumbs splattered as he spoke, finding their way to the front of his shirt.

Elizabeth eased herself into a kitchen chair. "I'm all right, a bit battered and bruised.!

"Christ, Mum, you look dreadful." His gaze was on her, his eyes roaming across her face, her hair. Elizabeth willed herself to stay still, not to pat at her hair, not to tug at the voluminous shirt she wore.

Knowing she couldn't shrug, she pulled a face, "You've already said that."

"What happened? Where's your car?" Gareth's hands were scrabbling for more biscuits.

Elizabeth minimised the accident and glossed over the trip in an ambulance to A&E, instead speaking about getting hold of a courtesy car, how she fully intended to return to the office the following day. "It's always wonderful to see you but I'm all right. Nothing to worry about."

Gareth shook his head, "Not according to Charlotte, you should have heard her. Banging on about you being in shock, about massive bruising. And looking at you, I'm more inclined to believe her than you."

"Oh, for goodness' sake. I'm entitled to wear what I want to wear. I don't need to dress up every day of my life, do I?"

Gareth held her gaze, "What happened? The truth."

"I've told you the truth."

"No, you haven't. Look, Mum, the thing is, seeing you dressed like that is on a par with seeing King Charles wearing shorts and a flip flops. C'mon, be honest with me. How bad was the crash? *Were* you hurt?"

Shaking her head, "Elizabeth whispered. "No, I'm a bit shaken, got a huge bruise, but I'm ok. I promise you I am."

"How did it happen? Were you speeding? Did you lose concentration?"

"No!" Her voice was louder than she intended. "I just took my eye off the road for a second, one second."

With Gareth's eyes fixed on her, Elizabeth squirmed, disliking his scrutiny.

He pushed the packet of biscuits to one side and, despite herself, Elizabeth saw he'd eaten half. His voice was soft, "Do you need anything? Shopping, milk, do you have enough food?"

For the third time that day, Elizabeth said she had enough food. "I don't need *anything*, but thank you."

"It's bloody hard work helping you, do you know that?"

"Maybe because I don't need any help."

"Right, have it your way." His hand moved towards the biscuits before he changed his mind and sat back.

Elizabeth knew her timing was skewed but she still asked what Gareth meant about his job. "Charlotte said something about you wanting to change."

"Oh, did she?" His head was down, fingers once again fiddling with the biscuits and Elizabeth tucked her hands under her armpits. She was itching to take the biscuits away from him. She looked at the top of his head, she saw the fine, silky hair parted, giving her a glimpse of pink scalp.

Gareth sighed. He looked up and smiled, "Don't seem to know what I want, Mum. That's the truth."

For a while, neither spoke and Elizabeth would have given anything to have Chris sitting next to her. Not to have to face, to *feel* the dread, the exasperation that Gareth's announcements always engendered, on her own. Gareth had been in and out of jobs since leaving school. He said he was searching for the right job, he said everything he'd tried had been boring. Boring? What was he expecting? For a while she and Chris had put up with him lying in a fetid bed, of arguments, of slammed doors before Gareth announced that he'd found a job working for a charity. "I'll be working with the homeless," he said, his voice full of self-importance.

Elizabeth had seen Chris clench his fists. He'd told her that the timing had been perfect. "Just about to throw him out," Whether he meant it, she didn't want to know.

That job lasted three months. "Conflict of interests," was all Gareth told them. He found another job, this time working at a music studio. "Learning the trade," he'd said and then he did leave home, sharing a flat with one of the sound engineers.

They'd gone to the flat on the pretext of taking a duvet to him. They told themselves that he hadn't been expecting them, that to drop in without warning wasn't fair. It took a long time for Elizabeth not to think about the squalor her son was living in, that he didn't care about his living conditions.

Then he left the studio, found another job, this time with a travel agency specialising in overseas trips for schools. Chris found it hard to cope with Gareth's aimlessness, his flippancy about what he wanted to do. The girls were high achievers, sailing through school, both attended university and Elizabeth watched Chris's face when he spoke about Gareth, believing that somehow, he'd failed his son. "They've all had the same, same chances, same education. We've brought them all up the same way." Of course, bringing up three children didn't work by osmosis. Two girls, one boy: had they treated Gareth differently? More than once she'd asked Chris if he expected more from Gareth just because he was a boy? Chris swore blind that had nothing to do with it. Elizabeth told her husband it was nothing they as parents had done or not done.

"We've got three kids, they're different that's all." Speaking with a confidence she didn't feel, she talked about Gareth's warm personality, his friendliness, telling Chris that their son simply hadn't found what he wanted to do. "He'll get there," she reassured Chris, aware that she didn't believe a word she was saying.

After his father's death, Gareth rallied for a while. He found a job in Oxford, working for a publisher. Elizabeth knew it was his affable charm, rather than any skill that kept him in employment. Fending off criticism from the girls, Elizabeth continued to defend Gareth. She had a barrage of phrases: "He's searching for the right job," "He's not found his niche yet." "He's keeping his options open."

What the girls didn't know because she hadn't told them, was that, after another failure, another walking away from a job, Elizabeth had offered Gareth a position in her company. She'd invented one just to put him somewhere where she could watch him, see what mistakes he'd been making.

He'd laughed, "No, not for me. Don't want to be working in the family firm. The girls can do it and good luck to them, but thank you and all that, but it's not what I want to do."

She'd wanted to scream at him, at the top of her lungs, asking him what the bloody hell did he want, Elizabeth never mentioned it again. Eighteen months ago, he'd found a job working for a company involved with recycling tyres and, up until this morning, that's where Elizabeth thought he was.

"Gareth?" she prompted him. "Tell me what's going on."

He moved, his chair squeaked and he bent down, his hands touching the battered satchel that he'd placed on the floor. He mumbled, "I'm sorry…"

"Sorry for what?"

"I'm in a bit of a mess."

"A mess?"

"Yeah, a big mess, really. But..." He lifted the satchel up, placing it on his knee. He looked at her.

And with that, the doorbell rang.

CHAPTER 4

I wasn't going to call in, telling myself there was no need, that Mum wouldn't want me there, you know, sticking my nose in. I'd spoken to her and, though the conversation felt a bit stilted, she sounded all right, in control. She said she didn't need anything, was crystal clear about that. Still, something made me leave the office early. I mean, I was concerned about her. I *was*, but it was more than that. It was as if something had shifted. Mum's always had things under control, took pride in that. Was it the car crash? No, well that might have been part of it but it was something else. I just didn't know what. Whatever it was, I found myself parked outside Mum's house, all sorts of craziness running through my head.

It was quiet on the street; school kids must have gone home and it was too early for commuters to be on their way back. I didn't see it at first, my head still full of trying to work out what I wanted to say to Mum. Not for one second did I think she'd want me there so I went over phrases, words, to let her know that I wasn't checking up on her even though, that was *exactly* what I was doing.

And then I clocked it. Gareth's car. What was he doing here?

His car, a battered Ford Focus, the driver's door in blue, the rest in white. It looked odd, as if an alien had arrived in suburbia. It was the sort of car that an over-zealous Neighbourhood Watch warden would have on the radar the second Gareth switched off the engine. Somehow that epitomises my brother.

I don't mind admitting, the fact that Gareth was there, with Mum, made me think of driving off, not seeing her. Who'd know? Only me, I'd know.

How can I describe Gareth? There's something about him that makes the rest of us want to shake him, yell at him. Of course we've all tried it: Mum, Kate, me and certainly Dad. But Gareth's Teflon, nothing sticks. Talking to him about taking control of his life, making choices – it's all a waste of time. Useless, he's useless. It's a bit like trying to educate a goldfish. You want to think that the words you use, the concern you have gets through. No, the goldfish continues to swirl aimlessly around, its mouth opening and closing and you realise that you'll never get over the language barrier.

Seeing Gareth's car flummoxed me. Should I go? Knowing that Gareth was there with Mum was infuriating. But why was that? Was I jealous? Oh, for God's sake. I'd been the one to pick Mum up from the hospital. I'd been the one who took her home, made sure she was ok and yet…yet what? I'd bee dismissed, told to go home. And I'd wanted to go home. She wanted to be on her own and I needed to leave her. But, in the middle of all that, was my guilt.

I went on and on about it to Jon, my husband. Over and over, telling him about feeling as if Mum had put up a barrier, keeping me at arms' length. "I don't feel she wants me anywhere near her. All I want to do is help."

He nodded, he's heard it all before and he said, again, that Mum is a fiercely independent woman, intelligent and forceful. "Your Mum is getting older and she doesn't like it."

"There's bugger all she can do about it."

"Doesn't mean she has to like it."

Yeah, well. Seeing Gareth's car, knowing he'd waltz in, charm her into thinking she's good for another seventy years, that's the bit I don't like.

I'd brought flowers. Ha! Bet Gareth hadn't brought anything. Only then did I realise I'd reverted to my childhood, wanting to get one over on Gareth, to better him.

Somehow, holding the flowers gave me courage and I rang the doorbell.

It surprised me when Gareth opened the door, not sure why. There was a tiny moment of silence as we stared at each other.

"Charlie," he stepped forward and we hugged. Men aren't good at hugging and Gareth's was tepid, half-hearted.

Seeing him had the usual effect, I went into bossy mode. "How's Mum? Hope you haven't tired her."

"Good to see you too, Charlie. Still the same, in charge of the world."

His tone irritated me, it *always* irritated me. "Why are *you* here? Why aren't you in work?" I didn't seem able to soften my tone or attitude.

"I'm here because of Mum. You phoned me, remember? I wanted to see if she was ok, if she needed anything."

He'd wrong-footed me. I was being unreasonable. I back-pedalled. "Ok, I'm sorry. I was surprised to see you, that's all."

"Apology accepted." His voice dropped. "She looks awful. Any idea how it happened?"

I shrugged, "She said she took her eyes off the road for a second. She downplayed it, said it could have happened to anyone. It's like trying to get blood out of a stone, she won't say anything else."

His voice dropped, "I've never seen her look so rough." He paused, "She's always immaculate, on top of things and now…" He shook his head. "She obviously isn't."

Before I could open my mouth, we heard Mum's voice, "Gareth, who is it?"

He glanced at me, I raised my eyebrows and, together we walked into the kitchen.

He was right, Mum looked awful. Her hair was all over the place and God knows where she found the shirt she was wearing. It *slopped* over her. I wanted to laugh, some hysterical reaction. I didn't, I moved towards her, the flowers out in front of me, like a shield.

"Don't, don't give me a hug," Mum smiled, "it hurts."

"Oh, Mum, I'm so sorry." I thrust the flowers into her hands, hoping they'd say it better. "These are for you."

"Thank you, sweetheart."

I was aware of an atmosphere swirling around. Mum must have felt it too because she busied herself faffing about finding a vase, opening cupboards, murmuring, "Now, where is the white vase?" Noise is easier than silence and Gareth and I stood there, watching.

She found the vase and, with her back to me, the sound of water muffling her words, said, "I'm planning to be back in the office tomorrow."

Gareth looked pointedly at me but I ignored him, "Are you sure, Mum? There's nothing urgent and, if there is, we can contact you. I have to say, looking at you, you don't seem ready to go back."

She turned, her hands clasped around the vase. "I think I'll be the one to decide whether I'm ready or not."

That put me in my place. I glanced at Gareth, he shook his head and then, somehow, he took over, asking if I'd like a cup of tea. I didn't but, for the sake of family peace, I nodded.

With that, Mum appeared to soften, thanking me again for the flowers, then the three of us sat in the kitchen. Mum asking questions about the office whilst Gareth stayed silent, his fingers laced around his mug of tea. As Mum spoke, I was aware of Gareth, his closeness. There's something *unfinished* about my brother. He's thirty eight but still dresses like a teenager: jeans hanging off his backside, a sweatshirt with a faded logo of a forgotten band. Apt I suppose, as far as I know he doesn't go to concerts or gigs. But then, how would I know? He's there on the periphery of my life, of his family's life. A presence, but out of reach. Not for the first time, I realised that none of us knew whether Gareth had a girlfriend, or even a boyfriend. He never talked about any romance, anything that might shine a light into the murky depths of his life. We certainly had never met anyone. He turned up to family events on his own. We accepted it I suppose. No-one teased Gareth about his love-life or lack of it. We just didn't.

A battered leather satchel was on the floor and I was aware of him pushing it to one side, his foot reaching out, nudging it out of the way. It looked like the sort of thing a librarian would own, something to shove books into, unloved, something that would spend its life hanging on a hook, under a pile of coats.

It's something I've thought of before but the fact that Kate and I work for Mum, the three of us together, always makes me think that Gareth is the outsider and sitting in Mum's kitchen, I saw how she tried hard to include him in our conversation. We were talking about a client, a builder who, in Mum's words, "had delusions of grandeur" and I laughed as I knew she wanted me to. She leant over, touching Garth's arm, "You should see this man. Drives a black Range Rover, tinted windows, all the bells and whistles. *He* thinks he's the real deal." She snorted, "He looks like an ageing drug dealer!"

Gareth's laugh was soft, polite.

And then something shifted, the temperature dropped. I looked up to find Gareth's eyes on mine. His gaze was unnerving and I knew it was time to go. Now it was my turn to feel the odd one out. Gareth didn't want me there.

Draining my mug, I stood. "Let me know if you want anything." I tried again, "I don't think it's a good idea for you to be in work but if you're hell bent on it, at least let me drive you in."

Mum eased herself up, "The garage has offered me a courtesy car but a lift would be kind, thank you. I'll ask the garage to bring the car to the office and then I can leave under my own steam."

God, we were so polite, *achingly* polite.

I told Mum I'd pick her up at nine, thinking she'd need extra time but no, she wasn't having any of it. "Eight thirty please, Charlotte."

"Right, eight thirty it is. Are you going to be around for a while, Gareth?"

He shrugged, "Not sure, got a few things to sort out…"

"Ok, well, good to see you. You must come and have supper, the girls haven't seen you for a while."

"I know, I know. I'll sort out a few dates."

That won't happen but I went along with the pretence and I left them to it.

I was glad to be going home and yet I was bothered about what I was leaving. For all Mum's tenacity, something was lurking behind Gareth's visit. He'd done something or was about to do something. After closing the front door, I thought about going back in. And do what? Say what? "Back again, Mum, just in case you need a human shield to ward off whatever Gareth has planned for you."

Oh, for fuck's sake. Instead I walked to my car.

CHAPTER 5

It was as if something had gone out of the room after Charlotte left, the kitchen drained, as if the air had vanished with her.

What does that mean? Elizabeth shook her head, pain jabbing at her shoulders. The thought of lying down, reading a book, not having to do anything was appealing – especially not having to sort out Gareth. Watching him as he put the dirty mugs into the dishwasher, the sight of his jeans, baggy and faded, hanging loose around her hips, granting a glimpse of navy blue underpants, irritated her. No, not irritated, infuriated her. *I can't, I can't.*

There was another ring on the doorbell and Gareth's eyes widened and Elizabeth had the odd feeling that he was expecting someone. But how could that be? This was her house, not his. Feeling apprehensive, Elizabeth went to the door.

A tall man, an angry man, stood on her doorstep. He barked his questions: "Is he here? Your son, is he here?"

Elizabeth touched the front of her shirt, hating the fact that she looked untidy, almost slovenly. "Who are you?"

"Me? I'm the person your son owes rent to. I'm the person who owns the flat your son was living in. I'm the person who put up with his useless promises to pay me what I'm owed, but not any longer. Is. He. Here?" He'd stepped forward and Elizabeth saw a brown suede shoe on her step.

"My son isn't here."

She had no idea why she lied; a part of her wanted Gareth to face this man, to sort out whatever mess he was in.

"Really?" The man pointed to Gareth's car. "What's his car doing here then?"

"His car?" Elizabeth turned to look at the car, "Well, yes that's his car but he left it here because the garage will be picking it up sometime today."

She kept her voice even, controlled, betraying not even a suggestion of the panic and anger she felt.

The man, pale-skinned with thick, curly hair crowding around his face, stared back at her. "And why don't I believe you?"

"I can't be responsible for what you believe. Now, please leave me alone."

As his gaze wandered up and down her body, Elizabet clutched at the neck of her shirt.

"You're safe with me, lady. Not my type and too old for one thing."

"You need to go, go now before I call the police."

"Listen, you tell that son of yours, that worthless piece of shit, that I'll be back for what he owes me." He took a step back, "If he can't pay, then look, you got money, got a house…either that, lady, or it's the courts, the bailiffs and I'm guessing you won't want that."

Elizabeth slammed the door, the noise echoing through the house. She waited until she heard footsteps retreating then closed her eyes. *Christ, how do I get through this? What the hell do I do now?* She was aware of Gareth sitting in the kitchen. He must have heard every word but hadn't come to her rescue, hadn't stood by her side when the man had threatened her. Balling her hands into fists, Elizabeth tried to control her breathing, all too aware that the pain had accelerated. *Shit, shit.*

When she walked back to the kitchen, Gareth was sitting ramrod straight, his eyes on her. "I'm sorry."

"Sorry for what? Did you know he'd knock on my door? That he'd threaten me? Try to intimidate me? He can't be your only problem. Listen, Gareth, you tell me all of it, don't leave anything out. Tell me the truth." Her shoulders throbbed with pain and she wondered why her voice was steady when all she wanted to do was shriek, to scream.

"I've got myself into a mess."

"I gathered that. What sort of mess?"

Without answering, Gareth bent down and picked up the satchel that had been underneath the table. Elizabeth had noticed the way he'd put it on the floor when Charlotte arrived. With the satchel on his lap, Gareth unbuckled the straps and sat, as if waiting. Elizabeth remained silent and, after a second, he took out a sheaf of papers. His breathing was rapid as he silently fanned out the papers in front of her.

"What is this?" She gestured, "What are you showing me?" She was scratchy, angry, frightened, not wanting to see, to understand what Gareth was showing her.

"Look at them, just look at them." His voice was low, his head bent down as if he too didn't want to see what was lying on the table.

Knowing she was delaying things, wanting to put off what she knew was coming, Elizabeth patted at her hair, searching for her glasses before she picked up a sheet of paper.

"This is a credit card statement, is this yours?"

Gareth nodded, avoiding her eyes.

"For Christ's sake, this is for over £20,000. I don't get it, I don't…" She looked at other papers. "You've got an overdraft of *how much? How* on *earth* did it reach this figure? What the hell have you been doing? What have you been *buying?*" The last word was more like a screech. "Tell me, tell me how bad this is. The truth, tell me the truth, all of it, all of it, Gareth, *now!*"

He mumbled something, his head down.

"*What?* I can't hear you. Gareth, how much?" The fact that she was shouting at the top of her voice didn't matter. Her head was full of a dull roaring.

"Um, it's a bit over "£100,000."

"Oh, my God."

Elizabeth felt pain slicing across her shoulder blades. Painkillers; she couldn't remember the last time she'd taken them. She stared at her son, his over-long hair, the faded sweatshirt. The satchel was still on his lap and she wondered why he'd put the paperwork, the *proof* of his debt, in there. Why? And then she wondered why it mattered. Maybe he thought that, putting it into something people used for work, for school, would signify to his mother that it was serious, *he* was serious. She shook her head, the figure of £100,000 moved around in there uncertainly. The first house she and Chris had bought; had it been, what, £8,000? Was it less than that? All of a sudden, she couldn't remember.

"Mum? Are you all right?"

She looked at him, "All *right?* What sort of a bloody stupid question is that?"

He flinched and Elizabeth's anger increased. "How the *hell* did it get to this? Why on earth did you let this happen? What the bloody hell were you thinking, Gareth?"

He shrugged and the gesture infuriated her, "Don't you bloody dare do that! Don't you bloody dare."

They looked at each other. Elizabeth understanding that, at that moment, she hated her son, hated him. Charlotte came into her mind; she'd know what to do, she'd support her mother and, in the same instant, Elizabeth knew she couldn't tell Charlotte about this, not for a while, not until she herself had worked out what to do.

Steeling herself, she spoke to Gareth, "Why did you bring it all to me? What do you want me to do? Bail you out?" Her tone was icy.

Gareth shook his head "No, no, that is, I don't know." He closed his eyes. "I don't *know* what to do, how to sort it." Glancing at her, he spoke quickly, needing, she thought to get his words out, to get rid of them. "There's also the fact that, right now, I'm homeless."

Christ. Why hadn't she worked that out? Feeling as if she'd been kicked by a horse, Elizabeth looked away, not wanting to see Gareth's face, not wanting to look at him ever again.

"Mum, I am so sorry, so sorry. You look pale, are you in pain?"

"I'm going to lie down."

"Do you need any help?"

"Not from you."

With as much dignity as she could muster, aware of the over-sized shirt she was wearing and the way she moved, painfully, slowly, Elizabeth stood.

Gareth cleared his throat, "What d'you want me to do?"

"I don't care."

Knowing he wouldn't move, knowing he still had that ridiculous satchel on his lap, Elizabeth left Gareth sitting in her kitchen.

Her bedroom was cool, curtains fluttering and the street was silent. Elizabeth lay flat on her back, eyes wide open, one hand resting on her chest. Her heart hammered, her mouth was dry. *Oh God.* She felt Gareth's haplessness, creeping towards her like a fog. But she also felt his blind faith in her, bringing her his problems, believing that, somehow, she'd make things right. Get him out of his mess. Pick him up, straighten him out, set him back on the road again. *How?*

Moaning, she turned her head.

Her hand crept out, touching the pillow next to her head, a

movement she'd made many times. Fingers splayed, she touched the cool cotton. "Oh, love, what *can* I do?"

The painkillers were downstairs. Knowing that Gareth was there, waiting, she willed herself to stay still, to focus on her breathing, to somehow *force* the pain away. She couldn't face the enormity of Gareth's mess. "No, I can't, I just can't."

When she woke up, the light was muted, the street light bringing amber tones to her bedroom. Her mouth was dry. She tested the pain, moving her shoulders, they felt easier, the pain less aggressive. The realisation calmed her – then there was a noise from the kitchen. Not understanding what she'd heard, all of a sudden, she remembered: Gareth. A second when she hadn't thought about him and here it was again, all of it, the whole bloody mess. He was downstairs, sitting there expecting her to sort him out. Her heart rate accelerated; she didn't have a clue how to manage the situation, to sort it, to sort Gareth. She was seventy three for Christ's sake! Did she still have to clean up after her son? And this wasn't sorting him out, this was huge, life-changing. *I don't know what to do.* She whimpered with anxiety and sat up. Hiding up here wouldn't achieve anything.

Moving to the wardrobe, Elizabeth tugged at her shirt and, slowly raising her arms, she took it off. Looking less like a bag lady would help; she needed to look like a woman in control.

Gareth was standing at the window. "Are you feeling better?" His voice was low, solicitous.

"Not really," Elizabeth turned the lights on and opened the fridge door, not understanding what she was looking for.

"Mum?"

"What?"

"Does it help if I tell you that I'm very sorry."

"No, it doesn't help."

Elizabeth didn't want to eat but feeling the need to be doing something, she lifted out a box of eggs. With silent hostility, she cracked four of them. "Are you staying for supper?"

"Um, thank you."

Elizabeth nodded at the table, "Clear it, get rid of that thing."

Gareth picked up the satchel, holding it to his chest and left the kitchen. The tension in Elizabeth's shoulder seemed to seep away and she knew she was on the verge of tears. Holding a fork, she beat the eggs into a frothy pulp.

When Gareth returned, she told him to lay the table.

"Are we having a glass of wine?"

"No, we're not. I don't think this is a cause for celebration, do you?"

Running water into a glass, she swallowed painkillers, hearing an angry *gulp* as the tablets disappeared. Once again, she thought about ringing Charlotte and Kate, telling them what their brother had done. *And what would that achieve?* Both girls thought he was useless, a waste of space and besides, Elizabeth didn't want the girls to know, not yet. Why? She wasn't sure who she was protecting, which of her children and why was that? She knew that both girls would want to protect *her*, their mother. They'd join forces against Gareth, tell her to let him stew, to sort out his own mess. Elizabeth thought of a phrase Charlotte used, "he's pissed on his chips," and felt an intense longing to be with her daughters, to sit in their homes, talk to the grandchildren, be part of family life. She didn't want this, this crap world Gareth was living in, flailing around, not knowing how to get out of it, to get rid of him. She heard Charlotte's voice, "He's a grown man, he's not a boy." But the truth was, he was neither, he was still wandering around in a half-grown universe of his own.

Giving up all pretence of making a meal, Elizabeth grabbed the back of a chair. Her legs felt wobbly and she found it hard to breathe. To be in debt was one thing, but a debt this size, oh God.

"Mum, are you all right? Do you need help?"

Turning to look at him, Elizabeth knew fear was paralyzing her, she couldn't think, didn't know how to deal with this. "What have you *done?*"

"Mum, I don't know what else to say. I'm sorry, I'm sorry, ok? I'm really sorry."

And then she howled, knowing that whatever she did, whatever she said, the enormity of his debt, the way he conducted his life would make little if any impression upon him. Childlike, he'd continue to run back home to her, expecting her to clean him up, kiss the end of his nose, telling him that everything would be all right.

Gareth stood wordlessly, watching as Elizabeth sobbed. The sobs hurt her, her shoulders throbbing with pain and he just stood there.

When the crying stopped, Elizabeth wiped her face with kitchen paper and blew her nose, her breathing ragged and harsh.

"Mum?"

"What is it, Gareth? What d'you want? Do you want me to say everything will be all right, that I'll bail you out again? I'm not doing it, not this time. I haven't got that sort of money, I haven't."

He took a step forward and she shook her head, "I mean it, Gareth. Not this time, it's not happening."

"But what about me?"

"You?"

"How can I...?"

"This is something you'll have to work out on your own, Gareth. I'm done helping you. I've lost count of the times you've asked for help with credit card debt, with loans you've taken out. I can't do it this time. I don't have that amount of money to give you, I just don't."

He looked at her, chewing his bottom lip. "Would you consider…?"

"Consider what?"

"The house, it's worth a lot…"

"You want me to sell my home? Is that what you're saying? Is that what you're asking me to do? Sell my bloody *house?*"

He flushed, "I mean, I thought you might want something smaller, to downsize…"

"Well, you thought wrong. I'm not going anywhere."

They stared at each other and, in that instance, Elizabeth thought how much like Chris her son was. Not in character, personality and certainly not in terms of work ethic, but physically, Gareth looked just like his father. She swallowed a sob.

"Do you want something to eat?" Gareth's voice was low. "I'm hungry. I haven't eaten much today."

She nodded towards the bowl of eggs, "Help yourself."

"D'you want…?"

"To tell the truth, Gareth. I don't even want to be in the same room as you."

"Do you mind if I make myself something?"

She pulled a face, "Go ahead."

"Mum, is it ok if I stay here… just for a few nights?"

No. She didn't want him in her house, not after this, not after an angry man had threatened her. She looked at him, trying to find something in him, something to make her feel that he wasn't totally lost.

She saw the pleading in his eyes and she felt her body sag. "Two nights, Gareth. That's all. Then you're out of here."

"Thanks, Mum. Thank you." The pleading had gone from his eyes, replaced by relief.

Without another word, Elizabeth left the kitchen.

CHAPTER 6

I drove home thinking about Mum. Jon would say that I think about her all the time. I argue with him, telling him it's not true, that I think about him, about the girls the whole time but I'm lying. I do think about my family, course I do, but I've got Mum in my head pretty much 24/7. I can sense her loneliness. It's just that she's all on her own…She'd hate me saying that, I mean, she's busy, she's running a company, she's dealing with people every single day. And she is, too damn right she is. But now, leaving her with Gareth and whatever he's got lined up for her, bothers me.

The thing is, when I get home, I'm with my family, you know, entering the familiar world of assorted shoes piled up at the bottom of the stairs, school bags left in a heap on the floor, coats hanging on the banister, a whole *world* away from Mum's ordered house. I know that I live in a unit, one of four people…it's not just me; Kate lives in her family unit and Mum, Kate and I work together and that's another unit and then there's Gareth. God knows what unit Gareth occupies. See, when we leave her, Mum's on her own. But why is that bothering me so much now? Like, she's been on her own since Dad died. Is it because of Gareth? Or is it because she's had an accident? Has that somehow left her vulnerable? Has it? Or is it more to do with me? Do I think she's vulnerable? Yeah, I know the answer to that! It's as if the accident has exposed something, a chink, a gap and, I don't know, I can see through it. I know what Jon will say: what did I expect? He'll say that Mum's getting older, that time will catch up with her whether she likes it or not. I know that's what he'll say, 'cos he's said it a million times. And then he'll say that I spend far too much time doing just this, this internalising everything about Mum, worrying, trying to shield her from what's ahead. And *what* is ahead? She's getting older. If I say it like that, it sounds like it will take forever, like a slow-growing tree. I mean, old age is still a long way off, right? The thing is, right now the company is doing well, you know, extremely well but we need to keep moving, maximising our strengths, increasing our customer base, taking on more staff. Like, we're getting bigger and we need to be on top of that, to cope with what that will mean for the company – but does Mum see that? No, she doesn't and sometimes I feel she's hanging on by her fingernails to what she still thinks is a small, family run concern and all that's associated with that. At times it feels like I'm trying to prise Mum's fingernails from the company, like, like…oh, God, what an image!

This is hard. Thinking about Mum in her house, I think about what it must have been like for her coping with the three of us, Gareth, Kate and I when she was working, starting out. Kate and I fought like tigers when we were younger and then she had Gareth to add to the mix. After Gareth came, the non-stop arguments between Kate and I got worse. We had to share a bedroom because of Gareth and we fought over every inch of that room. At one point, not too proud of this, I put a line of Narnia books down the middle of the carpet, daring my sister to cross the line; hey, I *loved* those books! When my daughters were born, I displayed them on the shelves in their bedrooms. They're still there thought I've got no idea when the girls last looked at them. Now, of course, it's my daughters that are fighting, they're ten and eight, and home life is like negotiating a slalom, skirting around one issue, trying to make sense of another. When Hannah and

Sophie argue, squabbling over a toy or some high octane grievance, I groan, wanting to tell them I've been working all day, please, cut me some slack...is this what Mum felt too? But all that's gone for her now, I mean, I've never asked her if she misses it. I know I sometimes wish the girls would hurry up, grow older, calmer, making *my* life calmer. Would I miss this, this *frenzy* of family life? Yeah, yeah, of course I would. Meanwhile, Mum has exchanged the relentlessness of family life for the life of her company. And now I want to ease her away from that. But what does that leave her with?

I reach home and sit in the car for a moment, trying to empty my mind of Mum and my thoughts, needing to concentrate on Jon and the girls.

Right now we're playing good cop, bad cop as we negotiate our way around the nightly argument: why Hannah has to go to bed earlier than her sister. Why it matters when they don't share a room, never fails to exasperate me. I look at Hannah, seeing her furious face, tears not far away as she demands, yet again, why she has to go to bed earlier when she's only two years younger. "I'm not a baby!"

Jon's voice is always soft when he talks to Hannah, "Sweetheart, you're not a baby, you simply need more sleep than your sister." His voice soothes her and she crawls into his lap, the threatened tears disappearing. I breathe a sigh of relief: at least one of my daughters is on her way to bed. When both of them are asleep, I'm going to have a glass of wine. It's been quite a day.

Later, I look at Jon, look at the way he sits in his favourite armchair. My husband never simply sits in a chair, he *inhabits* it, legs sprawled out, taking up vast areas of the room. Jon's eyes are on the tv screen, he's watching football, a wine glass close by.

There's a stillness about him I envy. What's he thinking about? Nothing more important than football I guess. I don't want to disturb him, don't want to tell him what I'd been thinking about, worrying about, the thing I *must* talk to Mum about. I sip my wine, wanting to empty my head.

I had a rubbish night's sleep, disjointed snatches of conversation, Mum's face, words I wanted to use, all of it floating about, making no sense. I'm glad when it's six, at least I can get out of bed, I can start the day.

Something about mornings makes me know it's safe to be on automatic pilot: insisting the girls have breakfast, sorting out their school bags, answering questions about a party they'd been invited to, none of making much impact. I kissed them all goodbye and left the house, ready to pick Mum up.

Must admit she looked better. She was waiting at the door when I pulled in. The second she saw my car, she walked down the path, smiling.

When she got in, her movements were slow but she didn't appear to be in too much discomfort, as if all signs of the dishevelled bag lady of the previous day, had disappeared. Like, she looked normal, you know? The signal was clear: back to business. I picked up my cue and we talked about a few things, nothing major.

There was a lull in the conversation so I asked about Gareth. "Hope he didn't tire you?"

Mum fiddled with the strap of her handbag, "He'll be staying with me for a few days."

"*What?* Why? What's the matter with his flat? Mum, you can't be serious."

"Watch the road, Charlotte."

"Never mind the road. Why is Gareth staying with you? What

is he? A schoolboy? Needs his mother to do his laundry?" God, I was furious. That's so typical of my brother. Selfish sod.

"Don't. He's got a few problems. I've told him he can stay for a couple of nights, until he's sorted himself out."

I glanced at her, "What problems?"

She didn't answer.

"*Mum?* What problems?"

"Nothing for you to worry about."

A phrase that drives me mad. "It's not *me* I'm worried about. It's you. For Christ's sake, he's running back to his mother when the going gets tough."

"It's a bit more than that." She took a deep breath, "Look, I can't pretend I'm happy about it, I'm not, but I've told him he has a bed for a few nights. Now, please drop it."

I opened my mouth but she lifted her hand. I bit my lip. I was outraged, how bloody *dare* he! Oh, sod him. Whatever Gareth was up to, it would have to wait. I had a full day, not to mention a whole raft of things to talk over with Mum. Instead, I changed the subject, talked about our nightly battles with Hannah and Mum, recognising the deliberate switch, sat back.

I'm not at all sure if it's a skill, a talent, but I've always been adept at keeping up a steady stream of conversation about bog all, while all the time thinking about something more complex. So, that's what I did: talking to Mum about the girls and lasagne and hair clips while all the time, thinking about what I needed to do in the office. And whilst I jabbered on, I went over, one more time, what I wanted to talk to her about. I mean, I'd discussed it with Kate and she was on board, thinking it's a great idea. But with Mum, well with Mum, I was sailing into choppy waters.

"She'll see the business sense," Kate had said. "It's perfect for us and you'll win her over, you always do."

Do I? Not so sure about that. I wanted to talk to Mum about

something I'd read in the Sunday supplements. One of those articles with endless photographs of pristine homes, improbably glamorous couples talking of their super-fast lifestyle, the impossibility of finding the time to deal with all those consuming details that come with a house move, always with the underlying meaning that they were above all that. I almost didn't read it, wanting to ask them, "What planet are you on?"

The company started up in America: *Smooth Operators*. I winced, remembering the song of the same name by Sade and that slinky, sensual voice, filling every home in the 80s. It sounded more like the name of a razor. However, what I read made sense, good commercial sense and I just knew it was something our company could, *should* do, not matter how full of crap the article was.

It went on about the fact that the idea had made its way to the UK. An enterprising couple near Reading had set themselves up in business and, actually, it was good, something we should be doing too. Whenever anyone decides to sell their property, we'll go into their homes, talk to the owners about what they wanted to take, cast our professional eye over items that maybe should be discarded, discuss buying new furniture for the new home and then, once the removal vans have taken everything to the new property, we'll set everything up, and I mean *everything*. Our team would sort out internet access, organise the kitchen, we'll fill the fridge and arrange the furniture, hang the prints. We'll even make the beds. In short, we'd make certain that, when the owners moved in, their new home would be ready and waiting. We'd have disposed of unwanted clothes, furniture, books, all the detritus which clogs up all our lives, giving them a clean slate, a new start, just what everybody wants.

I'd even thought about who would head up the team. Her name is Jess and she's got an amazing eye for detail. She'd be perfect.

She's been with us for about eighteen months and this was right up her street. I vacillated between wanting to tell her, just to see the enthusiasm on her face and keeping quiet – like, because of Mum. Each time I thought about telling my mother, *my mother*, my mouth went dry. And here's the thing: when Mum started her company (and we've heard that story a million times) she simply wanted to let prospective buyers see what could be done to the interior of any house. "To open their eyes to colour, to light and perspective." She said that all the time. And, as an aim, it's good, I mean, it's worked, working for a long time. But that was then and this is now. Our company needs to expand, to keep up with trends, to understand the pace that people live at today. If I'm honest, we need to do more, offer more. But, oh, God, telling Mum that: I can see the look on her face, the *distaste*, the shudder that will go through her. "Offering them what? Can't they do it for themselves? Need their backsides wiping, do they?" It's like she doesn't get it, the way the world has changed, the way money moves, shapes everything. She's still stuck in the early days of her company and although she drives a BMW, at heart she's still searching for the junk in her white van. I know that.

In bed last night, reading my book, hearing Jon's soft breathing, I found a phrase that summed it up perfectly: "arrested motion." That's it, that's it exactly. Mum's stopped moving, she's simply treading water. I shifted, wanting to tell Jon what I'd read but I didn't. I knew what he'd say for a start.

I know that, for a company, we need to think ahead, offer our services to people who are strapped for time, not strapped for cash. Listen: people who want their lives sorted will pay. For those people we can take away the drudge of organising the internet, of trekking to council tips, contacting utility companies. And that's where we come in.

I need to think of a name for the new set up, something that embodies the whole service that we'd offer. I need a name to impress Mum. Then – just maybe – all the other pieces will fall into place.

As I drove into the car park, I realised that neither Mum nor I had spoken for a while.

Mum's voice was low, "We need to talk about a few things, Charlotte. Would 10.30 be a good time for you?"

"Shall I come to you?"

"Yes, both of you, you and Kate."

When I reached my office, Kate was already there and, on her desk, was a small paper bag. She pointed to it, "For Mum, just arnica for the bruising and something to help her sleep."

"She won't take it, you know what she's like."

Kate smiled, "I'm sure she will."

Why was she so irritating? Was it because I hadn't thought of bringing something for Mum or was it Kate's belief in her powers of persuasion?"

When Kate and I walked to Mum's office, Kate held the paper bag and I held my iPad and a blue file. I'd worked hard, done my research, googled everything I thought would be important. My file held sheets of ideas for promoting the scheme and on my iPad were preliminary costings, promotional blurbs, things Mum would want to know. Quite deliberately, I'd not included the original article with its picture of fake-tanned couples beaming from their over-blown homes. I'd told Kate that I hadn't had a chance to speak to Mum and she patted my arm – "I'll be your back-up." I'd also told her what Mum had said about Gareth, about him living with her for a while. She rolled her eyes, "I don't believe him,"

When we walked into Mum's office, she was on the phone and

she mouthed *two minutes*. I couldn't swear to it but it seemed to me that her tone altered, became more business-like and I wondered who she was talking to.

"Bye, David. I'll be in touch," She put the phone down and smiled at us.

"Right girls, coffee?" Without waiting for an answer, she walked across to the coffee machine near the door. I saw no sign of stiffness, of slow movements.

Something felt weird. When Mum handed me a cup, she didn't even look at me.

The three of us sat there, eyes flickering from one face to another. I heard the crackle of the paper bag on Kate's lap. I opened my mouth, wanting to speak but Mum got there first. "I need to tell you about a new contract, a big one." She put a hand to her throat. "It's where I was before I had, before the car crash."

"Where were you?"

Mum's laugh was nervous, "At the Rosemount Retirement Complex."

"*Where?* What were you doing there? Are you thinking of moving there?" Even as I said the words, I knew how stupid they were.

Mum though so too, she pulled a face. "No! No, I'm not." She waved my words away, "God, no. I was there to meet someone. David Armstrong." She gestured to the phone, "It was him I was talking to."

I wriggled, impatient. "Well, who is he? Why *were* you at a retirement complex?"

Mum looked at me, then Kate, she was, I felt, working out the atmosphere, whether we would recognise, *appreciate* what she was about to tell us. "He phoned me, David, to ask if we'd be interested in working with his company. He's the Marketing Director of Ellis and James." She said their name, her head high, thinking we'd be impressed.

"They build homes for retired people, don't they? Have I got that right?" I'd worked out what was coming.

"Yes," Mum was nodding enthusiastically as if her enthusiasm could transmit itself to us magically.

Retirement. All that word conjured up for me, in terms of our business, was blandness, acres of beige, no vibrancy, utter conformity. No, no way – retirement homes wouldn't fit with the image I had for the company's future. I also knew that, by the look on her face, Mum thought she'd achieved a coup, that this was the way forward, prove she was still in charge.

Neither Kate nor I spoke.

"Well?" Mum's voice was hard. "Ellis and James, they're big, you know that. Surely you can see the potential in this, come *on*, what's the problem?"

Kate remained silent. *Coward.*

"Mum, I'm not sure that…"

"Not sure what? This is potentially a big deal for us, Ellis and James operate throughout the West Country, they're known for high end properties, for attention to detail, for Christ's sake, girls, this is *good* news."

Kate's hands rested on the paper bag in her lap.

Mum wasn't looking at Kate, she was looking at me. "Charlotte? I don't get it. This is a *huge* contract, it's prestigious, Ellis and James are rock-solid builders, their reputation is gold star. Listen, this will bring in a lot of work for us, it means security for the company."

I couldn't stop myself. "We're hardly *insecure!*"

Her voice was low, "Don't pick me up on my words, Charlotte. You know exactly what I mean, what I'm talking about. Security for the company, you can't tell me that's not important."

I couldn't speak, I looked at my shoes.

"You'd better tell me what your problem is."

My problem. I might as well have been in solitary confinement for all the use Kate was. *What's the matter with her?* I wanted to grab the bag of bloody arnica and…"

"Well, Charlotte?"

Here goes. "Mum, what you've done is brilliant. Ellis and James are big with a solid reputation…" I stopped.

"I heard the 'but', in fact that's all I'm hearing. Tell me what's wrong with this, this *impressive* contract, tell me why you don't think working with Ellis and James won't be a good thing for this company. Go on, Charlotte, tell me what's wrong with this, this… boost for our company?"

Oh, God, for Christ's sake, Kate, if there's ever a time to say something, it's now. Nothing, she didn't say a word.

"Mum, as good as the contract is, I don't think this is the way we should be going. Mum…" I took a deep breath, "Retirement homes, they represent people who are…*settling*, not, you know, searching, looking for new things, new outlets. They live in retirement homes, what does that imply? They've stopped working, they've lived their lives, they have done what they want to do…" I stopped, not wanting to say that for people living in retirement homes, their lives had turned full circle and they were back where they started. It was an ending, not a beginning. But how could I say that? I mean, Mum was past retirement age and still I ploughed on, not fully able to articulate what I wanted to say but jabbering away as if I had nothing to lose. "We need to focus on new trends, new ideas, projects that we're good at, that we can…and…"

I didn't know what I was saying. What I *wanted* to say was "not retirement homes, that's not the way forward. It bloody well isn't."

"I see." She pulled a face, "Is this because *I* did this? Does that bother you? Do you feel because *I* did this, *on my own*, that you feel it's not worth considering?"

Even before I could open my mouth, she lifted a hand, the action was one of *weariness*. I couldn't read the expression on her face.

She sighed and looked at the file, the iPad in my lap. "What have you got there? Something to show me?"

Part of me thought I should lie, bluff my way out, that whatever I showed her now, would be a terrible move on my part. Even if I said I'd got a contract to refurbish Buckingham Palace, she'd find fault with it, with me.

Then Kate spoke, *finally*, "Mum, you should listen to this, it's so good. Charlotte's done a lot of work and…" she too stopped under Mum's glare.

"Go on, I'm listening."

I sat forward and opened the blue file, knowing it would be futile, knowing that, whatever I said, Mum would dismiss it. I knew that because she was furious with me and Kate but especially me, furious that we hadn't jumped at the idea of this new contract of hers, fitting out bloody retirement homes. We'd reached an impasse: Mum wanting to keep the company in the mould it had always been, safe, secure, profitable, a high standard amongst the builders we work with. Solid. But – for me, anyway – that just wasn't enough.

"You won't like it."

I heard Kate cough and I sat back. What was the point?

"You'd better tell me, Charlotte." Mum put her head to one side. "Kate says you've worked hard on this, so I want to hear it."

Kate glanced at me, and in a low, flat voice, I told Mum about my thoughts, my plans, the way we'd need to set it up, how many people we'd need. "This is something entirely new. It's just arrived in the UK and, if we act now, we can be at the forefront of this,

this…" I trailed off, even to my ears, all this sounded ridiculous, something only an idiot would think about. And I was aware the whole time, of Mum's face on mine.

"I see."

Mum turned her head and, as she did so, Kate touched my arm. I didn't respond though – why should I? I mean, she hadn't exactly bent over backwards to support me.

Without looking at either of us, Mum said, "I don't think this is getting us anywhere. I *will* work with David. I will sign the contracts for the houses he wants and, with or without your support, I will see to it that this partnership with Ellis and James goes ahead. It is, after all, *my* company, *my* decision."

We sat there, Kate and I, like two dummies, unsure of what to do next. Kate was the first to move and she placed the paper bag on Mum's desk. "I thought these might help you," she said before leaving.

I followed Kate and left Mum's office. I was aware of a blinding sense of, of, I don't know what of: injustice, adrenaline, anger? Something had shifted, some line had been crossed and yet, the funny thing was, I still wanted to go back into Mum's office and say, sorry, apologise for not supporting her, to tell her that I didn't want to hurt her, that whatever she wanted, I'd go along with it. I didn't though. Instead I looked at the back of Kate's head. Whatever came next, now I was on my own.

CHAPTER 7

Perched on the end of her bed, Elizabeth heard Gareth moving around in the kitchen. Her radio murmured in the background, not turned to Radio 4, but rather to some unfamiliar station, one which had bursts of maniacal laughter, followed by music that Elizabeth had only ever heard from cars driven by lads aimlessly driving around. They all drove the same way: windows down, arms resting on the door of a souped up Golf or perhaps an elderly Subaru, music blasting. Every time she heard the steady *thrum*, Elizabeth winced – and now, here it was, right in her home. Gareth had been staying with her for three days and it felt as if, by coming back, he'd reverted to the life of a teenager with all its self-absorption. Elizabeth knew, even before she reached the kitchen, that Gareth would have *filled* it. He seemed unaware or maybe incapable of putting things back: boxes of cereal left on the worktop, containers of milk dribbled on the draining board, the sink hidden by a tower of crockery as he ignored the dishwasher.

Elizabeth closed her eyes, taking deep breaths in, trying to ward off her growing anger. She thought of the days when Charlotte, Kate and Gareth lived at home, when the house shook with different music from their bedrooms. It wasn't just the music, it was the feeling she had of navigating her way through their moods, their hostility. Elizabeth had a sense of being in the wrong: wrong generation, wrong beliefs, wrong words. *I can't do this again, I can't. Not now, I don't have the energy for this.*

But that wasn't the worst thing. No, the worst thing was that Gareth had shown no interest in doing anything about the debt he was in. He shrugged when Elizabeth asked if he'd done anything, spoken to anyone. "At least tell me you've spoken to the bank, that you've made an appointment with a debt counsellor, tell me you've done *something!* She screeched the last word and then he'd shrugged.

"No, I haven't. I'm sorry, sorry, ok?"

"*Sorry!* You're not three years old, Gareth, just saying sorry doesn't cut it any more. It doesn't bloody work!" Elizabeth's rage frightened her, stripping her of her vocabulary. She knew the words she should be using, words like 'responsibility', 'adult' and 'accountability' but the words made her freeze. Who or what was Gareth accountable to? No-bloody-one. He showed no interest in even being accountable to himself.

Chris had said, more than once, that Gareth behaved like Peter Pan. "Don't know what will make him grow up."

Well, how about a life-changing amount of debt? For *Christ's sake*. At least she could make him turn the music down and, with that, she left her bedroom.

"Turn it down!" The kitchen windows were steamed up, a small saucepan making bubbling noises on the hob.

Gareth switched the radio off, the sudden silence unnerving. "Morning, Mum. Thought you'd like a boiled egg for your breakfast."

"I don't. Just orange juice and a piece of toast."

"Oh, come on, soft boiled egg and soldiers. You always did those for our breakfasts."

"How *old* are you? Four *fucking* years old?" She saw the look on Gareth's face: if the Pope had used the expletive, Gareth could not have looked more shocked. And then, as if a pin had been stuck into her, Elizabeth deflated. A boiled egg? *Really?* Slumping into a chair, Elizabeth felt the full weight of Gareth and his problems, settle about her shoulders. "Gareth, you must…" She stopped, aware of the stricken look on his face. "You must get hold of your bank, you *must* make an appointment to see a debt counsellor, work out a way to pay this money back. And for God's sake, you need to find a job, one that maybe won't save the planet but you'll stay in for longer than a week."

Softening her voice, she said, "This won't go away, Gareth. Hiding here, pretending everything is ok, that's not the answer. This is too big to hide from." She lifted her head, "Look, this is *your* problem, not mine and you must find a way to sort it."

Even before he spoke, Elizabeth knew what Gareth would say. "Won't you do it for me? Please, Mum? Can't you pay the money and I'll …"

She looked at him. "No. Even if I had that sort of money lying around in a vault somewhere, I won't repay your debt." Seeing the way his shoulders sagged, Elizabeth tried again, "Gareth, all your life you've run away whenever things got difficult, didn't matter what it was: job, relationships, you took the soft option and simply walked away."

"Mum, I…"

"No, I'm not listening. All you ever do is promise that things will be better next time, that you've learnt your lesson, that the job wasn't working out, that your boss was a miserable bastard. Nothing has *ever* been your fault, Gareth. *Nothing*. It's always someone else's. This time it's your pile of shit and you need to sort it." She looked at him, "Every single penny of this bloody enormous debt is your responsibility."

Gareth stared at the floor, looking as if he was trying to work out what to say, searching for the right word to soften her, to plead for help.

"I'm sorry." He spoke softly.

"Yeah, you keep saying that. It doesn't work, it doesn't mean anything."

When he spoke again, his words hurtled from him as if they'd escaped before he lost courage. "Would you consider taking the money from the company? A sort of loan? I mean, you're doing well and I'd pay it back. I would, I give you my word on that."

Elizabeth's voice was icy, "No, I'm not prepared to do that. I run a design company and it not only employs your sisters but twenty other people, people who work hard, who have families, mortgages and who rely on me to pay their salaries. It's a world you know nothing about and I will *not*, under any circumstances put that in jeopardy because of your stupidity. How *dare* you ask me that, how *bloody* dare you!" With her heart thumping, Elizabeth knew, that for the first time in her life, she wanted to punch one of her children.

His sigh was loud, *whooshing* out of him. "Mum, at least think about it, please?"

"*No!* And don't ask me again." Standing, Elizabeth looked at him hard. "I'm going to get ready for work and you can clear up the kitchen. You've made the mess, your sort it out!

"What about your breakfast? You haven't had anything to eat."

"I don't want anything." And with that, Elizabeth left the kitchen.

Upstairs Elizabeth looked at her reflection in the mirror, seeing the angry red blotches on her neck and cheeks. Putting a hand to her chest, willing her heart rate to settle, she felt close to tears again. *Oh Christ, oh Christ.* She wanted to tell Gareth to leave, she didn't want him in the house under her roof. She wanted not to have to think about his debt, the mess he was in and she also knew it would never work; even if he left, his problems would stay with her, fill up her space.

Elizabeth knew it was fanciful, knew it was impossible, yet she could *feel* Gareth's martyrdom, his neediness rising from the kitchen to her bedroom. How *dare* he ask her to take money from the company, how bloody dare he! The fact that he had, made her shake with fury.

She finished dressing, putting on the clothes she thought of as her uniform, presenting an image, one in which she could work as an employer of a small workforce. She sprayed perfume, *Miss Dior*, on her wrists and her throat. She'd always worn it, Chris had presented her with a bottle each Christmas and, since his death, she'd bought one for herself, wrapping it and putting it under the tree, just so she could unwrap it and remember when he'd bought it. It made her think about Chris and that made her make a decision.

Running downstairs, she told Gareth that he would go into work with her. "There are a few things you can do, make yourself useful."

At first, he appeared startled. Then he nodded and smiled, "Ok, ok, whatever you want."

Of course. If he went into work with her, then he wouldn't have to do anything about his debt. But what else could she do? She couldn't bear to think of him in her home, alone.

"Right, come on then." Looking at him, she wanted to tell him to get changed, to look presentable but she kept quiet.

In the car, he was eager to talk, to ask questions about her BMW, about when she could get it back, about the damage, the crash. "Not like you, Mum, to take your eyes off the road."

Elizabeth recognised he was talking for the sake of it, talking about anything unrelated to his problem, talking to ease away from the argument they'd had. She told him that her car would be with her the following day.

"Bet you'll be glad to drive it instead of this thing," Gareth said.

"Of course." Was there a hidden message in his words? Or was she just becoming paranoid?

In the car park, she saw Charlotte's car, a white Volvo and, seeing it, Elizabeth thought of the argument she'd had with her daughter. They'd barely spoken since and now, with Gareth's unkempt presence, Elizabeth felt overwhelmed. *I'd like not to have to deal with any of them, at least for a while.*

When the car was stationary, Elizabeth watched as Gareth undid his seatbelt. He appeared untroubled, his head to one side as he fiddled with the belt. "You ok, Mum?"

No, I'm not. I don't want to deal with you or your problems. I don't want you here. Not now, not ever. Your sisters think I'm incapable of running my own business and right now, I don't want to be dealing with any of you.

"I'm fine."

There was laughter in Gareth's voice, "Ok, you're the boss."

"You got that right."

Knowing and disliking the fact that she derived pleasure from ordering Gareth about…"this coffee's cold, get me another one. Go down to the store-room, check the number of blue rugs…" Elizabeth felt unable to stop giving commands. In his eagerness to placate her, to ingratiate himself, Gareth scuttled from one task to another, hovering uncertainly, trying to work out what she needed. *Just like a puppy – ridiculous.* Now she knew why he'd never been able to hold down a job. *What's he equipped for? Nothing.*

"When did you last have a haircut?" Her question cut across Gareth trying to tell her about the number of rugs he'd found.

"What?" He pushed a hand through his hair. "I don't know, a

month ago, maybe two, why?"

"Because it needs cutting." Somehow the length of Gareth's hair symbolised exactly what was wrong with him. "You're a mess."

Even that didn't stop him grinning at her, as if having shaggy hair was part of his charm, proof that he didn't conform, that he didn't give a toss about his appearance, as if those things didn't matter.

What would he have done if he hadn't come with her? Waste another day, stare into space, listen to music, "contemplating his navel," was what Chris always said. Elizabeth wondered what Chris would have said about the mess Gareth was in now.

There was a time when Elizabeth could barely look at her husband. He'd said she was "going through a bad patch."

When he'd said that, she frowned, "A bad patch? That sounds like a stain on the ceiling."

"Ok, clever clogs, what would you call it?" Chris's expression was one of hurt and confusion.

"Not that, I don't know. I can't tell you what's wrong because I don't bloody know!"

And that was the truth. She didn't know, couldn't work out what the problem was. All she knew was that her nerve endings prickled with irritation whenever Chris came near her. She resented his attempts to fix whatever was broken by buying flowers, large boxes of chocolates. Each time he silently handed her his gift, she took it, leaving the chocolates or flowers on the table without comment. The *obviousness*, the banality of his gifts, seemed like part of the problem.

Whatever the problem was, it didn't have a name – not one she could come up with anyway. One minute Elizabeth had been content, busy, looking after the girls, happy to be with Chris and then things shifted and she wanted to scream in frustration, finding herself trapped in the life she had. She went off in her scruffy van, sourcing materials, working in the evenings, putting life back into the neglected furniture she found and it was on those trips, away from home, when Elizabeth was at her happiest. Although she'd never hurt or neglect Charlotte and Kate in any way, there were times when Elizabeth resented the hours she spent with them: being judge and jury during their arguments, hours in the kitchen preparing the food they liked, coaxing Charlotte to eat her vegetables. It all seemed pointless and Elizabeth knew that feeling had to remain hidden and she also knew that the following day, she'd have to do the same thing all over again. Only in her van was she free.

There was no way she could tell Chris. How could she tell him she thought she was drowning? What would he make of that? Elizabeth knew her husband would talk of "taking a break," or she was "overdoing it," and he'd suggest a day out, a visit to the cinema. The cinema? Oh Christ! Neither Elizabeth's mother or Chris's mother had worked outside the home and she knew Chris was floundering, didn't have a clue how to react to Elizabeth's coldness towards him. After she'd put the girls to bed, Elizabeth often stayed on her own in the kitchen, her arms wrapped around her chest, thinking about the way she lived. *I'm in the wrong life. This is someone else's life, it's not mine, it can't be mine.* She left the kitchen as soon as Chris entered.

But then, the mood, the dislocation that Elizabeth experienced, slipped away and when, one night, Chris put his hand on her shoulder, she turned towards him.

Looking at Gareth, wanting to snap at him each time he pushed his hair out of his eyes, Elizabeth knew that their son had disappointed Chris. Chris had an ideal, an image of his son: one who would enjoy football matches, one who'd meet him at the pub, one who'd be his mate, supporting him in a house full of females. Stereotypical as those images were, Gareth hadn't matched up. Every milestone in his life: walking, talking, reading, *everything* his sisters had achieved far earlier than Gareth. And Elizabeth had defended him! Over and over again. "Boys are always slower than girls at reading," "the girls smother him, he doesn't need to talk, they do it for him." Somehow, she'd wanted to cushion Gareth from his father's disappointment. But now, watching him trying to please her, to prove that he was a fully functioning adult, she knew she'd finally run out of excuses. They were all gone and oddly, she felt lightheaded.

The phone rang, she heard David Armstrong's voice. "Elizabeth? How are you? Have you had time to think about my proposal?" His laugh was practised. "The work related one, obviously,"

Elizabeth laughed as she knew she was meant to do.

With the phone in her hand, she saw a flicker of a smile on Gareth's face. *He thinks it'll be ok, he thinks I'm going to sort it, make it right for him.* Elizabeth felt a tightening in her rib cag and her tone was strictly controlled as she spoke to Armstrong, "Might be an idea for you to come here, David, to go over a few things?"

Gareth mimed drinking another cup of tea but she shook her head, turning away from him, instead making a fuss about finding a time and date to meet Armstrong.

She heard the squeak of Gareth's trainers, the sound of the door closing. She felt her shoulders slump even as her voice stayed bright and energetic.

CHAPTER 8

I drove home like a madwoman, ignoring all the rules: zebra crossings, give way on roundabouts, wait for green lights. Sod all that. Anyone who blew their horn or shouted, all they got was the finger.

Stupid thing was, I wanted Mum to be in the car with me. I *wanted* her to lift her foot as if to brake, to see her hand reach out to steady herself when I went too fast round a bend, I wanted to hear her voice, "For God's sake, Charlotte, slow down." But I couldn't slow down. I just couldn't. It wasn't as if I was in a tearing hurry to get home – it was more a gut feeling that I needed to get away.

I knew she'd react the way she had. Bloody knew it. Lips pursed, slight shake of the head. My suggestion, *my* idea, ignored. I saw the way she looked when she told Kate and I about her new contract, as if she'd pulled off the deal of the century. She's my Mum and it doesn't sit well with me to think these things, but bottom line, the word is *smug*. I mean, Mum's not stupid, she's astute, she's built up the company from tiny beginnings but she won't shift from the way she's always worked, but well, she operates on a 'don't rock the boat,' 'if it ain't broke, don't fix it,' sort of mentality. God, she might as well have all that printed on a tee-shirt.

Oh, Christ, whatever had made me drive like a lunatic, had vanished leaked away. I'd reached home but for some reason, I didn't stop. I kept going. No idea why or where, I just kept driving. The streets and houses near my home must be the same as streets all over the UK: neat, manicured lawns, glossy painted front doors, pots of whatever flowers are in season, maybe a bike or two leaning up against a wall, a pram waiting to be dragged through a door, mismatched Wellington boots left near the front step, a handrail to ease passage up steps.

The houses looked, what, what was in my head? What did the sight of all these *contained* homes say to me? Why was I doing this, driving around aimlessly instead of being inside *my* house? All I knew was that as long as I was outside, in my car, then I was a separate entity, I was me. But inside I would be…I don't know, something else.

I knew Jon would be home, it had been his turn to pick the girls up. Okay, okay, that's not a fair statement. It's usually his turn. My husband is a primary school teacher, something he says is in his DNA. He knew from an early age that he wanted to teach. Me, I didn't know what I wanted to do.

We met at university and I don't know what it was about Jon that attracted me. He's tall but that wasn't it. I guess it was the incredible aura of calmness about him. Nothing seems to faze him. I went to university because I thought I should, I mean, I had no pulsating desire to absorb all there is to know about marine biology or to be fired up by every aspect of sociology. To put it bluntly, I went because I didn't know what else to do. Dad sort of understood – he simply said that I should go "because it might give you time to think about what you do want to do."

I tried to tell him that having a job in Tesco would achieve the same thing but he wasn't having that. So, I went. I did English Literature only because I'd always enjoyed reading. And there was Jon, all 6'2" of him, committed, eager to learn, already so clear about what he wanted to do with his life. It both impressed and depressed me. I tried teasing him, telling him that he might change his mind, that he might discover a talent for painting or become a brilliant carpenter, but Jon wasn't having any of it.

I'm honest enough to admit that he's *far* better with the girls. Far better. You'd think that, after spending a whole day with other people's kids, the last thing he'd want to do is come home and do it all over again. But he does and he does it with a smile, with patience.

That's another reason why I'm driving around now, looking at other people's homes, 'cos Jon will have sorted out the girls' tea, their homework, their arguments.

Jon's better with Mum too. Somehow, he manages to both tease and flirt with her without sounding in any way weird, which is quite a skill. He's not like that with his own mother. Janet, my mother in law is five years older than Mum yet it could be five decades. Jon is an only child and Janet treats him as if he was four years old while, at the same time, conveying the impression that it's about time he started taking care of his parents. Derek, my father in law just does what he's told. He nods, he murmurs, he's beige, always in the background.

Jon jokes about the fact that I work for Mum, not in a cruel way, but in a funny way. After all, we both know that working for Mum, *with* Mum, was the best thing for me. I'd buggered about with other jobs, not settling, not understanding or even caring what I did and when Mum first suggested it, I laughed, "What would I *do*? I know nothing about decoration, got no idea about colour schemes." Truth was, the idea horrified me. Mum as my boss? Me, messing about with rugs and scented candles?"

I was between jobs, again, and she didn't let the subject drop and somehow she wore me down. I was all, "Well, just for a while, only until something turns up."

Turns out, Hallelujah, I'm good at my job. I leave the colours, the flair to Mum and I work on the contracts, long-term planning. It's hard to admit it, but working with Mum is the best thing I've done.

Janet, Jon's Mum, thinks what Mum does is weird. Running her own company? She won't let it drop, keeps going on and on about "at your Mum's age," as if being 73 is an excuse to stop living. The irony isn't lost on me: a large part of me thinks Mum *should* slow down, that maybe her decision making isn't as good as it once was and yet, another equally large part of me, is fiercely proud of her. I sing her praises to people like Janet, *especially*, people like Janet.

Last time I saw my in-laws, Janet was in full flow as usually, all about how the house was getting too much for her; she turns her head when she talks, looking at Jon's Dad as if she's including him in her conversation or maybe daring him to disagree with her. She was talking about moving to a bungalow. "The stairs are a bit of a problem these days." I can't help it but I always compare Janet to Mum, not only because of their physical differences: Mum's tall, elegant, walks with her head high, she always looks as if she notices what's going on around her whilst Janet is small, dumpy and God help me, nondescript. Who would want Janet as a Mum? Not me. Jon's parents would be the sort of people who'd move into Ellis and James' retirement homes. That made me smile, the thought of them doing that. I wanted to tell Mum, but I can't.

I've turned into my road now and there's my house, it looks like all the others.

When I opened the front door, I heard the girls' voices, something about a lost shoe, Jon's voice, "You'll need to find it before your Mum gets home." What am I? An ogre? A wave of guilt crashed over me and I made a silent promise that, from now on, I'd be a better mother, a better wife, a better daughter. I filled my voice with energy. "Hello? I'm home, where is everyone?" I flung myself into my family, determined to pull my weight.

Once the girls were in bed, I sat next to Jon on the settee, sitting close, wanting to feel his nearness, to feel I had his support. Or maybe something more than that, needing to let him know that we're a team, we do things together. I don't know.

I told him about the row with Mum, what she'd said, how angry I'd been. He listened to every word and when I'd finished, he was silent. He didn't look at me and that made me edgy.

"What? D'you think I'm wrong? D'you think I should have not told Mum about my plan?"

He touched my hand. "Charlie, listen to me. You're in danger of becoming obsessed…"

"*Obsessed?*"

"You know, with this whole thing: your mother's age, whether she's doing a good job, the progress of the company, your role in it…"

"No! No, I'm not." I put space between us.

"Yes you are. It's *all* you talk about." He hadn't let go of my hand and he was stroking the base of my thumb. I stared at his hand, thinking about what he'd said.

"That's not true," I heard the whine in my voice, hating it. "It's just that, what with Mum's accident and you know, her being secretive about where she'd been, not listening to new ideas…and don't get me started on Kate." I stopped, realising what I'd said, how I'd said.

Jon looked at me, a smile hovered. "See, I rest my case." He too looked at his hand, he kept up the rhythmic stroking. "Charlie, I saw you earlier."

"What? What are you talking about?"

"You were in the car, I saw you. I was upstairs searching for Sophie's shoe and, instead of coming home, you carried on. You drove past. Why did you do that?" His voice was low.

What could I say? That I wasn't ready to come home, that I

needed to clear space in my head before filling it with home life? But how can I say that to Jon who cheerfully leaves classrooms full of kids and their noisy demands and comes home to pick up the reins here? I mean, I can only work the hours I do *because* Jon picks up the slack. I rely on Jon for all sorts of things; he does more than his fair share of domestic duties and because he never questions the hours I work, the times I'm distracted. And now when I should have gone straight home to help, to be the girls' Mum and a wife, I took off. Jon doesn't have that luxury.

I squirmed, a mixture of embarrassment at being found out and guilt. I muttered something about wanting to "clear my head," and Jon sighed.

"Charlie, you're going about this all wrong. You'll alienate and upset your Mum and you're not doing yourself any good either." He looked at me, "It's not doing the girls any good either. Hannah has asked more than once if you're angry with her."

I yanked my hand away, "You're making that up."

"No, I'm not. Children know when they don't have your full attention."

That winded me. "Oh, God, I'm sorry." I thought about telling Jon about the promises I'd made, that I'd be a better wife, Mum and daughter but I kept quiet. He was *always* good. I was more a part-timer.

"I don't deserve you, you know…"

"C'mon."

"S'true."

Anyhow, the promise hadn't extended to becoming a better sister though and when I saw Gareth in the office the following day, I snapped. "What the hell are you doing here?"

He was holding a large green rug, "Hello Charlotte, always a pleasure. I'm here because Mum asked me to come in. She wants my help with a few things."

"What?" I looked at him. He's thirty-eight yet looks like a homeless person. The fashion for jeans hanging off your backside looked ridiculous on kids and, for someone Gareth's age, it's revolting. Sad thing is, my brother wouldn't have known that it was a fashion statement, he always looked as if he got dressed in the dark. I didn't give him a chance to tell me what he was doing, not sure I cared. "We don't have a dress down day here."

He laughed.

"I'm not joking, we don't."

"C'mon, give me a break. I'm just sorting through some stock, that's what Mum said." He looked down at his clothes: baggy jeans, faded at the knee, the tee-shirt he wore with a rip at the neck. There was something in his expression, surprise almost at seeing the clothes he was wearing, as if he had no idea who they belonged to. Oh, God, he's irritating.

"Mum says you're staying with her for a while, is that right?" I knew my tone was clipped but did nothing to alter it.

He shrugged, "Yeah, not for long, only until I get myself sorted." He was still holding the rug and he frowned at it, and there was something in his expression, as if he expected the rug to give him a better response.

"*Sorted!* What d'you mean, sorted?"

He shook his head, "Not now, look, I've got to go. We'll catch up later." And with that he walked away.

I watched the sway of his backside, the sagging of his jeans. Christ, it depressed me.

Going into the office, I told Kate that Gareth was working today. She frowned, "What, here? What's he doing?"

"Dunno, he said something about sorting through stock. Why Mum brought him in to do it, God knows."

Listen: whatever reason Mum had brought Gareth into work

with her, it wasn't for checking stock. Each time we move from one project to another, a few staff members go through what we've used: rugs, kitchen utensils, furniture, checking to se that nothing is damaged, that it can be used again. Anything broken or faded, we take to the council tip or offer it to a charity. The only reason Mum brought Gareth in, was to keep an eye on him.

Kate shrugged, "Perhaps he's at a loose end, perhaps he offered to help Mum, you know, after her crash."

See, that's another difference between Kate and me. She never thinks there's an ulterior motive. Jon said once that she's a quieter version of me, but I'm not sure I agree with that. He meant less defined, softer but I think she's woolly, always worrying whether she's upset people, said the wrong thing. I've seen her, *heard* her muttering as she stared at her screen, worrying about the wording of an email. *Just send the bloody thing!* And yet, I guess, this attention to detail, her constant checking of dates, amounts, makes her good at her job, which, to be honest, irritates me too.

Of course, I've not said anything to her yet about her lack of support when we had that meeting with Mum but I'm bloody furious. I need to think, need to work out what it means. Truth? I know what it means. Kate will hang onto my shirttails, she'll let me go into battle with Mum if that's what it takes and there she'll be, right behind me, offering to make cups of tea once the battle is over. Not for the first time, I wish I was more like Kate. She's, what's the word, sanguine, she can talk for hours about the benefits of eating a sensible diet, of restricting your alcohol intake .She's got her life compartmentalised. She leaves work at work and, when she gets home, she switches off and concentrates on her husband Dan and her son, Tom. There's no point in ringing her about office stuff when she's home – she couldn't care less. I wish I could do that. That's not all I wish. I wish I had her hair. Kate's hair is glossy, sleek, she's got hair like Mum's. My hair is like a mop, out of control, wilful and disobedient.

Kate and I didn't see Gareth for the rest of the day, yet I knew he was around which was bad enough. We didn't see Mum either which was unusual. Our offices are close and doors are always open. People are forever popping in, asking for something, showing us something but there was no sign of Mum. I told myself she needed time, *I* needed time but that wasn't it, not really. I thought about what Jon had said, about becoming obsessed. Then I thought about Gareth, that he was cloistered with Mum and that bothered me more.

At about four, feeling uneasy, thinking it had gone on too long, thinking about the promises I'd made. I was also thinking that, at the very least, I should behave like a grownup, I walked over to Mum's office and, unusually for her, the door was closed. That unnerved me and I hovered, unsure of what to do, should I knock?

And then I heard laughter, Mum's laughter, light, girlish. Who the hell was she talking to?

"Do you want to see Mum, Charlie?" Gareth's voice right behind me.

I turned, I'd been about to put my hand on the door handle.

"Mum's on the phone," his tone full of self-importance as if he was, I dunno, *guarding* her, keeping me at bay.

"I know that, moron. I can hear her."

With that he somehow pushed his way in front of me, shutting me out. "It's best if you come back later."

"What the fuck, Gareth! You her security guard now? I mean, for Christ's sake, you've been here, what, for half a day and you're telling me I can't see Mum. *Really?*"

Yeah, I was pissed off with him but I was even more pissed off with the way things were with Mum. And here he was, my idiot brother, dressed as if he'd come to clean the drains, stopping me!

I wanted to kick him in the balls in frustration but I didn't.

"She's tired, Charlie, can't it wait."

For a second I was lost for words. How bloody *dare* he tell me my Mum is tired! I know! She's seventy-three, she's running a business, she's working full time and…oh, what the hell. Talking to Gareth about business was like discussing applied physics with a tadpole.

I gave up. "Piss of, Gareth. Piss off back to where you came from,"

"Do you want me to let her know you wanted to talk to her?"

I didn't reply, just gave him the finger.

CHAPTER 9

Her car had been left in the car park. When it had been brought back, Elizabeth went out to look at it, to reassure herself that it was all right, that all signs of the accident had gone.

The valeted car looked new, its red bodywork gleaming in the sunshine. Elizabeth put a hand on the bonnet to feel its solidity and to reassure herself that it was ok, it was hers. With her hand on the bonnet, Elizabeth felt a shifting, a kind of transformation, as if the car had somehow restored her. *For Christ's sake, it's a car!* But that's how it felt. She smiled, the ache across her shoulders easing. Then she patted the bonnet before walking back into the building.

As she walked into her office, Gareth looked up, a smile plastered across his face. "Car ok? Bet it looks good."

Elizabeth nodded, unwilling to share her relief. "I'm calling it a day, going home."

"Sure there's nothing else you want me to do?"

She shook her head, "Tomorrow morning, Gareth, you will need to find yourself somewhere else to live." She turned, busying herself with picking up her laptop, her phone, bag and jacket, avoiding the look on Gareth's face.

"But I don't know…"

Elizabeth half-turned, "You don't know what?"

"I've got nowhere to go, I've got no money…"

Walking to the door, Elizabeth spoke crisply. "Those are your problems, Gareth, not mine." She looked at him. "I'm done, Gareth. One more night that's all. Are you coming or are you intending to stay here all night?"

He shook his head, his hair flying across his face. "I'm coming with you."

Elizabeth strode down the corridor, keenly aware of Gareth's movements behind her. She kept her head straight, avoiding any sight of either Charlotte or Kate and conspicuously avoiding having to look at Gareth. *Three of them here, all waiting to pounce.* Her thoughts confused her and she wanted to be home, the front door locked, keeping her inside and everyone else out. She heard Gareth's breathing and quickened her pace.

"Wow, Mum, the car looks great!" Understanding why his remarks angered her, Elizabeth remained silent.

He seemed unaware of her hostility and kept talking, "Must say, Mum, that not a lot of women your age would go for a car like this."

"*My age?* What car should I drive then? Something more in keeping with my advanced years?"

"No, that's not what I meant. Look, all I was trying to say was that…"

"Shut up, Gareth. I don't want to hear it. I just want to go home."

He sat forward, "Look, Mum, please let me…"

"Will you shut up?"

He slumped back and Elizabeth drove the car out of the car park.

As Gareth's martyred silence filled the car, Elizabeth thought back on the conversation she'd had with David Armstrong, there was something about him, about the way he'd spoken to her, that was niggling her, but what was it? Maybe his mildly flirtatious way of speaking, the slow speech pattern, almost as if he was carefully choosing words designed to flatter her. Or was he flirting? His words were designed to flatter her with an unspoken thread: *you're a woman in her seventies, you should be grateful*. Was that it? She shook her head, unable to pinpoint exactly what was bothering her. *Christ, I could murder a gin and tonic.*

Unable to bear Gareth's silence any longer, Elizabeth switched on the radio. James Taylor's voice filled the car, *Up on the Roof*. She saw the way Gareth flinched as the music registered with him. Elizabeth turned the volume up.

Upstairs in her bedroom, Elizabeth changed out of her work clothes. The white paper bag with Kate's gift of arnica was on the dressing table and Elizabeth picked up the bag. She looked at the tube of cream, sniffing at its contents. Normally she had little time for Kate's alternative therapies but, understanding that her daughter meant well, Elizabeth stroked the cream across the top of her shoulders. The bruising had intensified in colour and her skin felt tender and raw. When she touched it a jolt of pain went through her entire body and yet she kept rubbing the cream in, her movements hard, her breathing ragged. When she stopped, she closed her eyes, feeling pain in her shoulders. *Christ.*

She tugged a sweater over her head and her phone rang, so freeing herself, she picked it up: Charlotte.

"Hello?"

"Mum, it's me, just wanted to know if you're ok." Charlotte's voice was low, "I know Gareth's with you but …"

"I'm fine, thank you." Elizabeth spoke softly. "I'm much better, really I am."

"Good, glad to hear it."

The silence grew before Elizabeth spoke. "Are you still at work?"

"No, on my way home."

Hearing that, Elizabeth relaxed. "Are the girls ok? Jon, is he home with them?"

Picking up on her mother's tone, Charlotte answered the normal questions, "Yeah, everyone's fine. Usual drama about parties and lost shoes."

Elizabeth smiled, "Give the girls my love, and Charlotte…"

"What, Mum? Are you sure you're ok?"

"Yes, I promise. It's just that I won't be in until a bit later tomorrow…"

"Oh, I see."

"Nothing sinister. I've got a hair appointment, that's all."

Charlotte's laugh was one of relief. "Oh, good for you. We'll expect you when we see you."

Their conversation kept to a normal path of lightweight words.

"I'll see you tomorrow, bye." Elizabeth put the phone down. She wasn't sure what she was feeling. She lifted her head smelling onions. Gareth must be cooking. "Oh, God," she muttered, almost running from the bedroom.

At the door of the kitchen, Elizabeth stopped. He'd been home for what, fifteen minutes and he'd already wrecked the kitchen. The tiles at the back of her oven were splattered with what she hoped was tomato, an arc of blood red splodges looking like the interior of an abattoir. Gareth stood in front of the oven, a tea-towel draped across his shoulders, stirring something in a saucepan. An assortment of plastic trays littered the worktops and the smell of onions was overpowering. He hadn't heard her, Coldplay were on the radio and Gareth was moving to the music. *That* movement, the tea-towel draped across him, the way he stood, legs apart, standing in front of the oven, *her* oven, unnerved her. *He's taken up residence.* From nowhere she knew she was close to tears and she took a breath. She called his name, "Gareth,

Gareth, switch that music off."

He turned, his face open, wiped clean of any guilt or guile. He switched the radio off.

"Sorry, Mum, got a bit carried away." He gestured to the saucepan. "Thought I'd make Bolognese for supper. I found minced beef in the fridge."

"You've burnt the onions." Elizabeth didn't want to, couldn't let her guard down. "It won't be worth eating."

"It'll be fine. I've put in a lot of garlic," he stopped, aware of the expression on Elizabeth's face. "Mum, I've been…" he moved towards her and then stopped.

"Nothing's changed, Gareth." Elizabeth took a deep breath. "Look, why don't you get yourself packed and I'll clear this up." She waved a hand towards the fridge. "I've got some chicken and I'll …" this time it was Elizabeth who stopped talking.

"I wanted to make a meal for you, to say thank you, to say I'm sorry, to say…" Gareth pulled a face, "to say I'm sorry for being such a shit son."

Oh God, shut up, Gareth.

He shuffled, edging closer towards her and, despite herself, Elizabeth stepped back.

Gareth saw her movement and frowned, "*Mum!* I won't hurt you, I'd never do that."

"You *have* hurt me, it's that simple. You come home whenever you're in trouble, expecting me to clear up your mess but this mess is too big, I can't cope. Gareth, I don't *want* to cope with this. For Christ's sake, I'm seventy three, way past sorting out your crap."

She'd never done that before, not once, used her age to defend herself, as an excuse. She kept her eyes on Gareth's face, watching the penny slowly drop. Then she lifted her head and Gareth left the kitchen. His pace was slow and Elizabeth fought the impulse to say, "Stay, we'll sort it somehow. Don't go." Fortunately, she heard him close the door the bedroom before she could open her mouth.

Sitting opposite Gareth as they ate their supper, Elizabeth thought about asking him to choose some music; Radio 4, anything, any sound to lift the awkward silence between them. She'd heard an occasional *crack* of his jaw as he chewed the chicken she'd prepared. A few times she'd caught him watching her, his eyes dark and troubled and she wondered what he was thinking.

When Gareth put his knife and fork down, Elizabeth pushed her plate away and cleared her throat. "Gareth, I've transferred £1,000 into your account."

She watched as he lifted his head, his expression one of relief.

He opened his mouth but Elizabeth shook her head. "No, listen to me. That's it, the last time I give you money. I don't want to think about you sleeping in your car or on a park bench so that money is to find somewhere to live. It's for *that* purpose, Gareth. And there will be no more, *ever*. Do you understand me?"

He nodded, his voice low and breathy. "Thanks, Mum, I can't …"

"And you will leave tomorrow in the morning. I want your word on that. I'm leaving the house early for a hair appointment and, by the time I return home, you will have left. Do I have your word?"

He nodded and, pushing his hair away from his face, he spoke quickly. "Yes, I will, I'll be gone, thank you, I'll pay you back, I will, I promise. There's someone I know, Matt, he's a good bloke and he said that…"

His voice ran on and, watching him, Elizabeth thought her money had somehow recalibrated him, energised him and the thought left her cold and saddened. The thousand pounds salved her conscience, made her feel she'd done something for her son and yet she knew the money would leak away and he'd have learnt nothing. For that matter, neither had she, not really. She was his mother, that's what the money meant.

She'd not listened to a word Gareth said and realising he was waiting for her to speak, she lifted her head, "Sorry, I missed that. What did you say?"

"Just that I won't let you down. I won't. I'll make sure you get this money back."

Of course you will. "Let's drop it now, Gareth."

He nodded, "Ok," and he gestured to the table. "I'll clear this up."

Elizabeth knew she'd have to do it all over again but she agreed. "Thank you. I'm going to have a glass of wine." She poured one for them both.

Elizabeth awoke to the sound of birdsong and lay very still, listening. She loved the way one sound seemingly triggered another, then another. She knew very little about birds and certainly couldn't differentiate between the calls they made. A trill, high-pitched, then another. And then, as if from a distance, a *chirrup.* Elizabeth waited, wanting the call to be answered. She held her breath and then it came, a bird singing in reply. There was no pattern, it was all random and yet it sounded cohesive, as if they were discussing the day ahead. *What are your plans? Oh, dunno, thought I'd take a trip over the river, check out what's going on.* Elizabeth liked the thought of the birds being connected, interested in what each one was doing, as if they knew each other, sitting on telegraph poles, on trees. She loved the sheer joy, the exuberance of their birdsong, bursting from them unedited. It was as if each bird knew their calls would be answered. *So what happened then? Who did you see?* As if each bird knew their calls wouldn't be judged, criticised, simply enjoyed. Elizabeth stretched and got out of bed.

Later, walking past the door of Gareth's bedroom, there was no sound and, tapping at the door, she spoke rapidly, "I'm leaving now, Gareth."

His voice, muffled, sleepy, "Oh, right, give me a minute."

"No, I'll be late. Take care, Gareth."

"Ok, thanks for everything, Mum."

Knowing he couldn't see her, Elizabeth lifted a hand to wave before leaving the house.

Driving towards the salon, she thumped the steering wheel. "I should have stayed, I should have…oh, Christ."

Sitting in the chair, the itchy nylon gown tucked around her neck, Elizabeth only half-listened to the stylist's chatter. The voice meandering through her head, not meeting resistance, making no connection. "I told him, this time we're flying to France. I'm not sitting in a car all that way again, I'm done with that."

Carly had been cutting and colouring Elizabeth's hair for ten years and she hadn't batted an eyelid when Elizabeth asked for an early morning appointment. "Yeah, sure. What time did you have in mind?"

"7.30, can you do that?" Elizabeth didn't volunteer anything else. All she needed from Carly was a haircut, lowlights to hide the grey. Carly didn't need to know that Elizabeth had to go into the office with all guns blazing, needing to look the part.

Carly's tone had been neutral, "Sure, 7.30 it is. I'll have coffee ready."

The coffee had been placed near Elizabeth's chair and, when Carly put the small tray in front of Elizabeth, for the first time she noticed a black tattoo on Carly's wrist. Elizabeth looked at it, trying to work out what it was before Carly tugged the sleeve of her sweater down, covering the tattoo. Neither woman said a word and Elizabeth wondered why Carly had done that. What did that say about *her* – did Carly think she'd judge her, disapprove, that someone of Elizabeth's age wouldn't like tattoos? She drank her coffee thinking if Judi Dench could have a tattoo… Elizabeth pulled a face, thinking of Charlotte's reaction if her mother arrived at work with a skull and crossbows or a scorpion tattooed on her wrist. *Might just do it. I'd be worth it for Charlotte's expression alone.*

"Ok?"

"Sorry," Elizabeth hadn't realised Carly had asked a question.

"You ok for twenty minutes?" Carly patted Elizabeth's shoulder, a sort of soothing pat that made Elizabeth's teeth ache. She thought about shrugging, dislodging Carly's hand but didn't.

"Here," Carly put a magazine into Elizabeth's hand, "See how the other half lives."

Elizabeth flicked through the pages, aware that she didn't recognise any of the names of the celebrities. She looked at the glossy pictures of over-the-top homes, the tall crystal vases full of waxy, white lilies, the spotless, sterile kitchens where not even a kettle could be seen. A young woman wearing a long, floaty dress gazed adoringly at a man, his arm draped protectively around her shoulders. Elizabeth thought about Charlotte's proposal, *this is what she means, working for people like this, look at them! Why can't they get their hands dirty like the rest of us?* The sight of the couple, their vapid expressions irritated her and she put the magazine down with a thump.

As she waited for Carly to take her debit card, Elizabeth thought about staying where she was, *here* where she could drink coffee, make light conversation about holidays and not have to face Charlotte and Kate. She could stay in the perfumed confines of the salon, reading magazines, not thinking about Gareth, about his debt, about the train wreck that made up his life, let it all wash over her. She could spend her days not thinking about any of it.

Would that make her like the couples in the magazine?

In her car, Elizabeth looked at her watch, it was 9.20. But she wasn't ready yet to go to work. Instead ,she switched on the engine and called Charlotte. She heard her daughter's voice, "Mum? You ok?"

"Fine, just to let you know I'm running a bit late. See you later."

"Oh, ok."

"Bye," Elizabeth cut short the call and drove off.

The car park was empty apart from a white council van and, as Elizabeth got out of her car, she smelt newly cut grass. Clutching a bouquet of yellow roses bought from Waitrose on her way to the crematorium, Elizabeth took a deep breath and walked over to the area where she'd scattered Chris's ashes. After he'd died, she'd been bewildered about what to do with them. Her mind had run up and down various suggestions: at sea, at home in the garden, in the woodland where they'd taken the children to see the bluebells until finally, unable to cope with any further thoughts, she'd brought the spartan brown urn to the crematorium grounds and under the sombre eye of an official, had scattered Chris's ashes near a small mound of earth. She'd put a plaque nearby: *Chris Nicholls, (1944-2018) Beloved husband and father* and then she'd planted a yellow rose bush, Chris's favourite flower. The rose bush had since died and, instead Elizabeth brought fresh flowers whenever she visited.

Her eyes fixed on the small mound of earth, Elizabeth walked slowly. She whispered, "Sorry, sorry, love I've not been for a while. I'm sorry." What was she going to tell him? "I've been rushed off my feet, had a car crash, the girls want to take the company from me and, oh, yes, Gareth is in deep shit, again."

A bench was nearby, a bronze plaque bore the inscription: *For Rosemary Daniels with our love.* Elizabeth sat and gazed around. The crematorium overlooked the city and, from where she was sitting, she could see rows of houses, red-brick, white and pale cream, splodges of dark green gardens, as well as hearing the sound of a police siren. The cellophane which covered the roses, crackled in her hands and she looked at the yellow petals. The girls had told her that it was the perfect place for their dad. "He can see our house from here, Mum. He'd have liked that." Hearing the girls, hearing the way they'd tried to console her, made her chest ache. But the truth was, Chris was here because she hadn't known what else to do with him.

Elizabeth removed the cellophane from the bouquet and, standing up, she placed the long-stemmed roses over the grassy area. She looked at them, the soft, buttery yellow petals lying on the grass. His coffin had been covered in an enormous wreath of yellow roses. The girls had spoken to her, Kate holding her hand, Gareth sitting opposite, his face white with grief and shock.

Elizabeth couldn't remember much about the funeral service, only aware of voices, phrases: "Is there anything we can do for you? So sorry for your loss." All she thought about was the day Chris died. They'd been to the garden centre and he'd grumbled about the state of the boot of the car. "This will take forever to clean up."

Elizabeth had gone into the kitchen to make cups of tea and took little notice when Chris came in complaining about a pain in his arm. "Those bags of compost, should have bought smaller ones."

She'd put a mug of tea in his hand. "There you go, stop grumbling." She'd left him, eager to look at the trays of plants they'd bought. There, in the garden, she walked up and down, working out where the geraniums would go, should she have bought more fuchsias, would the colour of the begonias work against the fence?

A sudden, massive heart attack. That's what they told her but Elizabeth thought it couldn't have been that sudden. Chris told her his arm was hurting. Why hadn't she listened? Why didn't she call for help? She tried not to think about Chris's last moments. Had he been frightened, had he called her name, had she heard him, ignored him? She'd stayed in the garden, only returning to the house when her tea had gone cold. As usual, she'd forgotten about Chris, lost in her world of colour schemes, the best way to present her garden.

Elizabeth whispered, "Bye, love. I won't leave it so long before I come again."

As she was walking to her car, her phone rang. It was Kate and Elizabeth told her that she was on her way. "I'll be there in about twenty minutes."

Kate's voice was high-pitched. "Mum, I think you should know what Charlotte's done."

"What? What has she done?"

Kate stumbled over her words. "I don't want to tell you over the phone, just come in, please, Mum."

"Ok, I'm on my way." Elizabeth shook her head, was it still only the morning? Time seemed stretched out as if by a rolling pin. It had already been a long day.

CHAPTER 10

Christ, I wish I lived in Kate's world. Right now, I'd put money on Kate simply worrying about whether she should buy milk on her way home as if that was the most important thing in the world. Ok, ok, I'm a cow. I know I am. Kate works hard, keeps track of this company, does a brilliant job as Company Secretary and takes it all absolutely seriously. She's meticulous, practical and methodical and, best of all, she has the ability to leave the company and any issues behind her when she finishes at the end of each day. That's it, job done, now let's get the milk. I can't do that, my head's always full of *stuff*. Work stuff, home stuff, Mum stuff and somehow, they all bleed into one another. I feel as if I'm the only one who can see what's going on with Mum, with the company, with Gareth. To be honest, as far as my brother and sister are concerned, I feel as if I'm between a rock and hard place. Like, I opened my mouth, wanting to tell Kate that Gareth was guarding Mum and being a complete dick and I know, I just know he's with Mum because he wants to scrounge money from her again but then, for some reason, I kept quiet. Why? Who knows.

I'll ring Mum later. We haven't spoken since the Ellis and James argument and I don't want to talk to her whilst Gareth is nearby. I'll ring her when I leave work. I definitely don't want to talk to her when my witless brother is here.

Well, at least we're talking and the fact that she's going to the hairdressers tomorrow makes me feel easier as if she's carrying on, not stewing over things, you know, sweating the small stuff. No, Mum having a haircut, that's a good sign.

I drove home feeling better about things. We can sort this out, of course we can. But the sooner Gareth leaves, the better.

Back home, the kitchen table was piled high with paper and a large pot of glue, slowly leaking its contents. Jon looked up and grinned. "Bet you didn't know I was brilliant at cutting out butterflies."

Hannah's hair seemed to be stuck to her face and, when I tried to move it, she wriggled and told me to stop. "Don't Mummy. I can't concentrate."

I looked at Jon. "That's telling me." I then sat at the table, listening to the girls' chatter as they told me about their day. Jon too looked content and said he'd found something in the Sunday supplements that might be of interest to me. Jon likes the fact that we have papers delivered on the weekend. He says all the time that it doesn't feel like a proper weekend without the papers. I mean, I get my news from my iPad, from the radio, but Jon *devours* the papers, takes him a week to get through them.

Jon and I ate our supper after the girls wandered into the living room to watch tv. Their collages of pink and green butterflies were drying near the window and I looked at the way they'd coloured the bodies. Hannah, as always, scribbling outside the outlines, in a hurry to get the job done, whilst Sophie, ever cautious, took her time and each fat body was meticulously coloured. I thought about Kate, her attention to detail and my bull in a China shop approach to life, wondering if Hannah would ever view her sister the same way I viewed Kate: irritation mixed with love.

Jon and I chatted, usual stuff, part domestic and I also told him about the crap I'd been worrying about and I told him about

Gareth, how he'd guarded Mum and, as I did so, it felt as if all that stuff was disappearing in the rear view mirror, as if Jon had taken the worry from me.

We stood together, loading the dishwasher and then Jon touched my shoulder, "I'll get that article I was talking about."

I heard him in the living room, telling the girls that they had half an hour before bed and then he returned, holding a section from the Sunday paper. "Here, this is right up your street."

I often think Jon is impervious to my job. Oh, he listens and makes the right noises but part of me thinks he feels it's not a 'proper' job, one like his, educating children, doing something worthwhile. Truth is, I used to feel like that about what Mum did before I joined her and then, somehow, I got sucked in and before I knew what was going on, it had taken over my life too. The truth is Jon doesn't really care. And yet he does this, shows me something that might interest me, be of benefit to the company. It's one of those areas that I guess most partnerships have: neither one wanting to do the other one's job, yet knowing how much that job means to your partner. Either way, I'm not knocking it.

"Read it before the girls have their baths."

I looked at the article and at the photographs and felt a buzz of excitement. I glanced at Jon, "You've read this?"

"Of course," he ginned, "I do listen."

The article was headed: *Improve Your Chances of Selling Your Home*. There were the usual *Before* and *After* photographs, the *before* showing pictures of dingy bathrooms, tired kitchens, a lot of pine furniture and fussy carpets, while the *after* photographs were similar to pictures I'd seen many times: transformed kitchens, gleaming units and stripped back décor. The article made much of "depersonalising your home, make it appealing to someone else." There was a list of what to do and, at the foot of the article were names of recommended companies to help with the sale and there we were; E.N. Designers, Mum's company, *my* company, it was there in *The Times*.

"Oh, my God, this is brilliant! First time we've made the nationals."

Jon touched my hand, "Are you going to tell your Mum?"

"You bet, this is fantastic. I'll ring her now."

Just then Sophie came running into the kitchen, her face wet with tears. "Hannah's being mean, she said I can't…" and she hurled herself into my lap and I held her whilst Jon went into the living room to sort out whatever Hannah had or hadn't said.

The girls' argument wasn't new and it would happen again in different formats but it took up most of the evening as Jon and I tried to negotiate a truce between our daughters. It was only the following morning when I saw the newspaper article still on the kitchen table that I remembered. I grabbed it and took it with me into the office, wanting to show Mum, wanting her to know… know what? How well we were doing? She already knew that.

Part of me said that it was Mum's fault that, if she'd been in on time then I wouldn't have done it but that was rubbish. The truth? I did it *because* Mum came in later. I'd shown the article to Kate and if I said she was decidedly underwhelmed, that would have been an understatement. "Good to see our name in *The Times*." That was it, that was all she said. She was more impressed by the fact that it was *The Times*. Wonder if it would have made much difference if it had been *The Daily Mail?* Oh, Kate said stuff about our reputation, about being noticed, vague comments but it meant more to me than that, much more. This was proof, this was validation that what we were doing: diversifying, broadening our business base, was working. It bloody well was and I was determined not to let the momentum stop.

Anyway, that's why I told Jess about my new plan.

Jess is, well, I'm not sure just what's the best way to describe her. She's *bouncy*, full of enthusiasm and she's that rarity, someone who actually gets things done. Every job she's been given, she's gone the extra mile, staying late, making sure that our clients are delighted with her work and, if there's something they don't like, she'll sort it straightaway. That's what I mean when I said that Jess would be perfect for my plan.

"Wow!" She and I were sitting together at my desk, Kate going through her files, slamming the doors of her desk.

Kate hadn't been impressed when I told her I wasn't going to wait. I was going to tell Jess about my new idea. "Don't you think you should at least wait until Mum gets here?" She'd frowned at me. "Mum won't like it, Charlie. Maybe you should…"

"No! Can't you see…" I waved the newspaper article in front of her. "This is the right time to do this, our name is out there *now*. What are you saying, Kate? That we should waste all this free publicity?"

"But the publicity is for what we're already doing, not your new…idea." Kate's eyes were on mine, she didn't blink. "I think you should wait, Charlie…at least until Mum gets here."

"I'm just going to sound Jess out, that's all. I just want to hear what she thinks, I'm not going to do anything…" I was bluffing and Kate knew it but she said nothing else.

Jess perched on the edge of her chair, leaning forward as I outlined my thoughts and plans. "My initial thinking is that we do a small marketing plan first, a few press releases, sound out the idea, see what the reaction is and, if …" I glanced at Kate who was studiously avoiding having to look my way. "If the take-up is positive, we'll do a sort of trial run, offering our services, not necessarily free but at a reduced rate. Get the wheels in motion, a bit of carrot dangling." I spoke rapidly, trying hard to keep Jess interested as if the sheer force of my conversation would keep her motivated and stop me from dwelling on the fact that I was going behind Mum's back.

Jess's gaze was intense as I was going through my spiel and she looked across the room once or twice at Kate. Keeping her voice low, she asked, "Your Mum is ok with this, isn't she, Charlotte?"

Ignoring the throat clearing from Kate, I nodded. "She'll be fine. Mum will, as you know, take her time over things but she thinks this is a brilliant idea, a step forward for us as a company."

Why did I do that? I mean, I lied.

Jess pulled a face, "I just don't want to do anything that will upset your Mum."

I leant forward and touched her arm, "You won't, she'll be fine. I promised." I realised I'd said the word 'fine' more than once. "But it might be an idea to keep this to yourself for a while, Jess, just until I can sort out a way forward for us. Are you ok with that?" I gazed at her, willing myself not to blink.

"Oh, sure, if you think that's best." She stood and, with another glance at Kate, left the office.

Kate was glaring at me. "What have you done? You've got Jess involved now. Mum'll be furious when she finds out."

"You're such a bloody hypocrite, Kate. When we were talking to Mum, you backed me up, you said it was a good idea. Told Mum how hard I'd worked on it."

"But that's all it is, an idea."

"God, Kate, just once in your life, think outside the bloody box."

She didn't say another word, just shook her head as if I was beyond help.

Anyway, with that I flounced out of the office. I wasn't really angry with Kate, she was merely my whipping boy. The article in *The Times* had been the ammunition I needed to fire the starting gun. So what if Jess was involved?

Just down the road from the office, there's a converted bus selling coffee and cake. I marched down there, ordering latte for Kate and cappuccino for me and two blueberry muffins. Kate doesn't usually eat cake but I'll tell her these will be ok, as they've got fruit in them.

The girls who work there are nice people, neat in their red gingham aprons with their silver nose studs twinkling in the sun. "H'ya, how're you doing?"

"I'm good, thank you."

As I waited for the coffees, I watched them as they found a cardboard tray and chatted to each other. The bus had been painted red and there was an easel propped in the corner offered coffee and teas, all of them with an exclamation mark: *Camomile tea!* £2.90.

I could work here, I could wear red gingham and have a nose stud. Perhaps Mum would buy coffee from me each morning. How hard would that be?

When I got back, I pushed open the door and saw Kate, phone in hand, her cheeks flushed. "I've just spoken to Mum, she's on her way in."

The carboard tray wobbled and the latte fell, splashing its contents all over my black trousers.

Kate looked at me blankly, "You need to wipe that off your trousers, otherwise they'll be stained."

"No shit, Sherlock!" I thumped the tray onto the desk and once again, stormed out of the office. Inside the Ladies, I stood, heart thumping, trousers soaking wet and stinking of coffee. I wanted to go home, to hide, to not to have to face Mum. But I couldn't hide. I mean, I'd started this. Now I have to tell her what I've done.

CHAPTER 11

As soon as she entered the building, Elizabeth was aware of an atmosphere. There were the usual noises: voices, a door closing, a phone ringing but each one sounded stage managed, fake somehow.

The door to Charlotte and Kate's office was open but Elizabeth walked past, wanting to be in her office without having to speak to either of her daughters.

Pushing her door open, Elizabeth pulled a face. Her early morning escape from Gareth, the trip to the hair salon and the visit to the crematorium had already taken up most of the morning and now she had to face Charlotte, deal with her daughter's rebellion. Her stomach grumbled and Elizabeth took off her jacket and switched on the coffee machine.

Waiting for the machine to heat up, she stared out of the window, watching the clouds scudding past. There was something about the aimlessness of the way the shapes shifted, altered. Elizabeth sighed. The coffee machine was ready and she poured herself a mug full.

Switching on her pc and checking her emails, Elizabeth also knew that she had to talk to David Armstrong about his proposal. She put her head in her hands, not wanting to face any of it.

She heard a knock on the door and lifted her head, "Yeah, come in."

Charlotte and Kate appeared and Elizabeth saw the way Kate

tucked herself behind her sister. She also saw the look on Charlotte's face: defiance mixed with apprehension.

"Coffee?" Elizabeth asked before realising that Charlotte was holding a cardboard cup in one hand and a sheaf of papers in the other. Elizabeth's stomach knotted. *Oh God.*

She waved a hand at the chairs in front of her desk, "Will this take long only I've got a lot to do…"

She saw with sadness how Kate sat first and managed to turn her body to one side, away from Charlotte. By contrast, Charlotte sat down and brought her chair forward, directly facing her mother.

"Mum, I need to apologise for something I've done." Charlotte looked at Kate before continuing. "I know what you said and I know I shouldn't have done it but, before you say anything, look at this." She held out a sheet of newspaper and, without a word, Elizabeth took it from her.

Grabbing her glasses, Elizabeth read the article, conscious of both daughters watching her. She took her time before handing the article back to Charlotte. "I hadn't seen that, I didn't know…"

"Mum, this is big, really big."

"Not sure about that, it's a nice thing to see but…"

"Mum! This is fantastic. We're being mentioned in the nationals. Has it happened before? Come on, has it?" Charlotte's voice had risen and she was sitting on the edge of her chair. Elizabeth saw Kate glance at her sister before looking away.

Elizabeth shook her head, "I don't think so."

"Well then, we should make something of this, don't you think?"

To give herself time, Elizabeth sipped at her coffee, feeling Charlotte's eyes on her. "Is this what you're going to tell me, Charlotte? You've already *made* something of this?"

Kate looked at her feet and Charlotte's face was flushed.

Elizabeth sat back. "You'd better tell me what you've done, Charlotte." She glanced at Kate. "I take it you're here as shotgun?"

Kate shook her head, "No, no I'm not. I don't like what Charlotte's done but I thought I should…"

Elizabeth frowned, "Doesn't matter. Go on, Charlotte, I'm waiting."

Charlotte's words rushed from her. "I've asked Jess to work on my project."

"You've done *what?*"

Charlotte squirmed, "Mum, listen, please, just listen. This article, this mention we've had, is big for us. It'll get us noticed. I know it will. People will be thinking of us now when they want to sell their homes. We'll be up there, we won't be just a…"

"Just a what?" Elizabeth's tone was icy.

Charlotte shook her head, "I didn't mean it that way, what I'm trying to say is that this article will open a lot of doors for us. It will, Mum, I know it will."

Elizabeth drained her mug and looked at Charlotte. "What that article has done is to reinforce what I already knew." She spoke slowly and carefully. "We do a good job," she raised her voice, "At. What. We. Do. Do you understand, Charlotte? This article is *because* we've already got a good track record."

"But, Mum, we can build on this. We can afford to diversify, to go with the market trends and this, " Charlotte touched the newspaper article, "this can open even more doors for us."

"Aren't you listening? Doors might be opened because of our reputation. The article is a wonderful way of promoting our business but it's based on what we've already achieved. Charlotte, for God's sake, we can capitalise on this, bring in more customers…"

"Mum, that's what I've been trying to say to you. *Now* is the time for us to offer more, *do* more. Look, me asking Jess, well, ok, maybe I did jump the gun a bit but she's all for it and she'll be perfect. She's got the right mixture of enthusiasm and professionalism…" Charlotte stopped, her eyes on her mother's face.

"I know *my* staff, Charlotte, thank you." Elizabeth felt her heart knocking against her ribcage and she wanted both her daughters to leave. It was as if Charlotte's intensity was sucking the energy from her. She lifted her head, "Who else have you told?"

"No-one, only Jess."

Elizabeth looked at Kate. "You've been very quiet. What d'you think about what Charlotte's done? Do you think I'm missing an opportunity here?"

Kate shifted and shook her head. "I don't agree with Charlotte telling Jess," and for the first time since she'd entered Elizabeth's office, she glanced at her sister, "but…"

"But what?"

"I do think the project has some merit and it might be something for us to consider in the future…"

"Oh, for Christ's sake! You bring new meaning to sitting on the fucking fence, Kate." Charlotte's hair swung wildly as she turned to look at her sister. "One minute you're backing me and the next …oh, what's the point."

"Charlotte, that's enough. You can't steamroller this through by bullying your sister or trying to coerce me."

"I'm not! I just don't understand why you're so dead against this. Look, we won't be the first company to offer this service. It's already happening, all sorts of people are offering what I want us to do. Let's be one of the first to do it, to tell people we'll take the headache out of moving: the utilities, the internet connection, the getting rid of unwanted furniture. *Mum*, come on, this is a chance for us to be right at the forefront."

Elizabeth thought about the magazine in the hair salon, the

vacuous smiles of the couple she'd seen, their home awash with equipment and marble floors and a large piano in a corner of a room. The image irritated her and she shook her head. "No, it's not right for the company. We, *I've* built this up from nothing, from scavenging from furniture," Elizabeth was aware of the exasperation that flashed across Charlotte's face and she ignored it, "and I'm proud of the reputation we have. We offer a good service with professional standards and that's what we're known for. I don't *want* to show people with too much money how to manage house moves. For God's sake, Charlotte, you knew my thoughts on this and you've deliberately gone against my wishes. You'll have to tell Jess you've made a mistake. This isn't going to happen."

Elizabeth sat back and looked at her daughters.

Kate was chewing the ends of her hair and Charlotte's face was flushed with anger.

"Mum?" Charlotte spoke quickly. "Will you at least give this some thought? You've dismissed it out of hand and I don't think…"

"Right now, Charlotte, I'm not interested in what you think or don't think. You've adopted a high-handed approach to something I've not agreed to and in doing so, you've coerced a member of staff, *my* staff, to go along with your proposal and I bet you've told Jess not to mention it to me. You have, haven't you?"

Charlotte nodded and lowered her head.

"I've had enough, Charlotte. I'm bitterly disappointed in you and I don't want to think about this any longer. I've wasted enough time as it is. I've got a lot to do today and I also need to talk to David Armstrong." She waited, thinking Charlotte would react to Armstrong's name but her daughter kept her head down. Elizabeth continued, "*That* is a contract which will be viable for this company, it will mean steady work for all of us. Ellis and

James are a reputable company and it will maintain our profile…"

Charlotte lifted her head, "*Maintain?* That's the problem, Mum. We shouldn't be concentrating on maintaining, we should be lifting our profile. We should be diversifying, keeping up with the trends and instead, what are we doing? Treading water."

Her tone was bitter and Elizabeth flinched, "You forget, Charlotte that is my company and I make the decisions…"

"Your decisions are wrong, plain wrong! What, you want us to concentrate our efforts on…*retirement* villages?"

Elizabeth kept her voice steady. "And what's wrong with retirement villages? People are living longer, they expect the same quality in their homes as everyone else. Why shouldn't they have a beautiful home? What's wrong with that? Go on, Charlotte, you tell me."

"Because they're for *geriatrics* – we don't want to be thought of as a company who specialises in geriatrics, that's why!" Charlotte's voice was a shriek.

"Really, and have you forgotten that I too could be put under the banner of a geriatric? Has that occurred to you? Do you think of *me* as a geriatric?"

Elizabeth saw the way Kate flinched as the confrontation between her mother and her sister intensified. She saw Kate open her mouth as if to speak but then Kate closed her mouth. *Lost her nerve.*

Charlotte stood, her chair rocked behind her, "You're keeping this company back. I hate to say it but it's the truth. You're stuck in the same groove, won't take opportunities when they come our way. This is a brilliant opportunity for us and what are you doing? Nothing. It's the same old, same old for you, Mum. If we don't do this, others will and we'll have lost our chance."

Elizabeth stood and spoke quietly, "I think you should leave, Charlotte. I won't be spoken to in that way by anyone and I won't tolerate it from my own daughter. I'll give you time to calm down and I hope that you apologise for your behaviour today. Not just the outburst, but the way you've handled this, gone behind my back. You've overstepped the mark."

Kate stood too and stared at her feet, "Sorry, Mum," her words were muffled.

"Sorry for what, Kate? You neither defended me nor backed your sister."

Charlotte nodded and left Elizabeth's office. Kate hovered for a second and, with an anguished look at her mother, she too left the office.

Elizabeth slumped back into her chair and closed her eyes. *Oh Christ.*

She'd waited until she'd eaten a sandwich before ringing Armstrong, unwilling to talk to him on an empty stomach. Her head was stuffed with Charlotte's words and the whole time she listened to David's conversation, she knew she wasn't paying proper attention. "So, Elizabeth, what d'you think? If I get a contract sent over, do you think you'll sign it or do you think you and I should meet up again, just to make sure we're on the same page…"

There it was, that odd tone in his voice and Elizabeth forced herself to concentrate, "Maybe once I've seen the contract, that will be the time to meet again. You know, in case there are any issues."

"Oh, I'm sure there won't be any *issues*. It's a straightforward enough contract. I'm sure you've seen enough of those over the years."

Was that it? Was he making a veiled reference to her age? Was that what was bothering her each time she spoke to him or was that paranoia?

Elizabeth gave a non-committal laugh. "Well, yes, I've seen a few in my time but I treat each one with the same amount of respect." She winced, *Oh, sod it. I sound pompous and up myself.*

"Of course, Elizabeth. I meant no harm." His tone had reverted to one of politeness and they agreed that, if there was anything Elizabeth needed to discuss, they'd arrange a meeting.

The afternoon dragged on, various members of staff knocking on Elizabeth's door to give her updates on contracts already underway, though each time a hand knocked on her door, Elizabeth wondered if it was Charlotte's hand. The phone rang and emails appeared and she worked her way through them all, knowing that she wasn't operating on all cylinders. Instead, she felt the weight of her problems: Gareth, the argument with Charlotte, the ache in her spine.

She was in the middle of replying to an email from a customer asking for a quote when Elizabeth stopped typing and looked at the screen, not seeing what she'd written. Outside a door closed and she heard laughter, a woman's laughter. Elizabeth took a deep breath and thought about what she'd done that day. Had anything brought her happiness? When had she last felt happy?

She shifted in her chair, looking away from her laptop. But was that a stupid question? What did it *mean* to be happy? Free of worry, having a sense of excitement? Finding joy in something or someone? If that was what being happy was all about, then she was unhappy. Was it that simple? No, it can't be.

She thought about when the children were young, how uncomplicated their lives were and, by contrast, her life then had been full of anxiety. She thought about the way she'd always been on edge, worrying about them, about their safety, whether they were getting enough sleep and whether she was being a good mother. She thought too about the times she'd been in her van, ricocheting around the countryside, the furniture she'd found, her delight each time she'd sourced something she knew she could restore. She thought of the way she'd left the house each morning, free of the demands of her children, happy to be on her own, doing what she loved best.

She *had* been happy, she'd loved that van, its smell of damp and oil, the rust in the floor. She'd loved what it had represented to her, freedom.

There must have been other happy times surely? She'd loved Chris she loved her children and her grandchildren, they'd brought happiness to her. But what was the difference?

Elizabeth stood, rubbing the small of her back. What the hell was the matter with her? All this angst. She walked to the window and stood looking out. The clouds had gone now and the sky was a perfect blue. The question wouldn't leave her. Should she have been *aware* of the times she was happy? Made a note of what time, where it was? Is that what you did? Clear a space in your life: *Today between the hours of 10 and 12, I was happy.* She should have treasured those times, enjoyed them more. Was that what it was? Being in the moment? Why wasn't that taught at school? Why did no-one ever say, "Treasure this, this moment when you're truly happy. Write it down, keep a note."

"Oh, God, I'm knackered."

She returned to her desk, completed the email and made a few notes for the following day, writing them on yellow *Post-it* notes and sticking them to her laptop, Charlotte had been on her case about keeping everything on her phone but Elizabeth didn't see any reason to change what she'd always done.

Glancing at her watch, she saw that it was almost 5.30. Feeling a strange sense of wanting to defend herself, she muttered, "Sod it, I'm leaving now. I've had enough."

Walking towards the girls' office door, Elizabeth took a breath and stepped inside.

Addressing her remarks to the space between Kate and Charlotte's desks, Elizabeth said briskly, "I'm going home. I'll be in at the usual time in the morning. Goodnight." She left without waiting for a response.

As soon as she left the building, Elizabeth paused. How childish was that? She half-turned, thinking she should return, go into the girls' office to…what? Apologise? She'd been abrupt but…No. She'd been doing far too much thinking, far too much. Instead, Elizabeth walked towards her car.

The car, with its leather upholstery and gleaming dashboard relaxed her and she felt in control again. She turned the radio on, thinking she should listen to the news but then, shaking her head, she found a music station and sang along to *Sweet Caroline*. As she sang, she thought about her house, the fact that it would be empty, hers again.

When she reached her house, she frowned. Gareth's car was still in the driveway. "What the…"

Maybe he couldn't get his car to start.

Opening the front door, Elizabeth could hear voices, one of which was Gareth's. She heard him laugh, she heard the sound of glasses being *clinked* together. She heard whoever was in her kitchen say, "Cheers."

"Gareth?"

Why was Gareth still here and who was he with?

CHAPTER 12

Even after Mum had done her visiting Royalty act, dipping her head as she left, I knew my anger hadn't disappeared. It was still with me, bubbling away. I wanted to run after Mum and scream at her, tell her what a mistake she was making, how stubborn she was being, how, because of her *bloody-mindedness* we could miss out on a potentially lucrative market.

But I didn't run after her. Instead, I watched from the window, seeing the way she walked, upright, as if she knew I was looking at her. Not seventy-three but a middle-aged woman, a *professional* woman.

Afterwards, Kate had a go at me, accusing me of swearing at her but I didn't care, she *always* sits on the fucking fence. She's like Mum, not wanting to rock the boat, both of them thinking that, as long as our normal contracts keep coming in, why change things? Because we bloody well should, that's why. The business we're in isn't static, it keeps moving, evolving and we should do too.

After watching Mum drive away, I emailed the staff, all of them. All except Kate.

I said there was something I needed to discuss with them and would they come in a bit earlier tomorrow. I said it wouldn't take long.

When you tell people you've had a rubbish night, that you tossed and turned and didn't get a wink of sleep, why do they insist on saying that you probably slept more than you think? That's crap. I know it's crap because I kept looking at the clock radio. What's the point of that? Why do I do that? Why does *anyone* do that? All it does is tell you that four minutes have gone since you last looked. Jon either slept through it all or did a good impression of someone asleep. Or maybe he was awake and just didn't want to talk.

I'd made a mistake, I miscalculated. I'd told Jon what had happened, what Mum had said and then I told him I'd asked the staff to come in early.

"Why?"

"Why what?" I knew what he was asking.

"Why did you do that? What are you up to, Charlie?!

"Nothing!"

"Cut the crap, Charlie. What's this about?"

We were in the kitchen, the girls had gone to bed and I picked up a cloth and began polishing the taps, not wanting to answer Jon, not wanting to tell him what I'd done. There, in the office, it felt I had no option than to call the staff in, to tell them what was going on. But now, here, in my home, it felt wrong. I felt wrong.

Jon moved towards me and took the cloth from my hand. "Charlie, what have you done?" He gripped my shoulders and steered me towards a chair. "Sit down. Does your Mum know you've asked everyone to come in early?"

I shook my head, "No, she doesn't."

Jon sat opposite me and spoke softly. "You can't go behind your mother's back, Charlie. That's not fair, it's not right. It's *her* workforce, she should know what you're doing, what you're saying to the people whose wages she's paying."

"Oh, for Christ's sake, Jon. You don't know anything."

Jon's eyes widened. "Don't I? Let me tell you what I do know.

Your Mum's company is hers. She started the company from bugger all." Jon shook his head. "*Christal!* She gave you and Kate a job and you, you in particular, Charlie, owe her a lot. Have you *forgotten?* Are you so far up your own backside, hell bent on having your own way, that you can't or won't remember what she did for you? Jesus Christ, Charlie, you're going to *destroy* your mother, there's no other word for it."

"That's bullshit, sheer bullshit! I've tried, you've no idea how hard I've tried to get Mum to see sense. We're just treading water – we can do so much more and she won't bloody see it. God, Jon, I wish you'd understand a bit more about what I'm trying to do! This company is capable of so much more and Mum can't or won't see it. She's getting too old for the job…" The second I said it, I knew what Jon's reaction would be.

"No! Jesus, Charlie. Please tell me you haven't said that to your mother. Tell me you haven't said she's too old."

Jon's voice was high with anger and I tried desperately to soften what I'd said. "No, I didn't…"

"Charlie! For fuck's sake…Your mother does a phenomenal job. She's built up a company from scratch and her attitude towards work has *made* the company what it is. What the *hell* are you doing to her?" He slumped back in the chair. I heard his sigh of exasperation.

"For God's sake, Jon, just because your own mother acts as if she's half-way into her grave, you put my mother up on some bloody pedestal."

Jon stood and looked at me, "Sometimes I don't think I know you very well."

With that, he turned and left the kitchen. I wanted to go after him to say I was sorry, I shouldn't have said that about his mother but instead I didn't move an inch.

I don't know how long I sat in the kitchen. I listened to the random sounds of the night: a car driving past, a dog barking, the sound of Jon getting into bed. Everything around me felt normal.

When I got into bed, Jon was lying on his side and didn't say a word. I went along with that. I wanted to sleep, to get the day over.

But I couldn't sleep. I felt miserable and I wanted to ring Mum to apologise and I wanted to turn over, to touch Jon's arm but I couldn't do that either. Jon and I never talk about that thing that happened. It's not a conscious decision: we simply never mention it. It would be wrong to say I'd forgotten about it – perhaps I'd airbrushed it out.

Now though, in the middle of the night, that part of my life, the part that no-one ever mentions, somehow re-emerged as if a searchlight had found it in the gloom.

I was in university, taking English literature – or that had been the plan. I'd gone partly because I didn't know what else to do, not so much aimless as completely clueless. I'd gone to Durham thinking that leaving home was one thing, but going to the other side of the country, well that might work in terms of putting distance between me and what was familiar and what was new, but otherwise it made no sense. Mum had been worried that I'd end up drifting, rudderless but I didn't listen. What did I care? She talked endlessly about having a plan, a focus and none of it meant a thing. It was Dad who suggested it, like an escape route. So I went. My grades were ok and I'd always loved *Middlemarch* and I don't know, just…because.

Anyway, everyone there seemed positive, hell bent on having the time of their lives and for ages, *months* I felt as if I'd wandered into a party without knowing a soul. It never occurred to me that I was sending out the wrong signals – you know, those *piss off*, *leave me alone*, sort of signals. Anyway, I went to the lectures, wrote things in a notebook, but none of it made any sense. I felt more and more dislocated. And then I met Richie, the type of boy, the type of man, who didn't doubt his place in the world. I'd never come across that before, that inbuilt assurance. Richie said I intrigued him – what the hell did that mean? He spoke with a London accent, his hair was too long and never very clean. His clothes had once been expensive, only he wore them as if he'd picked them up from where he'd thrown them the night before – and I was right about that. And then, for some reason, he pursued me, *cornered* me. Is that the right word? It sounds as if I had no choice, no will of my own, that I allowed myself to be caught. Maybe that was about right too. University was just somewhere else to be, it didn't really *matter*. Richie told me he was at Durham because his father had insisted. He spoke vaguely about allowances, about family money; we didn't go to lectures, we spent most of our time in Richie's bed. I got used to the dirty sheets, the fetid, unaired smell in his room. The slovenliness of it all sort of felt right. I mean, I never liked him, not really. But being with him, ignoring everything else, meant that I didn't have to think, didn't have to make decisions. I still didn't want to make decisions when I realised I was pregnant. The pregnancy lurked in my head. It took on a shape, dark, strange and I pushed it away although I knew I'd have to do something about it. I didn't tell Richie, there was no point. Instead, I phoned Mum.

All she said was, "I'm coming up." She drove through the night and I waited for her. I don't know what was going through my head. But then she was there, tired, her face pale.

I never knew what she said to the university but when Mum and I went home, she said I could defer. At first I wanted to say that I didn't want to go back, it hadn't worked out but, looking at Mum, her hands steady on the wheel, I kept quiet.

She sorted it, all of it. She'd told Dad but they didn't tell Kate or Gareth. Mum and I spoke to the GP, Mum doing all the talking. I remember the doctor looking at me and nodding, like he'd heard it all before – of course he had. Mum drove me to a discreet clinic, no plaque on the door, just shiny blue paintwork. Inside the carpet was thick, the walls pale cream.

I sat there while Mum registered me. Neither of us spoke although Mum held my hand until my name was called. We both stood and Mum whispered, "It'll be fine, I promise." She told me she'd be waiting and I followed a woman in a white uniform.

When we drove home, I remember looking at women and girls on the pavement, standing at a bus stop, coming out of shops. I looked at their faces trying to work out if they'd ever done the same thing. Would it show? But I could read nothing from their expressions and I'm not sure now what I was looking for.

Mum told Gareth and Kate that I'd had a minor operation, the tone of her voice implying that it was best if they didn't ask any questions. Dad simply accepted that I'd find my way again.

I returned to Durham, Mum driving me again and it was understood that I was going back and I'd have to work hard. We stopped at a service area, sitting in an anonymous café to eat. Mum was grumbling about the packaging of the tuna sandwiches we'd bought. "Why are these things so bloody difficult to open?"

Then she stopped tearing at the package and looked at me. "There was someone. His name was Adrian. Your Dad doesn't know."

The words came out in a rush and I gave up all pretence of eating. "*What?* When? Where did you meet him?"

Mum shook her head, "It doesn't matter now. It was a long time ago."

"Mum, you can't…" I wasn't sure what I wanted to say: did I want to know?

"Why are you telling me this now?"

Mum sighed, "Not sure really." She straightened. "Forget I said anything. It's water under the bridge."

And that was it, she wouldn't say another word. For a long time, I wondered why she'd told me. Was it some sort of female solidarity thing, or wanting me to know that, even though she's my Mum, she too had made a mistake over a man? Whatever the reason, it stayed with me. I looked at her differently. Perhaps I still do.

Just then Jon muttered something but I couldn't make out what it was. He was sleeping, his breathing steady, even. That was the one thing I never told Jon, Mum's confession or admission. It hadn't been mentioned again, not by me nor by Mum.

Back at Durham I felt guilty about the abortion, guilty about what Mum had done for me so I threw myself into university life. I avoided Richie although I think it fair to say that he avoided me. Didn't matter. I got a 2:1 which pleased Mum and Dad and that was enough.

At home I floated, not getting on with anything, not knowing what to do with my degree. I had some half-baked thought that, having graduated, things would slot into place. Then, one weekend, Mum suggested that I join her in the company. I didn't want to, had some woolly views on nepotism, about wanting to do things under my own steam, but what those things were, I had no idea. And the thing was, I *owed* Mum. She wanted to sort me out, again. I said I'd do it for a while. I wanted to please her and perhaps let her think that I was ok, that I wasn't totally useless. I know on the first day I went in to work with Mum, I felt superior. I didn't think the job was for me.

And here I am, still there. At the start I admit it felt as if I was repaying Mum, but that's not the case anymore. I've earned my place there and I *know* the company can do more, the workforce can do more but, with Mum at the helm, we're not making progress. None.

I turned, bunching the pillow under my head. Oh, God, let me sleep. I resented Jon for sleeping and thought about digging my elbow into his side.

I tried again, squeezing my eyes shut, feeling the muscles in my face tighten with the effort. I remember reading an article about relaxing your body, starting with your feet, making a conscious effort to let go of any tension. I tried that but then I had cramp so I had to change position.

I thought instead about what I'd say to the staff tomorrow, *today?* I knew they'd wonder why I'd asked them to come in early. I'd suggested the boardroom. *Boardroom!* It's just a funny room next to the kitchen where people go to try out paint colours on the walls. The room is clean but the walls are covered in daubs of paint: *Arctic Blue, Daffodil Yellow* and my all-time favourite: *Garrison Green.* Somehow, even with the uneven lines and blobs of colour, the room is a good place to be.

Oh God. Once more I turned, feeling that if I kept my eye shut, I had half a chance of getting to sleep. This time though, I saw Mum, hair all done, back straight and wearing her red suit. She called it her *kick-ass* suit. She'd told me once that, when she wore that suit, when she drove her red BMW, people saw her coming. Truth is, I've always loved that about her. Her sheer *in your face* attitude. I've never been able to do that. Ok, I can act tough, "talk the talk," but I'm not confident, I don't have that attitude to life that Mum has. Here's the thing: I would give *anything* to be like Mum. She had an idea, a plan and even with three kids and no money, she made that plan work. Kate and I pull faces when she witters on about how she started. God knows how many times we've heard that story of the rag and bone man, the driving around in a knackered old van. We tease her, grumble about hearing the story over and over but the truth is, Mum knew what she wanted and she went for it. I've never had that, that vision, that drive. All I did was bugger about, making a mess of my life and now, whatever I've achieved, is because of Mum, what she gave me. And what have I done to repay her? Was Jon right? Am I trying to destroy Mum? Or was I only doing what Mum did? Seeing an opportunity and going for it? Maybe, but what Mum did doesn't compare with what I'm trying to do. How can it?

I opened my eyes not wanting to think any more. I picked up my phone, wincing when I saw the time: 3.22. I scrawled through text messages. One from Mum, months old. *Would the four of you like to come for lunch on Sunday? There will be wine!!.*

I looked at the words, the exclamation marks. We all loved going to lunch with Mum. We all love her. But, at the same time, there was something else lurking in the back of my brain. Mum's had her day. It's someone else's turn and that someone is me. I know, I know…how can I *feel* like that after everything she'd done for me? I've asked myself that a million times and it doesn't make any difference. I want her job. And that's not the worst part. Mum's done the slog, the hard in part building the company up. I just want to take it from her.

I put the phone back and I whimpered, hoping to wake Jon so he could hold me, tell me that it would be all right, that he had my back. At the same time though, there's something about lying still in the middle of the night, feeling as if you're the only person awake in the whole world, that crystallises your thoughts and emotions. It all gets stripped back. I have to make this right. I have to do it.

Once again, I turned over, looking at the back of Jon's head, seeing the shape of a 50 pence piece where his hair has thinned and his scalp shows through. He denies it but it's there.

I must have slept because the next time I looked at the clock radio, it was 6:10 and I needed to get started. I had to be the first one to arrive at the office that day. It had to be me.

CHAPTER 13

Elizabeth walked into her kitchen, both apprehensive and furious at the same. *Why was Gareth still here? And who was he with?*

Gareth was sitting at the table, two men flanking him, Elizabeth's home laptop in front of all three. Their heads were close together as they looked at something on the screen.

"Gareth!"

Gareth's head jerked, his face flushed. "Mum, I didn't hear you come in."

"I gathered that." Elizabeth felt unnerved. Neither of the two men sitting alongside Gareth looked at her, their gazes still fixed on whatever was on the screen. "Would you like to tell me what's going on? Why are you still here and who are your guests?" Her tone was cold. She was aware that her breathing had quickened and, in an attempt to disguise it, she took a few deep breaths.

"Oh, yeah, right." Gareth half-rose and he touched the shoulder of the man on his right. "Mum, this is Myles, he and I…" he glanced at the other man. "Well, we've known each other for a while."

Myles remained seated and put his hand out, "It's Myles with a 'y'." His tone was one of amusement and Elizabeth ignored his outstretched hand.

Gareth nodded to the other man, "And this is Sean." The second man stood and smiled at her. "Hello," he said, keeping both hands at his sides.

Not liking the sensation of feeling like an outsider in her own home, Elizabeth stepped back. "Gareth, a word please."

He pulled a face, "Now? We're in the middle of…"

"Now! Gareth, right now."

She didn't catch what Myles said to Gareth, his voice was low, but she saw the frown that crossed Gareth's face and she waited until her son had moved away from the two men.

"In the living room, please."

When they were both in the living room, she closed the door and she faced Gareth, keeping her hands by her sides.

"What are you *doing?* Who are those men and *why*, for God's sake, why are they in *my* house and why the hell are you still here?"

"Mum, listen, please, just listen."

"*No!* I bloody well won't listen! Gareth, we had a deal, you promised you'd leave this morning. You told me that, when I got home today, you would have left. And you haven't, in fact you've brought…who are these men? Why the hell are they here, Gareth, you gave me your *word!*"

"I know, but Mum, listen, please, just listen. Look, stay here, don't move…"

Elizabeth watched as Gareth opened the door and returned to the kitchen. There was a murmur of voices and she had a peculiar sense of waiting for a play to begin. She shook her head. She *hated* the thought of the two men, whatever their names were, the pair of them sitting in her kitchen, as if *they* and not her, had a right to be there. Her fists were clenched as Gareth returned. In his hand he held a sheaf of papers.

"Here, look at these." He thrust them at her but Elizabeth kept her hands still.

"What? What is this all about?" Her voice was shrill. Whatever Gareth was showing her, she didn't want to look, she didn't want to get involved, she wanted the three of them out of her house.

"Mum, just look, please. Just look at them, that's all I'm asking."

"No, it's not all you're asking, Gareth. For God's sake, just tell me. Let's get this over with."

"Sit down, Mum. Have a proper look at them." Gareth touched her shoulder and she flinched.

"I don't *want* to sit down. Tell me you're leaving and taking those two men with you. Please, Gareth, just leave." Elizabeth struggled to keep the tears out of her voice. *Just go, for Christ's sake. Please, just go.*

Gareth stood in front of her, his eyes mournful and dark. "This could be the thing that will turn my life around, Mum. I really think it could."

Oh my God.

"What are you talking about?"

"Mum, please, just look. Please." He held the sheaf of papers in front of him.

In silence Elizabeth took them from him and, aware that Gareth was watching her, sank down into an armchair.

Gareth moved, stood behind the chair and Elizabeth could hear his breathing as she flicked through the sheets of paper. Each one had a photo of a dilapidated barn or rundown cottage, the buildings set amidst fields of vines or rows of scabby bushes. Not wanting to look at any of them in detail, Elizabeth rattled the page. "What the hell is this? What are you showing me? You want to be a *farmer* now, is that it?"

"No, no, I don't. Mum, look at them properly. They're all in Italy, near Umbria."

Elizabeth shook her head. "Gareth, I'm beginning to feel I'm lost in some sort of parallel universe. What the bloody hell are you talking about? And for Christ's sake, stop loitering behind me. It's driving me mad."

Gareth moved and his tone was low, soothing, as if he was talking to a child. Elizabeth wanted to hit him.

"Mum, the authorities in Italy, this area in the photos, they're asking for people to buy these buildings." His fingers touched the papers in Elizabeth's hand. "And the best thing is, Mum, they only want one euro each! One euro! I mean, that's got to be..."

Feeling disadvantaged by sitting down, Elizabeth stood and shoved the papers at Gareth. "That's got to be, what? A con, a disaster, a scheme to pull in idiots, those with no brains or acumen? Tell me, Gareth, where do you fit in? For Christ's sake, you don't have a pot to piss in right now. Where are you going to find the money?"

"No, Mum, you're not listening. They only want one euro for them as the authorities want to bring people into the area, it's under populated, youngsters won't stay there, they want to move away so the town mayor or, or..." Gareth glanced at the papers as if searching for the answer. "or whatever his title is, wants to attract people into the area. These properties need rebuilding so they hope that by offering them at stupid money, people will stay and live in the area."

Elizabeth looked at her son, hearing the way his words tumbled from him, as if by speaking quickly, she wouldn't hear the flaws in his argument. Or did he speak like that so *he* wouldn't hear them either?

"Oh, Gareth." She shook her head, "When are you going to grow up?"

"*Mum*, that's what I'm saying to you. This is my opportunity, I can do this. It's got my name written all over it. Mum, please, this is what I've been waiting for."

"Houses for one euro each? Is that it? And then what? You or other people like you, rebuild them, making them habitable and what happens then? Do you stay there or do you sell them on hoping to make a profit, have I missed anything out?"

Gareth nodded, "That's it, that's it, Mum. Sean and Myles came up with the idea and we've been talking it through and we think we should go out there and…"

"Where? Out to Italy?"

Gareth nodded again, "Yeah, we think we should take a look, check out what's available…"

Elizabeth moved over to the window. "So, let me get this right, with the money I've given you, Gareth, the money that was purely intended to keep a roof over your head, you plan to fly out to Italy to look at these rundown properties?"

"Well, yes. I thought I could use the money for the flights and somewhere to stay when I'm over there."

"I see. And where do the Chuckle Brothers come into it?" Elizabeth jerked her head in the direction of the kitchen.

"Um, well, they want to come too and we thought…"

"You thought what? Oh, I think I know the answer to that. You thought and those two obviously thought it too, that as your mother has given you £1,000, that would come in handy for a trip to Italy on some bloody, wild fucking *goose chase!*" Inwardly she flinched, knowing her use of expletives had increased.

Her voice had risen and Gareth stepped forward, his hand out as if to silence her. Elizabeth glared at him. "Don't you dare, don't you bloody dare! This is my house and I'll do what I want in it. And, Gareth, right now, I want you and those two morons in there to go. D'you hear me? Out, all of you. Right now."

"Mum, please…"

She looked at him. "Go, I don't want you or those two in my house. That's it, Gareth. Just go."

"Um, well, the thing is, Mum, I thought, to be honest…"

She looked at him. "What did you think, Gareth? That I'd allow my home to be used as a nice, clean place for the three musketeers to sleep in? Is that it? Is that what you told those two? Oh, Christ, I don't believe you, I don't bloody believe you." Just then something occurred to her, "You came here with those two spongers to sound me out, didn't you? Oh, my God, you thought I'd invest, you did, didn't you? Jesus Christ, Gareth, you thought I'd *bankroll* your stupid idea. Oh, my God, I'm right, aren't I?"

She thought for a moment that he'd argue but then Gareth turned and silently left the room. Elizabeth stood close to the door, listening to the murmurs coming from the kitchen. She heard a harsh laugh and her stomach knotted in anger. Then footsteps ran up the stairs, she heard the sound of a toilet being flushed, a door opening, footsteps on a squeaky floorboard. Elizabeth kept still, one hand to her throat. Someone ran down the stairs and something bashed up against the banister.

A voice called, "Come on." It wasn't Gareth's voice and then she heard the sound of the front door closing. Elizabeth counted to ten and walked out of the room. In the kitchen, the table held three crystal tumblers, remnants of whisky coloured the bottom of each glass. Her laptop was still there and Elizabeth realised she half expected it would have been taken.

Outside a car started, then the engine spluttered and died. She held her breath, waiting for it to start up again. It did and then there was the sound of the car moving away. Elizabeth opened the back door and, positioning her chair near the doorway, she sat down facing her garden, not understanding what she was looking at.

She had no idea how long she'd been sitting there but, at one point, she'd poured herself a glass of wine. She looked at the table, at the three tumblers left there and, hating the sight of them, the smeary marks of fingers, she hand-washed each glass, allowing the water to run freely, scalding her hands. Then she carefully dried each glass before replacing all of them back into the cupboard. Feeling chilled, she closed the back door and sipped at her wine.

How had it all come to this? Was it because Chris was gone? In the weeks following the funeral, she'd not know what to do, how to do *anything*, and it had been her children even Gareth, who'd stabilised her. They'd taken it in turns to sit drinking endless cups of tea, putting plates of food in front of her, urging her to shower, to get dressed. With their help, she'd got through it.

When Elizabeth returned to work, the entire workforce welcomed her back. Some were hesitant and nervous but she knew from their stumbling phrases of sympathy, that they were glad she'd returned. She knew she wanted to get back to work, in her office, her company, where she was once again in charge. Weeks later, taking a call from a company she'd worked with many times, attention wandering a little, Elizabeth gazed out of her window and, out of the blue, she realised she'd not really understood how grief had affected her children. She'd hugged them and they'd cried but had she really grasped what their father's death might mean? As the voice droned on about the Scandinavian influence on colours, Elizabeth knew that her grief had swallowed her up, leaving no room for anything else. Only later had things shifted, recalibrated. Chris's name was spoken, stories were repeated, jokes shared and his loss became part of their lives. But at the time, she'd been too caught up in her own desolation.

What she *had* understood though, was that Chris's death had tightened the bond between Elizabeth and her daughters. Gareth, initially supportive and helpful, faded away as he'd always done, while the girls grew closer to their mother. She'd thought, more than once, what a great team they were.

But now that was all gone. Charlotte was hell bent on

destroying it and Kate, as ever, Kate the people pleaser, vacillated between wanting to support her mother and her sister, unable to make up her mind. And as for Gareth…Elizabeth pulled a face and drained her glass. She wanted to get changed, wanted something to eat and wanted to rid herself of any thought of Gareth.

When she reached the landing, she frowned. Her bedroom door was wide open and she knew she'd closed it before leaving that morning.

She hadn't seen Gareth and his friends leave, what if one of them was still here, lurking? Would Gareth have allowed that? She didn't know the answer to that. With her mouth dry, Elizabeth walked softly int her bedroom and then stopped.

All the drawers in the tall chest of drawers, were wide open. Her underwear had been pulled out, lace bras and pants were draped over the edges of the unit. There was something about the way her underwear looked as if it had been *displayed*. The sight horrified and distressed her. *Who?*

She almost ran to the chest of drawers, scrabbling to get her underwear back, to hide it. She had no idea if anything had been taken, the thought repulsed her and she didn't want to know. Once everything had been jammed in, she sat on the edge of the bed breathing hard. *Christ.*

Who had done that? One of those two men? It couldn't have been Gareth, surely he wouldn't have done that, would he?

Facing her dressing table, Elizabeth frowned. The top of the unit looked different and she wasn't sure why. She kept a pretty Limoges dish that Chris had found for her in a French flea market, on the top and it looked as if it had been moved. Living on her own, Elizabeth knew that meant she had an almost photographic visual of her house, where everything was, or should be. The dish had been moved.

She kept very little in it: odd pairs of inexpensive earrings, a few rings that she'd found in various junk shops when she first started scavenging, two necklaces that she'd been meaning to get repaired, a silver brooch, the word *Mum* outlined in paste diamonds, something the girls had bought for her years ago. Nothing of any value.

A sickening thought made her open the smaller top drawer. She kept her jewellery in that drawer. All of it: the pearls Chris had bought for their 30th wedding anniversary, the diamond stud earrings he'd presented her with one Christmas, the sapphire ring he'd insisted she had when the company celebrated its first birthday. Other pieces she'd treasured: amber earrings, a jade bangle, an emerald eternity ring that needed a stone. It had all been in a black leather jewellery roll. Gone, it had all gone.

Knowing it was futile, Elizabeth grabbed at every drawer in the dressing table, yanked each one open, her hands scrabbling through the contents. She upended the drawers, shaking out half-used pots of hand cream, old diaries, boxes of paracetamol, a box of *Lemsip* with two sachets left inside. Once everything was on the floor, she dropped to her knees and pushed the items around, searching for the jewellery roll. It wasn't there. Of course it wasn't there.

She rested her back against the bed and looked at the bedroom floor. The assorted detritus appeared to mock her. Had Gareth done this? Had he stolen from her? Had he been so furious because she hadn't taken him or his half-baked plan seriously, that he'd taken her jewellery? Had he? Was he going to sell it? Elizabeth felt a pain in her rib cage and she rubbed at her chest. *Take a breath, take a breath.*

She had Gareth's number, she could ring him, she could ask him if he'd stolen her jewellery. She could do that.

What if he hadn't? What if it had been one of those men, that reptilian Myles who'd stolen her jewellery? Somehow and knowing it was skewed thinking, Elizabeth understood that she'd rather know that Myles had taken it than her son. Did it matter who'd stolen it? It had been stolen. Yet, somehow, it did matter.

Her phone was downstairs and Elizabeth made her way to the kitchen. Picking up her phone she hesitated. Police? And say what? That it might have been her son who'd stolen her jewellery and it might not have been. Charlotte? Kate? What would they do? Relations were so bad and Charlotte in particular might view this disaster as yet more proof that she, Elizabeth, couldn't cope on her own.

Elizabeth held the phone to her chest and she paced the floor, not knowing what to do. Amongst the indecision was outrage that someone had gone into her bedroom and not only stolen her jewellery, but had displayed her underwear in that obscene fashion. That had been deliberate, she was sure of it. And with that realisation, she knew it hadn't been Gareth. He would never have done that.

That had the effect of calming her and she dialled Gareth's number. It went straight to voice mail. *Now what?* She had no idea where he was and, because of her refusal to help him, he might be ignoring her.

Elizabeth felt tears on her cheeks and whispered, "I don't know what to do."

The weight of her *aloneness* felt heavy and, putting the phone down, she sat in a chair in her kitchen and wept.

CHAPTER 14

Part of me wanted to stay at home, to be with my daughters, put things right with Jon and I and part of me was itching to start the whole process of sounding out the workforce – no, is that right? Part of me was itching to ease Mum out. That's something I don't want to voice. I can't. Who can I tell? Jon won't listen to me. God, he won't even *talk* to me. This morning was all icy politeness done for the girls' sakes, presenting a united front. I left before they all went off to school and, for the first time, I wanted to tell Jon that his job was a *doddle* compared to mine. I didn't because, well, what was the point?

The drive into work took no time, no holdups, no excess traffic, even the lights were in my favour and I pulled into the car park aware that I was the first one to arrive. Even without any sleep I was buzzing with – well, who knows, excitement, nerves? Oh, God, the questions going through my head: would there be a backlash, would the workforce walk away without agreeing to anything I said to them?

I sat, looking at the office building, wondering what I was doing when a car parked next to mine. It was Jess's car and she waved when she saw me. I waved back and we both got out and went inside.

The Board room, ha, what a stupid, bloody name. Mum always said it with emphasis, mocking the word, its implications, but sitting there, facing everyone as they walked in, I wished I'd suggested somewhere else. With its messy blobs of colour, the room looked like a nursery and we were toddlers waiting for the first game of the day.

The staff meandered in, some clutching cardboard mugs of coffee, some with bags or rucksacks over their shoulders. They yawned, smiled at me, their expressions showing mild curiosity. Jess sat near the front where I'd asked her to sit, needing her support, I guess. Back-up. Right then, all I wanted was to be somewhere else, *anywhere* else, rather than be sitting in front of Mum's workforce telling them I wanted them to work for me and not for Mum.

I'd arrived with a file full of information, with press cuttings and print outs of spread sheets. Why had I brought them? Some sort of comfort blanket? It wouldn't matter one bit what I showed them, I knew that. This was about transferring Mum's workforce over to me. It was that simple, that devastating.

I waited until Greg arrived, he pulled a face and I smiled, acknowledging the fact that he was always the last to arrive for anything. Then I stood, asking him to close the door.

At first, I spoke rapidly, my words falling over themselves whilst I tried to sell this new venture to everyone. I saw a few heads turn, people checking to see how others were responding. I didn't stop, just kept going. I told them about the articles, about the press coverage and a few heads nodded as if in agreement. Then I took a deep breath and told them what I thought that we, as a company, could do. "This is just taking off here in the UK, the Americans got there first." I glanced at the copy of the newspaper I was holding. I didn't need to read it again, I knew the article off by heart. "Guess what the Americans called one company? Smooth Operators!" I expected laughter, it came and I heard their comments, "Yeah, they would. Typical Americans, they got that wrong, sounds like an advert for razors." There was more laughter and I wanted until it had died down before speaking again.

"They probably didn't get it right, who knows, but what I do know is that we can do this *and* with a better name. Our company is more than capable of this venture. We can offer a whole package, the lot, not just moving, but making the whole thing as painless as possible. We'll offer *everything*: sorting out each room, the internet, the stocking of the fridge, the making of beds, hanging prints on walls, the faffing around with the utility companies, you name it, we'll do it. We will take the whole lot off their hands." I stopped, aware of all the faces looking at me.

In the silence and just as I'd asked her to, Jess spoke up. "It'll mean a lot of work, putting together teams to focus on the various elements of this. These people who will be asking for help might have money but they don't have time. And that's where we come in…" Her cheeks were flushed and I gave her a smile.

"What about our other work?" That came from Phil, he'd been with Mum almost from the start. "We've got a lot of contracts right now, can't afford to lose them because of this…" his hand lifted and he trailed off but I knew he wasn't impressed.

"We won't lose them, we'll just need to juggle a few things. Listen, at first, it'll stretch us but I'm confident that before long, there'll be more than enough work and we can expand the workforce. I *know* this will work, this is what we're good at. Going forward, we need to be doing more things like this."

That wasn't all. I had something else to talk to them about, something else I'd been thinking of. An article in a magazine had caught my eye, a trend in London where people could rent furniture, such as a sofa, armchairs and rugs, paying for them to be in their homes for as long as they wanted and, once they'd grown tired of them, they'd return them and rent something else. Dear God, what a way to live but I wasn't there to pass judgement,

I wanted this to be something else we could do, something else in which the company could get involved in. We had stock, masses of it and maybe we'd need to rent larger premises, a warehouse to contain it but, oh, what the hell, this was something we could, we *should* get involved with.

But, looking at their faces, something stopped me from going any further. There were whisperings, heads were bent, eyes lowered and, conscious of the time, I decided to go for it. I lifted my head, "So, the thing is, I need to know if any of you would be interested in working on the start up project with me. I give you my word, nothing will change as far as your employment is concerned, your jobs are safe but, as this is a new venture, I'd like to know if any of you are interested in helping me set it up. Be with me, right from the start." I stopped and took a breath, "I want us, this company, to be at the forefront of all these new ventures. I want us to be more than a company specialising in dressing new builds, much more. We're more than that, we're *better* than that." *Oh God, had I gone too far?* There was, not sure what it was, a ripple, a shockwave and I took a step back.

Of course it was Phil who asked the question, "How does your mother feel about this? Can't help but notice she's not here with you this morning."

"No, she's not." *Now what? What do I say?* I looked at him, "Mum will be focussing her attention on the contracts we already have and those that she's currently working on to maintain the company's long-term security." What a pile of crap. Phil knew it. I could see it no his face.

He nodded then said he'd continue to work with Mum.

There was a pause and I sensed Phil's comments had rattled them. "Look, you don't have to make a decision now, think about what I've said and," I glanced at my watch, almost 9 o'clock, "perhaps sometime later today, you could let me have your thoughts. Ok?"

I couldn't leave it there. "Come and talk to me, we can have a chat...my door is always open."

I shouldn't have said that because at that precise second, the door to the Board room opened and Mum stood there.

"Would you like to tell me what's going on, Charlotte?"

Her tone was icy but that wasn't the reason I shivered. As if on a signal, everyone stood. I heard the squeak of chairs, the sounds of bags being lifted. I saw their faces, tense, uncomfortable, their movements jerky and awkward. Jess was the last to leave and she glanced at me before walking past Mum.

"Close the door, Jess." Mum said, keeping her eyes on mine until we heard the sound of the door being closed.

Mum moved towards the chair that Jess had vacated and in silence, deposited her bag, laptop and coat. Her shoes looked new. God, why did that matter?

"I asked you a question, Charlotte."

I looked at the random marks of paint covering the walls. Why did I choose this room?

"Charlotte! What have you done?"

I motioned to a chair, "Shall we sit, Mum?"

"I'd prefer to stand." She was upright, head back, her eyes dark.

"Ok," I looked at her. *Oh God, here goes.* "I've asked the workforce to join me in setting up the new project. As soon as the words were out, I wanted to claw them back. Mum looked as if she'd been punched. I heard her intake of breath and I wanted to apologise, to tell her I'd made a mistake. I didn't mean to hurt her, all that, but it was too late, far too late.

"You had *no* right to do that. This is *my* company, these people are employed by me and I instruct them on the contracts to work on..."

I thought she'd stopped so I opened my mouth, not having a

clue what I'd say but Mum lifted a hand.

"No, you keep quiet, Charlotte. You've deliberately ignored my wishes, you've gone behind my back and you've talked to the workforce about something that is so far off the scale that…"

"It's *not!* You're wrong, so wrong. This is not some half-baked idea I've come up with, this is what other people are already doing and we need to be there too, we need to be at the forefront of this. Mum, if we don't, we'll be left behind, simply plodding along, same old, same old. For God's sake, Mum, we're stagnating and you can't or won't see it!" *Oh Christ.* "Mum, these people are not evil, they've got money that's all. You've been concentrating for too long with the same companies, treading the same path. We need to diversify or, if we don't, we'll be left behind, we'll be known as a museum piece." *Whoosh.*

My words hung in the air like a speech bubble.

"I see, I knew things were difficult between you and I, Charlotte, but I didn't know that they had reached this stage."

Shit, shit, shit. Then I wanted to tell her I was sorry for hurting her, to give her a hug, tell her it didn't matter, none of it mattered, could we have a cup of coffee, have a chat, make it right. She's my Mum.

But I couldn't, it had gone beyond that. I couldn't think of anything else to say to her and we both knew that a line had been crossed.

Mum bent forward to collect her bag and laptop. I watched her, looking at the way she draped her bag across her shoulder. She then turned and left the room and I heard the door close, very, very softly.

I stayed for a while, waiting for my heart rate to settle and because I needed to wipe the tears from my face. I peered into the mirror that hung lopsidedly on one wall. I looked awful, pale, my skin grey with tiredness, redness under my eyes, the mascara I'd applied earlier, already smudged and clumpy. Whatever came next, I needed to look in control. Picking up my stuff, I also left the Boardroom, hoping that the Ladies would be empty so that I could salvage my appearance in private.

It would have to do, *I'd* have to do. Those who knew me well and I was thinking then of Jon, would say I looked awful, knackered but I'd done the best I could and I walked into my office. Kate was there and she glared at me. "What the hell, Charlie? What on *earth* made you do it? And to do it in secret. Who the hell d'you think you *are?*"

"What was the point in telling you? You didn't want to know. Don't come across as holier than thou, Kate. Don't you bloody dare!"

She made a show of shaking her head to let me know she washed her hands of the whole thing, of me and then she said, "Mum's really upset. She said she doesn't see any point in talking to you."

Brilliant. "So, what does that mean, Kate? You've gone toadying into her office, offering tea and sympathy and I'm the wicked witch of the west? Christ, you make me sick."

And then I lost it. No excuse, didn't matter that I was knackered, that I was frightened about what I'd done, that I was worried about Mum and couldn't say or do anything to help her and, for the second time that morning, I let rip. "For *fuck's* sake, you don't get it, do you? As long as you can come in every day, do what's expected of you, nothing more, nothing less and then go home and play happy families, that's it for you, isn't it? Job done! Well, it's not enough, not anymore. The world is changing, it's moving rapidly and you, like Mum, will be left behind." In that second, I hated her. I hated *everything* about her: her prissy clothes, her neat hair, her undemanding life…and once more, I knew I was crying.

Instead of arguing back, she went off to get me a cappuccino, a muffin. She ignored the phone and, from inside her handbag, she found enough makeup to make me, if not presentable, then passable. She listened to my hiccupping apologies, my incoherent jabbering about what I'd done, *why* I'd done it. God, I even told her about the row I'd had with Jon and I never do that, *ever!* Kate's marriage is straight from the pages of *Good Housekeeping*. Jon and I laugh about the way Kate and her husband, Dan, operate. They're neat, their roles clearly defined and, God help me, I've laughed at my sister's marriage, but then, crying and wiping my snotty nose, wondering what sort of mess I'd made of everything, I wanted to be Kate. I did. At least she wasn't in the shit I was in.

"Is Mum all right, how did she look?"

Kate pulled a face. "Difficult to get much out of her. She's furious with you but…"

"But what? What did she say?"

Kate shrugged, "She was doing her best to be in charge, to let me know that it was business as usual but she's rattled and very angry."

I moved and Kate touched my arm. "Don't."

"Don't what?"

"Don't go and see her. She won't talk to you."

Slumping back, I looked at Kate. "I didn't mean to hurt her. It's just that…"

"You're so much like her."

Kate and I jumped when we heard a knock on the door and Kate looked at me. I nodded, "I'm ok."

Kate opened the door and Jess came in. She looked troubled and her words came out in a rush. "You told me that your Mum knew all about the new project. She didn't, did she?"

"She did but she didn't like it. I'm sorry for misleading you, Jess. I got carried away with the whole thing and I should have been honest with you. I'm sorry." I glanced at Kate who moved towards her desk.

Jess perched on the end of a chair, shaking her head. "I don't like going behind your Mum's back. It doesn't sit right with me. She's my boss, she's a good boss and I…"

"I know, I know." I knew enough not to say anything else to Jess.

She wriggled and looked at me. "I don't want to upset her, Charlie but…"

"But what?"

She frowned. "I'm still interested in your project. God, I feel awful."

"No, don't feel awful, this is *my* mess, not yours and it'll be sorted one way or another. It won't affect your employment here, I give you my word on that." I paused, wondering whether to ask but went ahead anyway, "Do you still want to head this up?"

Jess turned to look at Kate who held her gaze in silence and Jess sighed. "To be honest, Charlie, it's all I can think about. I've got so many ideas and…yeah, I do."

"Ok," I leant forward and touched her arm. "Put these ideas down, send them to me and we'll have a chat about, well, all of it."

Jess's smile was brief. "Ok, I will." She stood and, with one more glance at Kate, she left the room.

"Now what?" Kate's voice was loud. "What happens next?"

I shrugged, "Dunno, I told everyone if they were interested in my idea, then they could come and talk to me but after Mum's appearance…who knows, it might all go down the pan."

Just then a head appeared around the door, it was Greg wearing his usual lopsided grin. "Charlotte? Have you got a minute?"

The whole day was weird, no, that's not the right word. It was surreal, barking mad. They all came to see me, all except Phil. His absence spoke volumes but I sort of knew he'd never be on board. That's ok.

I saw the same expression on faces: embarrassment, unease tinged with a hint of bravura, as if they didn't fully understand why they were doing it but they were doing it anyway. I heard the same phrases: "We think your Mum's great but..." "I saw the article, I did wonder whether..." There were questions about when it would start, about whether there would be enough interest in the project. I answered every single question as honestly and truthfully as I could. The whole time I sat there and it took pretty much all day, I was conscious of Kate. She'd kept quiet, her back to me as she sat in front of her laptop.

"What d'you think?" I needed to hear her say something.

She turned, "Honestly? I don't know, it's a gamble, Charlie but..."

"But what?"

She opened her mouth and closed it again.

"Kate! What?"

"Dan said..."

"Dan said what?" I couldn't work out what on earth Dan had to do with anything. As a brother-in-law, Dan was almost invisible. Jon said once that Kate needs two handbags, one for her purse and makeup and one to keep Dan inside. That's a bit harsh but I know what he means. I can't remember Dan ever voicing an opinion about *anything*. At family gatherings, he just sits there, nodding, smiling, rarely making a contribution to the conversation.

"Dan says it's time Mum stood back from the business." Her words were stilted, rehearsed.

My first thought was, what the *fuck* does Dan know?

"Why? Why does he think that?" My voice was sharp and Kate

winced.

"He's thought for a while that Mum's struggling to cope."

I wanted to defend Mum, to say, "No, she hasn't. He's talking crap." But instead I asked, "What does he mean by that?"

Kate shrugged, "He says that it's obvious she's tired and, well, Dan thinks it's time she stood back or aside, let someone else take over."

If there's one thing I know about my sister, it's that no subterfuge ever lurks within her and, looking at her face, I knew that, whilst she was troubled by the way things had gone with Mum, she thought that, just because Dan said so, then it must be right. I didn't know whether to envy her or pity her. I looked away.

"What?" Kate frowned.

"Sorry, my head's all over the place. I'm knackered and it's been one hell of a day."

Kate wittered on about me drinking too much coffee and maybe it was time I drank camomile tea and I switched off. I wanted to go home.

Driving home, I knew and it was a stupid thought, but the one person I wanted to discuss things with, wasn't Jon, I wanted to talk to Mum. We've always talked things through: long-term planning, staffing levels, stock levels, all of it. Now she won't talk to me and I can't blame her.

God I was tired.

I had a thought. Maybe I should go and see her this evening. Perhaps have a glass of wine, a cup of tea and just talk to her. Tell her I never wanted to hurt her, to undermine her in any way. Was that the truth? I have never, *ever* wanted to hurt her. But I had, undermining her in the most spectacular fashion: in front of her entire workforce. *Oh, Christ.*

Of course, even if I did go and knock on Mum's door, she

probably wouldn't let me in so maybe if I wrote to her, a note, a letter of apology, that way I could put it through her letter-box and she wouldn't have to see me. It also meant that I wouldn't have to see her either. My thinking was off kilter but somehow the thought of *telling* her that I was sorry, whether in person or by letter, made me feel a little better. What did that make me? A coward and a child. A child who still needed to know that whatever I'd done, my Mum still loved me.

CHAPTER 15

As Elizabeth pulled out of the carpark at speed, her shoulders were rigid, her jaw clenched. *How bloody dare she!* She could make no coherent sense of the anger that coursed through her, a primeval, overwhelming sense of hurt, rage at the way Charlotte had plotted behind her back. Plotting, that's what it was, something clandestine, vengeful and whatever way you turned it, it always came back to the same thing: Charlotte had betrayed her. *Betrayal.* It was an appalling word. Then, out of nowhere, she had an image of Charlotte as a small child, two, maybe three, sitting in a pale, blue paddling pool in the garden, sunlight on her damp hair, squeals of excitement as she splashed the water with a wooden spoon. Elizabeth's eyes widened, *where had that come from?* She tried to dislodge the image but couldn't. Why would she think of that now?

Elizabeth shook her head, focusing instead on the scene in the Board room, seeing the startled faces of her staff, Charlotte's guilt. What Charlotte had done was force a wedge between Elizabeth and her team. Elizabeth pulled a face, Charlotte had made her feel like an outsider in front of her own staff! She knew what her reputation was, not only amongst her workforce but amongst the people she worked for: fair-minded and honest, redoubtable but professional. Those things mattered, they were *her*, the person she was. And now Charlotte was undermining all that, trying to destroy the things that Elizabeth most valued about herself. The realisation prickled against her skin, her hairline. "No, she won't!" Elizabeth spoke loudly. "It won't happen, I won't let it."

She failed to see the lights change, stopping just in time. She lurched with the force, hearing the squeal of brakes and she sat back, closing her eyes for a second. Not again, not another accident. She needed to be calm, focused. Afterward, she drove carefully, aware of traffic, of zebra crossings, of people wandering into the road, feeling as if each of her nerve endings was rubbed raw, exposed.

Outside her house, she collected her coat, her bag and she struggled to find her house keys.

"Oh, God, where is the bloody thing?" There, she found it and opened her front door. On the mat was a battered Jiffy bag. Elizabeth dumped her bag on the bottom step of the stairs, picked up the bag and turned it over. Gareth's childish writing in lurid purple ink. Her fingers scrabbled, trying to open the bag. Her jewellery, he'd returned it.

She sat on the stairs and emptied the contents of the Jiffy bag into her lap. It was all there: rings, necklaces, earrings. Peering inside the bag, Elizabeth thought there might have been a note, an apology but there was nothing. She touched the pearls, her fingers stroking their smoothness, uncertain about her reaction. Gareth? Had he taken them and now returned them?

Putting a hand to her face, Elizabeth felt wetness on her cheeks. Her nose was running and she sniffed, wiping her nose on her sleeve. She felt utterly desolate. Her children, all of them, one by one had let her down.

Afterward, she'd eaten a meal, going through the motions, with no appetite or enjoyment of what she'd eaten. In front of her, on top of a pile of newspapers, was her jewellery. It felt wrong to leave it all there but, for some reason, she was unable to move it.

The phone rang and she ignored it. It rang for a few seconds and then stopped. The silence grew, filling the kitchen, amorphous, threatening. *Christ.* She sat as still as possible, her breathing shallow, rapid, waiting for the feeling to pass. "Come on, get a grip."

Finally, she rose and left the kitchen and returned with a notebook and pen. A list, she needed to make a list. Pros and cons, the simple act of writing things down might help. She didn't know what else to do. She stood, the notebook close to her chest and listened. The house was silent, the hum of the fridge/freezer there in the background but, apart from that, there was no sound at all.

The silence felt alien, harsh and she thought about the noise in other people's homes: children squabbling, conversation between couples, the sound of doors opening, closing, the sounds in her own kitchen when the children were all at home. Agitated, she switched the radio on, a voice, something about animal welfare issues. Yes that would do and she sat down and put the notebook in front of her. She needed to think about what Charlotte had done, what the implications were.

Pros: Talk to the workforce, tell them about new contracts in the pipeline. Talk about loyalties, remind them who pays their salaries!!

Cons: Risk losing their support?

"No, no." Elizabeth stood and ripped the page from her notebook and then tore it into tiny pieces before pushing them all into the bottom of the kitchen bin. Stupid! She knew no-one would ever go through her bin but she didn't want anyone to see what she'd written.

The voice on the radio talked about the cost of animal feed, "fluctuating primarily to the changing cost of raw materials,." "Oh, shut up." Elizabeth found a music station and instead she heard the voice of Karen Carpenter singing *Close to You*.

Sitting down, Elizabeth went over the day: the discovery of the theft of her jewellery, the sight of her entire workforce listening to Charlotte as she urged them all to swap sides, to abandon everything that she, Elizabeth, had worked for. Had all this happened in one day? Elizabeth groaned and wrapped her arms around her chest and rocked from side to side. She didn't know what to *do*, how to find a way through. She'd spent the day in her office, her door shut, talking to customers, discussing long-term plans with builders but she knew she'd padded the day out, making unnecessary calls in an attempt to bolster her ego, convince herself she was still in charge. She resented Charlotte even more because of it.

She should talk to Charlotte and Kate, she should. No, she shook her head. "No, I can't, not yet." Her anger with Charlotte hadn't dissipated and she knew there would be little point in talking to Kate. Kate would, as ever, go with the flow, trying to placate her mother and yet wanting to support her sister.

Elizabeth breathed out. *Christ, what a mess.*

Standing, she poured herself a glass of wine and, as she sipped, she thought about the way Charlotte had spoken to her in the Board room. The difference in her two daughters always caught her out.

A woman...Elizabeth closed her eyes. *What was her name?* Useless, although she could see her, tall, messy red hair. She saw her sometimes at the school gates on the days when Elizabeth picked up the girls. They waited together for the avalanche of small children hurling through the open doors. This woman once told Elizabeth, whispering like a shameful secret, that out of her four children, her elder daughter was her favourite child. Elizabeth had been horrified. How on *earth* could anyone think that, believe that? She treated, loved her children equally.

Gareth, pudgy knees bent, a rapt expression on his face as he searched for crabs in rock pools on the beach at Perranporth, his excitement each time he found one, running to show her, his red plastic bucket slopping water as he ran. His utter absorption in counting the crabs, not understanding why he couldn't take them home. His pleading, his promises that he'd take care of them. His tears when they died and his insistence on a burial.

Kate, her eyes dark, earnest. Framed with silky lashes and the way she gripped Elizabeth's hand whenever they walked anywhere. Her serious questions: *Why is the sky blue? Where does the sun go at bedtime?* She always held her head at an angle whenever her questions were answered and if they were not, her voice rising. Tell me, tell me! The way she sat, waiting until Elizabeth came out of the bathroom, picking up the conversation as if it had never stopped.

Elizabeth took another sip of wine, remembering Charlotte's first day at school, the way she'd marched off, her new leather satchel banging against her small shoulder blades. Her thoughts shifted to Charlotte at university, the abortion, the fear in her eyes, her insouciance, trying to pretend she was all right, that she was coping. Elizabeth hadn't interfered, she'd just put Charlotte back on track, nothing else. Any mother would have done the same for any one of her children. *Was* Charlotte her favourite? No! She'd loved them all, treated them all in the same way. She had. *Christ!* How on *earth* would there have been time to have had a favourite? Bringing up three children was like being on an assault course, one crisis was averted and then, before she had time to catch her breath, there was another one looming, something else needing her attention.

She sighed, what the hell was she doing? She was skirting the issue, avoiding what the day's events would mean to her in the long term. Her head was all over the place. She glanced at her jewellery. She should put it somewhere safe, that she could do.

Elizabeth stepped out of her skirt, running her hands over the fabric before hanging it on a padded coat hanger. When she'd dressed that morning, doing up the zip on her skirt, she'd felt distressed, angry at what Gareth had done, the loss of her jewellery, only the knowledge that she was going to the office had soothed her. There, amongst her staff, she'd always felt invincible, strong. But not today, Charlotte had ruined it.

She put her skirt into the wardrobe and her eyes fell on the other clothes: the business suits, the silk shirts in jewel colours, the wool, the cashmere that made up her working wardrobe. Her hands went out to touch the clothes, to revel in their extravagance, their femininity. *Stop it*. She shut the wardrobe door with more force than she needed then sat on the edge of the bed.

Old people, she'd never liked them, being around them. Even as a child, she'd loathed their loose, unstructured bodies, the sense of decline. When Ruby, her grandmother went into a nursing home, she'd done all she could to make her comfortable, making up for her mother's indifference, but at the same time, she was honest enough to admit, it had all been an act. She detested the sight of Ruby's hands, the papery skin, freckled with blotchy age spots, had gritted her teeth when Ruby failed to hear what was being said to her, her incessant "eh?" her frown of confusion. The sight of Ruby's clothes, the Velcro to make dressing easier, the bunion distorted shoes, her pale pink scalp visible underneath a cap of wiry, thin hair, she didn't want to look at any of it. Elizabeth's mother regarded the transfer of Ruby into someone else's care, as something that needed to be done, rather than something to be feel agitated or guilty about. Faced with her mother's coldness, some part of Elizabeth wanted to soften her mother's attitude. She wondered if she was seeking recognition, praise for her concern towards her elderly grandmother, something her mother would thank her for. If so, it hadn't materialised. Elizabeth's mother made infrequent visits so Elizabeth went instead, armed with flowers, boxes of biscuits knowing that Ruby would dribble her tea down the front of whatever faded dress she wore. Elizabeth sat there on a sticky, vinyl covered chair, glancing at her watch, checking to see when she could legitimately say she had to leave. Once outside, she'd draw in huge gulps of air, trying to rid herself of the smell of old age. During the time Ruby had been at the Home, Elizabeth had listened to the nursing staff, the carers telling her how "wonderful" Ruby was, what a character, what a sense of humour. All Elizabeth saw was her grandmother's bony fingers, plucking constantly at her clothes, answering in monosyllables whenever Elizabeth asked a question. After each visit, she'd tell her mother that Ruby was "all right", enjoying life at the Home. Why did she lie? Did she think she was somehow absolving her mother from *her* guilt? Well, good luck with that! Her mother wasn't interested either in guilt or Ruby's well-being. Driving home after each visit, Elizabeth felt a maelstrom of emotions: guilt, relief, sheer *joy* at being able to leave, to return to her family. She'd never admitted how she felt, not even to Chris but Elizabeth knew that, for her, growing old filled her with nothing but disgust.

Of course, since her grandmother's death, her own mother's death, life for the elderly had changed enormously, people living longer, healthier lives, still working in their 60s and 70s. She knew all that, she'd read the papers, listened to the radio and heard the arguments, the discussions. Of course she knew. She'd read the patronising articles in newspapers: *OAP Mrs. Edna Hughes, at 82 years old, still walks on the Downs every day! Charlie Porter, in his 90s volunteers at the charity shop!* All these articles, all these exclamation marks. What did they indicate? Was it, that for their age, these people were doing well? Hallelujah! They can still function, put one foot in front of the other. *Sod that, sod that. Anti-ageing*, an ingredient on face creams sounded like an organisation, a march to stop the unstoppable. She'd seen Helen Mirren, Jane Fonda on tv, she'd heard the slogan, spoken with irritating coyness: *Because you're worth it*. Why? Because you're older? Not for any other reason? Ruby had never used anything which had *anti-ageing* on the label. She'd simply accepted that she was old, knowing there was nothing to be done about it. Elizabeth however, bought those creams, peering at herself in the critical light of her bathroom mirror, convinced they'd made a difference. The bathroom shelves held an assortment of creams, serum, moisturisers, all promising *younger looking skin*. Why did it matter? Yet it did. She didn't want to be like her grandmother, ageing fast, accepting her fate, nor did she want to be like her mother, not giving a toss about anyone or anything. Elizabeth thought she'd been a good mother, she was *still* a good mother. She hadn't walked away from that responsibility.

Ruby. Her grandmother's one nod to vanity was drawing on thick, wobbly lines with a *Rimmel* eyebrow pencil, her unsteady hand framing her watery blue eyes with harsh, black colour.

Still sitting on the edge of her bed, Elizabeth thought about David Armstrong, his company, the homes he built for the elderly. Not once had she ever thought those homes concerned her.

Oh God. Elizabeth stiffened. Ruby was 78 when she entered the Home. Elizabeth was 73. No, no way. She stood.

She wore an old pair of jeans and a sweater that Chris had bought her. She didn't look at herself in the mirror, deliberately turning her head. She'd put her jewellery away and, as soon as she could, she'd buy a wall safe. She told herself she should have bought one before. She paused, thinking about a safe, about the need for one, about who'd know how to open it, another new code to remember.

Downstairs, Elizabeth poured another glass of wine and her thoughts, cushioned by wine, were darting wildly around. Snippets of conversations and memories swirled about her, nudging up against each other in no chronological order. She pictured Chris standing in the garden, his face shiny with sweat as he stood over a barbecue. Charlotte, or maybe it was Kate, next to him, holding out a paper plate wobbling under a pile of blackened sausages. *When was that?*

She looked at the collection of family photos: Charlotte's graduation, Kate wearing her gown, her cheeks flushed. Gareth on his first day at school, arms crossed, freckles splashed across the bridge of his nose. Finally, she looked at her wedding photo. She and Chris gazing at each other, self-consciously posing for the photographer. The photos meant a lot, they were proof that her family life had been successful, that *she'd* been successful.

When she'd introduced Chris to her parents, her father had glanced at him telling Elizabeth later, "You won't do better than him." She'd never asked what he meant: was it a compliment or was it derogatory? It didn't matter, they went ahead with the wedding, her parents leaving before the rest of the guests. "We've done our bit." Elizabeth's mother told her.

Elizabeth threw herself into her marriage, using her parents lives as a warning as she tried to be the sort of wife she'd read about: caring, loving, making a home into a sanctuary, the sort of home her mother had mocked. It worked for a while but when the children were small, when Elizabeth was weary of motherhood, of being a wife, not having anything of her own in terms of dreams or goals, she told Chris it wasn't enough. "But what else d'you want?" He'd looked at her, looked around him at their living room. "Don't we have a nice home, a nice life?"

What could she tell him? Yes, they had, they did but was that *it?* She wanted something of her own, something away from the children's constant demands, away from Chris too. She loved him, he was easy to love but she wanted something less smooth, if not abrasive, then at least with obstacles, edges, variations. Most of all she wanted bright colours. Once, taking the children to the park to feed the duck with stale bread, Kate tugged at Elizabeth's hand. "If I was a colour, what would I be?"

"What?"

"What *colour* would I be?" Kate's voice was insistent. "Mummy, you're not listening to me."

"Um, you? Maybe blue, the colour of the sea, always moving, changing."

Kate had run off to tell her brother and sister. Charlotte's voice immediately rang out. "I'm purple. I'm a witch's cloak."

Without a child hanging on to her, Elizabeth increased her pace, deep in thought. *What colour would I be? Green, colour of nature, of grass. No, I'm not green, I'm not placid enough.* She thought about Chris, about an argument they'd had, a silly one: it had been his turn to empty the kitchen bin and he'd forgotten. *He's beige, bland.* She'd pulled a face and corrected herself. *No, that's not fair, he's a deep cream, rich and gentle.* But the beige wouldn't go away.

Gareth had run back to join his mother, "What am I? What colour am I? I want to be yellow, like custard and ice-cream."

Elizabeth smiled, "In that case, we'll eat you for tea." She grinned as he ran to tell his sisters.

She met Adrian at a café. He wore a canary yellow jumper.

She'd taken the kids to the play area in the local park and, when the rain started, she'd steered them into a small café, the windows steamy and the air smelling of wet coats, shrill voices of children clamouring for cake. Elizabeth found a table and, telling the three of them not to move, she made her way to the counter. A woman, hair scraped back into an untidy bun, barked, "What d'you want?" as Elizabeth reached the front of the queue.

Raking her eyes over the array of cakes, Elizabeth asked for toasted tea-cakes and lemonade. The woman nodded, telling Elizabeth she'd bring a tray to her table. As Elizabeth turned, she bumped into a tall, dark-haired man. "Oh, sorry."

Smiling, he stepped back. "It's ok. Now it's my turn to approach the dragon."

Elizabeth grinned, "Be careful, she bites."

Sitting with her children, listening to their chatter, Elizabeth was intensely aware of the man sitting at a table near the window, a small boy wearing dark framed National Health glasses next to him.

When she rose to leave, the man smiled and Elizabeth knew she'd breathed in, hoping her stomach was flat. He said, "We survived the dragon."

During the following week, Elizabeth thought about the man, wondered what he was doing in the café midweek, with a small boy. All the men she knew, worked, they didn't spend time with children in cafes. Where was the boy's mother?

She knew she was thinking about him in the same way she thought about receiving a gift, savouring the anticipation. She limited herself to thinking about him just once a day.

Understanding why she did it, Elizabeth took the children to the café the following week, telling them it was a treat, not knowing if he'd be there.

He was and he was sitting at the same table, wearing the same yellow sweater and the young boy was sitting next to him again.

He smiled as she pushed the door open and Elizabeth felt her stomach knot.

Adrian, he told her his name when they sat in the café, moving two tables together so the children could talk. They hadn't. Elizabeth's three staring mutely at Adrian's son, Will. Elizabeth had glared at Charlotte, daring her to snigger, to whisper *willy* to her siblings.

The conversation was stilted and awkward, both of them trying to include the children, trying to make their children think that it was normal.

Somehow, Elizabeth couldn't remember how, Adrian had pushed a piece of paper towards her, his phone number written in neat numbers. "Please call me," his voice was hoarse. "I'm home in the mornings with Will."

He'd told her he was divorced, that his wife worked as a solicitor and, between them, they were doing as much as they could to look after their son. Adrian worked as an engineer and, as a shift worker, he was able to have Will during the summer holidays.

Elizabeth took the piece of paper and jammed it into her pocket. Of course she wouldn't ring him, what would be the point?

She called from a phone box, not wanting to ring from home, telling herself that it was safer that way. Going behind Chris's back was one thing, calling from their home was something else.

Had it been an affair? Didn't an affair mean sex in cheap hotel rooms or on the back seat of Adrian's Citroen? Did an affair mean they wanted to be with each other, that they were willing to give up their families, to wreak havoc on other people's lives?

Elizabeth didn't know and she didn't want to break up any family but Adrian asked her to leave Chris, to be with him. She couldn't. It was an episode, a chapter in her life, just that. At the same time, she longed to talk to him, to hear his voice, his views, his beliefs. Being with Adrian was the only time Elizabeth felt truly present, that she had a place in the world. At first, feeling like that had saddened and shocked her. She was Chris's wife, a mother but what else had she been? Adrian had listened to her, talked to her and Elizabeth stored things up, something on the radio, an article in a newspaper, an overheard conversation, waiting for the time she could talk to Adrian, hear what he had to say. She'd sit opposite him in a quiet pub they'd found, heads bent together, Adrian a kind of catalyst, somehow making sense of everything she'd stored up.

It had been Adrian who'd suggested she could do something with the furniture she restored. He told her that her energies, her intellect were rusting. "Don't let family life drain you." He'd told her she was capable of so much more. "You're quite extraordinary, Elizabeth." Was she? She hadn't thought so but she thought about what he'd said.

Adrian told her she could do more with her life when she told him she couldn't see him again. He'd said he'd grown tired of skulking, of hiding and he wanted her to go with him to a cinema in the next town. She'd baulked, nervous about being seen but he'd been insistent. He spoke with passion of Jean-Luc Godard, of films she'd never heard of, telling her what she was missing, what she'd enjoy.

Frightened by the number of lies she'd told, of the convoluted plans for picking up the children, of being *caught*, Elizabeth sat in Adrian's car as he drove to where he said they could watch a matinee. "And maybe have an early supper together."

She sat forward in the seat, unable to relax, to feel anticipation. Adrian glanced at her, putting a hand on her knee. "You'll enjoy this, you really will." All Elizabeth knew was that her mouth was dry and her heart was pounding.

When Adrian parked the car, Elizabeth looked right and left, worrying that someone might see them, want to know what she was doing, who she was with.

Walking towards the cinema, Elizabeth was aware of Adrian's coat brushing against her leg. He was taller than Chris and

Elizabeth was light-headed with nerves.

Needing to cross a road to reach the cinema and, waiting for traffic, Elizabeth grabbed Adrian's hand. He looked at her, smiling. She yanked her hand away. She'd been thinking of her children, of warning them about crossing the road, of being mindful of traffic. It had been an instinctive reaction faced with a busy road. She told Adrian she wanted to go home.

Sometimes, when Elizabeth went out in her van, scouring towns and villages for furniture, she thought about Adrian – did he ever think about her? She wanted him to know that she'd listened to him, that she wasn't wasting her life. She was making something of herself.

Elizabeth closed her eyes. She had no idea why she'd told Charlotte about Adrian when they sat in that soulless café at the service station. What prompted that? Charlotte didn't need to know. Was it some sort of misguided need to let Charlotte understand that she, Elizabeth, hadn't always been efficient in all aspects of her life? That she too had cocked things up?

She knew the moment she'd said the words, it had been a mistake. Adrian was locked away, she never brought him out, it was safer that way.

Christ, I've had too much to drink. Her back ached, her shoulders throbbed and she had a headache.

She made her way upstairs, grabbing hold of the banisters to pull herself up.

The bathroom illuminated Elizabeth's face and she winced, lifting her head, seeing the skin on her neck tighten with the movement.

In bed, Elizabeth turned on her side, facing the window. She didn't want to go into the office tomorrow. Let Charlotte and Kate interpret that any way they wanted. She needed to think, to sift through what had happened. It wasn't her mess. No, it was Charlotte's.

She tugged the duvet up to her chin. The wine had left her feeling maudlin. What if she didn't wake up? *Who'd know?* And then, a second thought, one which left her sobbing – who would really *care?*

CHAPTER 16

If someone that morning was nosy enough to look through our kitchen window, what would they have seen? What did we look like: a family of four talking about which cereal was better, *Coco Pops* or *Cheerios?* a mother talking to her younger daughter about whether she needed a haircut, or a father making jokes about the size of his feet? To an outsider it all looked and sounded normal, maybe boring. At least I hoped so.

Jon stood up, "Come on, girls. Time to go." His eyes slid over me, his words innocuous yet full of meaning. "See you later."

I hugged the girls, burying my face in their hair, smelling their shampoo. I heard the bang of the front door then the house was quiet.

After the door closed, I busied myself as best I could, stacking the dishwasher, wiping down surfaces, wondering why it was important to me to leave my kitchen spotless. Because of Jon? He wouldn't care less. I even polished the draining board, rubbing furiously at the marks that had been there for ages. Leaving the kitchen, I ran upstairs, grabbed as much dirty washing as I could hold. Downstairs I listened as water filled the washing machine, watching as my family's clothes sloshed one way, then another.

And then I wrote a letter to Mum.

I wrote it because it seemed easier to write down the things I was feeling. I didn't want to take the risk of saying them to her face. What does that make me? A coward? Yeah, I was, I am. I found the last of the *Basildon Bond* paper and, using a proper pen, I said how sorry I was, how much I regretted what had happened. I told her how proud of her I was, what a great job she'd done, both as a mother and as a businesswoman. I wrote about the respect people had for her, the respect that Kate and I had. I said she was truly inspirational and I felt privileged to not only be her daughter, but her employee as well.

It was awful, crass, self-serving, vacuous and smarmy, a get out of jail card.

I vacillated between pushing it through Mum's letter box and then running away, or ringing her doorbell and handing it to her. I chose the first option. Leaving it on her desk didn't feel right and I didn't want to hand it over in the office. I'm not sure why I felt that way, but I did.

I dressed carefully knowing how much emphasis Mum places on appearance, a bit *knock 'em bandy*. Jon's a fan of *Only Fools and Horses*, watches endless repeats and that's what he always tells me whenever I make an attempt at looking smart or posh. What difference would it make how I looked? Mum wouldn't see me, yet I wanted to look good, professional.

I felt such sadness. I didn't know whether Mum would be in the office today or whether she'd stay at home, working out what to do next. Stupidly, I wanted to send her a text, something jokey like the texts I've sent after we'd faced a problem together. *Sorry I've been the daughter from hell. You could always return me and get your money back.* But I couldn't send that. I mean, I'm pretty sure if Mum could swap me for someone more malleable, less competitive or ambitious, she'd do it in a heartbeat. Then Kate popped into my head. She wasn't competitive or ambitious. Kate operates in my slip stream. I'd known that for a long time. And before that? She'd worked with and behind Mum, in her slipstream. So why had she changed tack? For the first time I realised that, at no point, had Kate suggested she might be unhappy with Mum's performance, her decision making. She'd used Dan, her husband's comments to jump on my bandwagon. Why was that? Why hadn't I thought abut that before? I thought about Jon, about his comments about the way I was taking everything from Mum. And then I thought about Gareth, how he just takes from Mum, gives her nothing. And what does Kate give her? Total commitment, that's what. Never questions, never challenges. How does Mum feel about that? I don't know if it ever crosses Mum's mind. But what about me, what have I done? I've bullied Mum, pushed her because I'm so hell bent on taking control of the company. I didn't feel good about myself. All of a sudden, I didn't want the letter in my hand any longer.

Mum's car was on the driveway. She'd parked it too close to the bushes and I had to squeeze my way past. I had the strangest feeling she was watching me. I looked at the windows, imagined her there, watching as I inched my way past her car. Then I looked away and shoved the letter through the letterbox, running away like a child playing *Knock, knock Ginger*. I didn't want Mum to know that I'd been to her house. How stupid was that? The minute she saw my handwriting, she'd know and she'd know that I'd delivered it myself, too much of a coward to face her. Blinking back the tears, I pushed the thought aside and drove to the office.

Kate seemed *fluttery*. She kept asking if I wanted a cup of coffee, *did* I want a coffee, repeating the question even after I'd said no, twice.

"Kate! What on earth's the matter? You're jumping around like a..." I paused. She looked incredibly tired. "Are you all right?"

She shook her head, "No, not really. I couldn't sleep. Didn't matter how many cups of camomile tea I had. I was awake for hours."

"Me too. I tried wine but that didn't work either." I looked at her, seeing the fine lines around her eyes, the shine on her hair. She's *neat*, my sister. Nothing out of place, not a lost button on her clothes or an overflowing laundry basket at home. Everything's under control. Apart from this. I'd introduced an enormous spanner in her works. I felt as if I was unravelling and making Kate unravel with me.

"Kate?" I touched her hand, "Tell me honestly, how you're feeling about all this." I waved my arm in the direction of the door. "We've got a workforce out there, waiting for news, waiting for…" I shrugged. "Waiting for something." I took a deep breath and steadied myself for the question I wanted to ask her. "Is this *honestly* what you had in mind when you said you agreed with me?"

Kate fiddled with her hair and looked at her feet.

I waited, "Kate?"

She pulled a face, "Dan said it's time Mum stepped back." Her words were flat.

My first thought: *sod Dan, never mind what he thinks, what d'you think?*

"Dan says it's been obvious for a while that Mum's tired and well…Dan thinks it's time she took a backwards step and let someone else take over."

"And what d'you think?"

Kate glanced around and took another breath. "To be honest, Charlie, I *hate* all this. Seeing Mum upset, things all over the place."

Just as I thought she'd finished speaking, she lifted her head.

"But the truth? I think Mum needs a break, some time off, away from the business…"

Again, she trailed off and I knew these weren't Kate's words, they were Dan's. She was hiding behind her husband's rambling thoughts. *She hides behind everyone: Mum, me, Dan…she has no original thoughts of her own.* I really was on my own.

But despite that, I felt a kind of tenderness towards her. I mean, she must feel utterly lost by all this.

"Charlie, d'you know if Mum's coming in today?"

"Got no idea." I looked at my desk. "Whether she does or not, we've got to sort this out, Kate. We have a workforce who will be wanting to know what happens next." I looked at her, "Oh, Kate…" I couldn't, *couldn't* ask her for help. It wasn't her fault.

Her smile was brief and for the third time that morning, asked if I wanted coffee. This time I said yes.

After that I had to go into Mum's office. We have a centralised system for every contract, every project, but for some reason, it wasn't up to date and several entries were full of gaps where there shouldn't be any. Mum's diary – the big red one she keeps on her desk – was there and, in her handwriting, I quickly found most of the jobs that should have been on our system, not all of them but enough.

I sat at her desk, close to tears, what was *wrong* with me? It was here, the thing I'd been dimly aware of even though I couldn't put a name to it or wouldn't face up to. I mean, Mum could use technology, she'd been doing so for years; it had been her idea to set up the office system so that each one of us knew what was booked in, what was nearing completion. And yet, she'd been what – using her diary as a back-up? Distrusting herself?

Oh God. This felt all wrong, almost as bad as rummaging through Mum's bank statements. *No, it was worse!* I mean, maybe Mum felt better writing things down than using our high-tech system. After all, I do it. I put things in my phone: haircuts, dental appointments, car service and then I write everything down again on the calendar on the wall in my kitchen. Jon does it too. So why is *that* different from what Mum has been doing?

I sat back, placing my hands on the armrests, thinking of the times I'd seen Mum do the same. I heard the usual sounds coming from outside Mum's office and I knew the company was functioning. Kate and I had talked to the staff or at least I'd done most of the talking. We'd re-assured them that we were still operational, that it was business as usual. And here I was, in Mum's office, checking up on her, spying. But I also felt a peculiar sense of vindication. I was right. Things had gone beyond Mum's capabilities. The company had outgrown her.

Maybe Jon would understand now. He'd talk about Mum's vulnerability, about how hard it must be for her to keep going, to keep abreast of the changes she'd seen, changes threatening to swallow her up, leaving her with nothing to show for her hard work. He'd remind me about how hard she'd fought for her company, how she had set it up. I picked up my phone, wanting to hear his voice but then put it down. I know, I *know*.

Mum's desk was neat and organised, unlike mine. This was where she worked, where she felt in control, it represented everything she'd worked for. And here I was, invading it, invading her, stripping her of her identity, taking away everything she'd worked for. What was the phrase? She *owned* this. In that moment I knew I shouldn't be here. I needed to go back to where I worked.

When I returned to my office, Kate was on the phone gesturing for me to take the call. "My sister is here now, she'll explain." And with that she handed the phone to me.

Mouthing *who is it?* I said, "Hello?"

"Charlotte, it's Alison Clarke. Wanted to check with you about something we've heard."

Alison worked for Harper Buildings, one of our biggest customers. She handled the dressing of their homes and we'd worked together on a lot of projects. A tough nut to crack. No bullshit.

I glanced at Kate before asking "What have you heard?" Kate shook her head in reply.

Alison's laugh was light, without emotion. "Oh, there's talk, Charlotte. You know the sort of thing."

"Not sure I'm with you." I closed my eyes. "What sort of thing?"

"It's just that there are a few rumours, bit of gossip about splitting the workforce. We've tried to get hold of your Mum but apparently she's not in today."

And how does that look?

"Gossip, Alison? Mum has a day off, she's been working hard, you know her. Meanwhile, we're taking on more staff, we've got new contracts coming in all the time and, as far as this company is concerned, it's all go, it's all good." How did my voice sound? Confident? Evasive?

"Oh, glad to hear it. It's just that someone mentioned that your Mum might be stepping down."

Christ. My laugh was brittle. "God, no! You know what Mum's like…"

Alison duly laughed. "Yes, of course. I thought it was odd."

"Actually, Alison, now you're on the phone, I wanted to talk to you…" I launched into a made-up enquiry about a contract and the question of Mum faded. I hoped it had." I was conscious of Kate's gaze on me.

Alison's call wasn't the only one. This industry is like any other and a network operates, vultures listening out for business failures, board room fall outs, redundancies, the Chinese Whispers of business.

Kate answered calls, repeating almost word for word what I'd said to Alison. Each time Mum was mentioned, I felt what was becoming a familiar mixture of emotions: pride, a need to protect her and an even bigger need to tell people that, from now on, I'd be taking over. I didn't like myself very much.

Mum sent me a text. She said she wanted to see me after work. Would I call in? I said yes of course, *I'll be there about 5.30 Is that ok?* She didn't mention my letter and I had an insane hope that she hadn't read it. I fervently wished I hadn't shoved it through her letter box. Why had I done that?

I wanted to ask if she was all right, was there anything she needed, thinking that if I took a bunch of flowers, a bottle of wine, *something* it would make things if not better, maybe less awkward. Needless to say, I turned up empty handed.

"Charlotte," her face was blank as she held the door open and I walked in.

We didn't hug but then what did I expect? That she'd grab hold of me, laughing, crying, telling me that we should forget all about it, a stupid row, nothing to get upset about? I didn't deserve a hug. And it hadn't been a stupid row.

We sat in her living room and I tried hard not to look at Mum. I knew that if I did, I'd burst into tears and I didn't want that.

"Charlotte," her voice was low, controlled. "I've decided to take some time off. I'm going on a short holiday."

I remained silent.

"I need to think things through, think about…"she trailed off. Her head turned and she closed her eyes. "I need to put some distance between you and me, you and the company."

"Oh, Mum." I stopped myself from reaching out to touch her. "Would it help you to know that I'm so terribly sorry."

"Not in the slightest."

The silence was painful and all I could do was ask where she was going.

"To Dartmouth."

Her tone implied that she had no intention of telling me anything else but I persisted. "How long will you be away?"

Mum didn't look at me. "Probably a week."

"Mum…"

She ignored me and talked about the meetings she'd cancelled. "I've re-arranged most of them but you will have to see Peter Hopkins and Martyn Evans." Her face was impassive. "They're both important, don't mess things up."

Shit. That hurt and I pulled a face. "Mum, I won't, you know I won't. Please, the company means too much to me to…"

I had to stop. She was staring at me, her eyes cold, "Really?"

I felt words crashing around in my head and I thought of testing out a few: *forgive, sorry, love, commitment.* I didn't say anything. I couldn't put them into a coherent sentence and anyway, she wouldn't listen. She'd tell me that I hadn't behaved with love or commitment and honestly, who could blame her?

She stood and so did I. When I faced her, she looked away.

"Will you at least tell me where you'll be staying?"

"No, I don't see the point."

So that was it. I walked to the front door, conscious of Mum behind me. As I reached the door, I turned and whispered, "I really am incredibly sorry for hurting you."

"Yes, you've already said that."

"Mum, the letter…"

She lifted her head. "I think it's best we don't mention that, wouldn't you agree?"

The door closed almost as soon as I'd stepped out.

Sitting in my car, I felt broken. I'd managed to cause what seemed to be irreparable damage to all the most important relationships in my life. *Oh God, what have I done?*

I rested my head on the steering wheel. Lack of sleep was

finally catching up with me. I'd been operating on coffee and adrenaline all day and now, seeing Mum so bitter, so angry, I was wrecked.

Earlier I'd sent a text to Jon letting him know I'd be late. *Going to see Mum after work.*

His reply had been terse: *Thank you for letting me know.*

All this politeness! I tried to imagine Mum, screaming, waving that pathetic letter in my face, telling me what a bitch I'd been, maybe Jon should have yelled at me too. He cared about Mum, admired her…but even as I thought this, something inside me shifted. Mum had done things her way for a long time. She believed that as long as she kept doing what she'd always done, everything would be fine. Why wouldn't it? Jon, with parents like his, without any drive or ambition, thought Mum was unique in building a small empire on her own. He'd never met anyone like her before. Neither my husband nor my mother thought things should change, ever: why rock the boat? But this boat needed rocking. There were avenues to be explored, discoveries to be made. What I *hadn't* done was make sure that Mum – or Jon for that matter – understood. I'd handled this all wrong, *all* wrong.

I switched the engine on, I needed to be home.

The phone rang as I turned into my drive. It was Gareth and, not wanting to talk to him, I ignored it. Then a text arrived.

I need to see you.

Fuck off, Gareth. I don't want to see you.

I jammed the phone into my bag and went into the house.

The kitchen smelt of chips and I grabbed a few from a dirty plate. Stone cold but they tasted good.

CHAPTER 17

Elizabeth knew why she'd chosen Dartmouth. She remembered Chris's mother, Enid, talking about Dartmouth when Elizabeth mentioned a honeymoon. She'd squirmed with embarrassment when Enid said that they must have one.

Enid had said *honeymoon* with exaggerated facial expressions, winking at Elizabeth. "After the excitement of the wedding, you'll want to be on your own." Terry, Chris's Dad, nudged his son in the ribs and Elizabeth had watched the flush on Chris's face reach his hairline.

Dartmouth? Elizabeth thought it would look like she was running away. So what?

She'd spent the day going over options, thinking about buying the girls out of the company – yes, Kate too. Both girls had been given shares in the company when they reached forty, a special birthday dinner, everyone dressed up, champagne in crystal flutes. She'd looked upon it as giving them a reward, bestowing them with something precious to her. And now? Now she wanted to take it all away from them.

She'd phoned her solicitor, listening to his tales about the pressure he was under. "God, Elizabeth, it's never-bloody ending. I'm in the middle of a long-drawn out case and just when I thought…"

She'd waited until he'd drawn breath and, in a rush, asked him if she could buy the girls out.

"The girls? Both of them? Why d'you want to do that?"

"It's not working out, Phil. We want different things and well, to be honest, I'd like to be on my own again. After all, it's my company."

There was silence, "Phil? Are you still there?"

"Yes, I'm here. Are you sure about this, Elizabeth? I must admit it's taken me by surprise."

"Yes, I'm sure." Elizabeth spoke with a confidence she wasn't feeling. "I think it's for the best The girls are young enough, they can start again. They've learnt a lot from me and I'm sure…" To her embarrassment, she realised she was crying. "Oh, Phil, I'm sorry, I…"

"Elizabeth, please don't apologise. This must be distressing for you. Might I suggest…"

"What?" Elizabeth sniffed loudly. "Are you going to suggest that I take a few days to think about this? Do you think I *haven't* thought about it?"

"I wouldn't *dare* suggest such a thing." He paused and spoke softly, "I don't know what's gone on, Elizabeth, that's your business but what I *do* know is that you're a woman of principle and, as your solicitor and also as a friend, I'd strongly suggest that you take a bit more time to think about this."

"I've just told you, I…"

"Well take a bit more time. That's my professional advice to you."

"Oh, for Christ's sake, Phil. Do you talk to all your clients this way?"

"No, only a few, those I like."

"Oh, right."

"When did you last have a holiday?" Phil's voice was low. "I'll bet you've not been away for a while."

"I can't go away. I just can't. There's so much going on right now, it would be impossible for me to take time off."

"So, the world would stop, the company would grind to a halt if you had a few days off, is that what you're telling me?"

My world would stop. She couldn't say that to him. Irrationally she felt annoyed that his suggestion had been so banal, so *obvious*. She tried to mask her annoyance, "It's not as simple as that, Phil. It would take too long to explain but things are decidedly difficult right now."

"Can't remember a time when life wasn't difficult but that doesn't mean you can't take time off. Elizabeth? Elizabeth, are you still there?"

"Yeah, I'm here. Sorry, Phil, this is awkward for me. I'm not sure…"

"Take time out, give yourself some space. Elizabeth, you're a remarkable woman but you're not made of concrete. Stop beating yourself up over whatever has happened."

Again, she felt tears and wanted to apologise for them.

"Phil, I'm sorry to have bothered you. I'll be all right, I'll talk to you soon. Take care."

Without waiting for his response, Elizabeth put down the phone. After that she googled Dartmouth, saw the Dart Marina Hotel, made a booking. She'd leave in the morning before she had time to change her mind. Yes, before another voice told her something she didn't want to hear.

She spent the rest of the day packing, telling her neighbours she'd be away, watering her garden, clearing out the fridge and, each time she heard her phone *ping* she ignored it. When she did pick it up, she saw missed calls from Kate and Gareth. He'd sent garbled texts: *Mum, where are you? Can I come, can I see you? Mum, please?*

After Charlotte's visit, Elizabeth sank into a chair. She sat completely still, waiting for her heart rate to settle.

She'd booked a room with a balcony overlooking the estuary. On their honeymoon, she and Chris had walked past the hotel, gazing up at the rooms and he'd said, "One day, we'll come back and we'll stay here." And now, here she was.

For both of them, the Dart Marina Hotel represented much more than a hotel. It was something Chris used to say. "We'll stay in posh hotels, we'll eat meals at proper restaurants, those which have white linen cloths on the table, roses in a vase." Elizabeth knew that those places, those things, were important to Chris, not in any flamboyant way, merely that they were what he wanted for Elizabeth, things that he, at that time, couldn't give her.

They'd stood in the car park of the hotel, looking at the lights, the couples on the balcony and he'd held her close and he'd told her that, "one day, that'll be us up there, looking at the view."

After she'd checked in and her case had been brought to the room, Elizabeth sat on the bed. She frowned, it felt soft. The walls of the room were tiresomely nautical. She sighed. Now she was here, she didn't know what to do. She unpacked, hung up her clothes, put her toiletries in the bathroom: all this had taken ten minutes. Maybe a drink, that would fill up time.

The bar of the hotel overlooked the estuary and, with a glass in her hand, Elizabeth watched the boats moored at the jetty, the hulls bobbing up and down with the rise and fall of the water. A man and a woman approached a boat, both holding bags and coats. The man reached the boat first and held a hand out to help the woman onboard. Elizabeth saw the smile on her face and she watched as the couple made preparations to cast off.

Squinting, Elizabeth tried to see the boat's name but gave up. She saw the woman jump off the boat and untie the ropes before stepping back onboard. The woman joined the man, putting a hand on his shoulder and then the engine started, churning up the water and the boat moved off. She wondered where they were going, neither of them looked back.

Elizabeth sipped at her gin and tonic keeping her eyes on the boat before it disappeared from view. She finished her drink and thought she'd walk around Dartmouth, see how much it had changed.

"Everything all right, madam?"

Looking up, Elizabeth saw a young waiter.

"Thank you, it's all good." She looked at him, seeing the signs of a recent haircut, the skin on his neck looked raw, exposed. "First time I've stayed here. I used to look at the hotel from the outside when my late husband and I were on our honeymoon. Not been back since and it doesn't seem to have changed…" She stopped, aware of the expression on the waiter's face: she knew that expression, she'd seen it before. Wordlessly, she signed for her drink and, collecting her bag and jacket, she smiled at the waiter and left.

Elizabeth wondered what other people saw when they looked at her. Did they see a mature woman with well-cut hair, stylish clothes? Someone who's age was difficult to guess, or didn't they see her at all? Now, hearing the harsh cry of the seagulls and seeing the sun's rays on the water, Elizabeth felt more alone than she'd ever felt.

This lack of purpose, of direction threw her. For as long as she could remember, she always knew what she had to do next. Now, she didn't have a clue. She saw an unoccupied bench and sat down, facing the water. Everything around her moved: the boats, people, seagulls, all going from one place to another. Even the birds seemed to have a purpose, a motive for their flight. Elizabeth heard snippets of conversation: "Can't face another plate of fish." "How d'you feel about a boat trip tomorrow?" She sat there feeling disconnected. The phone in her handbag rang and, longing to hear a voice, someone, *anyone* if only to give her a sense of belonging, she answered, not knowing who was calling, the sun shining on the phone.

"Hello?"

"Mum! Where are you? Are you ok?" Kate's voice was high with anxiety.

"Yes, I'm fine. I'm in Dartmouth for a few days."

Elizabeth closed her eyes: the sound of her daughter's voice brought her close to tears.

"Thank you," she whispered the words.

"What for? Mum, are you ok?"

Elizabeth straightened. "I'm fine, I promise. I just needed time to myself, that's all."

"You worried us, going off without telling anyone where you were going."

"I told Charlotte, Kate. I'm a grown-up, I don't need permission to take a few days off."

Kate's voice was soft, "Just as long as you're ok."

"I am, I promise. I'll let you know when I get home."

Kate's voice altered, she sounded brisk, business-like. "Good, take care, enjoy your break."

"Thank you, I will."

She replaced the phone and sat back. Her feelings of being apart, disconnected had eased and she watched the movement of the water as boats went past, hearing the soft *chug chug* of engines and the flapping of sails.

A man dressed in a white shirt and a captain's cap, approached her. "Good afternoon, may I interest you in one of our cruises?" He held out a leaflet, "Two hours exploring the River Dart."

Taking the leaflet, Elizabeth smiled and she told the man that she'd think about it. He walked away and, shoving the leaflet in her bag, Elizabeth stood. As brief as it had been, the conversation with Kate had restored her and now she wanted to explore, see what she could remember of Dartmouth.

Bella Vista, The Waves, Seaview what had the B&B been called? She remembered giggling with Chris, thinking of the evening they'd spent in a pub coming up with alternative names for the Victorian end terrace house: *Mon Repos* and Chris had frowned, "Not with that mattress." She'd suggested *Sea Winds, Ocean House*, until Chris pointed out that there was no view of the sea unless they stood on chairs and put their heads at an angle.

There'd been no view and the only smells they detected were not from the sea but from the kitchen where the smell of bacon lingered all day.

Elizabeth stopped and looked to the right, the road looked familiar, snaking its way up a hill.

She turned and walked, passing the street sign: *Fair View Road.*

She felt a knot of memory unravelling. *That's it! That's it, it was called Fair View.* She stopped, delighted with herself especially because she remembered Chris saying it hadn't been a *Fair View.* "We could get them under the Trades Description Act."

Walking on, she thought of the times that she and Chris had slowly made their way up the hill, not because they were out of breath but because they were dawdling, too scared to get back to the B&B before nine at night. The landlady, Elizabeth frowned, *Oh, God, what was her name?* She'd made it clear that guests were not welcome before then. Elizabeth shook her head. She could see her, a dumpy woman with frizzy dyed black hair, a floral apron wrapped around her, fingers stained yellow with nicotine.

Elizabeth stopped. *Mrs. Harrison!* That was her name, Betty Harrison. She'd never allow her guests to call her Betty but Chris had overhead a conversation between their landlady and the man who delivered bread. "I think he fancies her."

She'd laughed, telling Chris that the bread man must have nerves of steel. "Can you imagine her with that apron off?"

Elizabeth couldn't remember how much a week at the *Fair View* had cost. She did remember how they'd pooled their money, carefully eking it out, paying for fish and chips and an ice-cream on their last day.

She'd reached the B&B. It was still there but wasn't the same. The dull, brown paintwork had been replaced with gleaming white. The small garden was a riot of late summer colour and, looking upwards, Elizabeth saw the room where she and Chris had stayed, stepping back to get a better look. The tiny window had gone and, in its place, she saw a large picture window, no sign of the cheap net curtains which had effectively blocked any view, sea or otherwise. Elizabeth closed her eyes: *there*, she could see the arrangement of stiff, dried flowers cluttering up the narrow windowsill. Each time they pulled the curtains at night, the brittle flowers disintegrated even further, leaving a fine dust on the windowsill. Elizabeth used to wipe it away with the sleeve of her cardigan, hoping Mrs. Harrison wouldn't notice.

This part of Dartmouth was quiet, away from the harbour and Elizabeth realised that the house didn't appear to be a B&B any longer. The sign, *Fair View* had disappeared and the hand-painted card which hung in the front window with *No Vacancies* written in shaky white letters – that had gone too.

The realisation distressed her. Her memories were fading and with them that sense of what – adventure? She remembered telling Chris, lying on the lumpy mattress, the slippery pale, lilac eiderdown wrapped around them, how lucky they were, that no-one else felt the way they did.

Chris pulled her close, kissing the top of her head. "Don't you think most honeymooners feel like that?"

"No, they don't, they can't. We're special, we're not the same as everyone else."

Chris laughed and Elizabeth didn't say anything else, realising he wouldn't understand. Nevertheless, that sense of wonderment, of excitement stayed with her for a long time.

Now, looking at the sun shining on the windows of the house where she and Chris had honeymooned, Elizabeth felt weary. *Stupid idea to come here. What was I expecting? Mrs. Harrison wearing the same bloody apron?* Why had she come? Trying to resurrect the feeling of excitement, the sense of beginning something new? Revisiting old memories?

She looked at the house. What if she knocked on the door, what if she asked if she could look at the top bedroom, one more look, one last time?

No, what would that achieve? Best to leave things alone, leave her memories intact. Instead, she wandered through the town, stopping to look at shop windows, peering into galleries, eyes widening at the price of paintings hung on plain, white walls, knowing she knew where to find prints to match them, much cheaper. All around her people moved, jostled, laughed. She saw sleepy toddlers in pushchairs, women still wearing summer clothes, determined to hang on to the last vestiges of summer.

Stopping for a cup of tea, Elizabeth delved into her handbag, fingers searching for her purse, needing coins to leave a tip. She found the crumpled piece of paper the man in the captain's hat had given her. Smoothing it out, she read the blurb: *River Trips! See Agatha Christie's house! See Walter Raleigh's boatyard!*

All those exclamation marks, all that excitement – Elizabeth felt weary just reading it. Glancing at her watch, she saw it was only 3 o'clock. The next river cruise started at 3.30.

Sod it, it will kill some time.

The man in the captain's hat asked if she'd like the senior rate and, prickling with resentment, Elizabeth nodded. Sitting at the back of the blue and white boat, she watched as holidaymakers made their way to the front deck or the upper deck, nearly all clutching phones and bulging, misshapen rucksacks.

Elizabeth lifted her head, she closed her eyes, feeling the sun's rays on her face. She was enjoying the smell of the boat's engine, the tang of the water.

"Good afternoon!" The voice startled her and she opened her eyes.

"Thank you all for joining us onboard the *Cardiff Castle.*"

She smiled, wondering why the boat was called the Cardiff Castle and then, she gave up all pretence of dozing. The voice was loud, steady and, despite herself, Elizabeth listened intently to the information about the scenery surrounding them.

"To your right is Agatha Christie's home, *Greenway*, now owned by the National Trust."

She remembered reading the Poirot mysteries to the children and how she'd also enjoyed the books.

"Directly in front of us lies Dittisham, a picturesque village much loved by artists."

Elizabeth stood and, with her phone, took a picture.

"To your left is a new development, the subject of much discussion by our council. The plans include a spa, holiday apartments and new homes."

She stood again and took more photographs, aiming the phone at the board on the site with the name of the developer. Sitting down, she wondered why she'd done that, was it a reflex: see a development, a new possibility? Was there any point? The thought bothered her and she put her phone away, with a sense of embarrassment.

Elizabeth glanced at her fellow passengers, she was the only solo traveller. That wasn't what marked her out though, she knew that. She was over-dressed.

She sat back and looked at the rows of houses lined up behind the harbour, the colours on the brickwork: pink, white, blue. She watched the car ferry make its stately progress between Dartmouth and Kingswear, smiling at the thought of the commute some people must have. She wondered how she'd feel about taking a ferry to work. Would it become the norm or would there always be a sense of adventure?

When the boat stopped and the crew helped the passengers off, one dark-haired man told Elizabeth to be careful, "Them steps can be lethal if you don't watch yourself."

Thanking him, Elizabeth made her way up to the harbour again.

Sitting out on the balcony outside her hotel room, a glass of wine nearby, Elizabeth scrolled through her phone. Messages from Charlotte: *Hope you're ok. All good here. Let's talk when you get back?*

All good where? Office or home or both?

One from Kate. *Hope you're having a good time. Miss you.*

"Course you do." Elizabeth picked up her wine glass.

A message from David Armstrong: *Looking forward to our meeting.* Bloody man. She'd called him to organise a meeting, all the time listening to that odd tone of voice of his, trying to work out why it bothered her.

"Elizabeth, the ball's in your court. You name the day and I'll be there."

Was he flirting with her? Was that it? No, no, he was far too young for her to be interested in him. Or him her. No, he was just patronising her, mocking her. His flirtatious manner was his way of telling her that maybe once, when she was a younger woman, he might have been interested, but not now, not at her age. He was letting her know she was no longer of any interest. Past it.

She'd cut through his conversation and asked, "Wednesday 24th, 2.30. How does that sound?"

He laughed and Elizabeth gritted her teeth.

"Yes, certainly, you're the boss."

"Good, that's settled. I'll see you at my office then."

"You wouldn't prefer to come here?"

"No, I think it's best if we meet in my office, don't you?" Her voice was clipped.

"If that's what you'd prefer."

"It is. I look forward to working with you." And she'd put the phone down. Arrogant shit. Not wanting to think about David Armstrong, Elizabeth turned her phone over. No, she didn't need to see any more messages, not now. And yet, a few seconds later, she picked it up again, this time looking at the photos of the new development on the banks of the river. It looked bigger than she remembered it. It would incorporate moorings for boat owners and when she looked at the layout, she pictured where the new homes would be built, all those with fine views of the river. Without consciously thinking about it, she wrote down the name of the developer.

The following day, Elizabeth took a trip to Kingswear, going on the small ferry, hands gripping the sides as the boat eased away from Dartmouth.

From where she stood, she saw Dartmouth Castle and though she'd walk up the hill to see it, thinking it would use up a morning. She knew what she was doing: filling her head with *things*, all designed to stop her thinking, worrying about what had happened. It was futile of course; watching the shifting shadows on the buildings in Dartmouth harbour, she saw Charlotte's face, heard the condemnation in her words, felt her daughter's distrust of what she, Elizabeth was capable of. That hurt the most. The knowledge that her daughter thought she was past it, that she'd exceeded her sell by date. Oh God, that hurt.

Elizabeth made a noise, unsure whether it was one of distress or anger. Whatever it was, the boat's engines covered it and no-one glanced at her.

When the ferry stopped, she walked up the hill towards the town. A line of green fencing encircled a large, derelict building, a board fixed to the fencing. Elizabeth stopped. The name of the developer was the same she'd seen the day before. She stepped closer, looking at the photos of apartments, reading the blurb: *Extensive views of the estuary. Large high-ceilinged rooms, original features, fully-fitted kitchens. Concierge, secure parking.* She saw the prices and whistled. The photos showed walls with stripped back brickwork, soft honey-coloured wooden flooring. Sunshine flooded through large windows. Taking her phone from her bag, Elizabeth took pictures from every angle. Her mind was buzzing.

Back at the hotel, Elizabeth sat in the restaurant, her phone in front of her. She'd phoned the developer, Charles Heywood and Partners and she'd spoken to the marketing director, "My name is James," he'd said when she'd introduced herself.

His voice sounded young and Elizabeth wondered how her voice sounded to him. She spoke briskly, telling him of her company's projects, the builders they'd worked for and, not giving James a chance to interrupt, asked if she could meet him. "I'm here in Dartmouth for a few days and would be happy to meet you wherever is convenient for you."

"Where are you staying?"

"At the Dart Marina."

"I could meet you there tomorrow at 11. How does that sound?"

"Sounds fine. I look forward to meeting you."

Before she'd spoken to James, Elizabeth googled the name of the builder, looking at the developments, the areas they'd worked in. She trawled through photographs of sites, of completed houses and apartments. It was impressive, although relatively small, they were obviously prestigious. "See, this is what we need." Elizabeth muttered. She glanced at her phone, wondering whether to send Charlotte a text: *Look what I've found.* No: best wait until after she'd spoken to James. She had a good feeling about this. Coming to Dartmouth had been the right thing to do.

James was tall, his chin fuzzy with gingery bristles and, although he tried hard not to show it, he seemed taken aback at the sight of Elizabeth.

She'd dressed carefully, aware that, when she'd packed, it was with no thought about meeting potential clients. She wore a pair of well-cut navy blue trousers and a matching jacket. Looking at her reflection, she muttered, "Oh, God, I look as if I work in a car salesroom."

When James walked towards her, she smiled and asked if he'd like a cup of coffee.

Sitting in the lounge area of the hotel, the cleaning staff moved around them. Telephones rang, receptionist voices repeated the same phrase: "Dart Marina Hotel, how may I help you?" A querulous voice could be heard, "Where the hell is my *Daily Telegraph?*"

Smiling brightly at James, Elizabeth found to her horror that she was gabbling, trying to jam her entire working experience into a rushed sales pitch, wanting to make this young man (*how old is he for God's sake?*) understand, be impressed by her years of experience, make him realise that she was capable and efficient. At first, he looked at her with blankness, then sitting back, he looked as if he was watching something on television, a drama unfolding, a spectacle, as if he was being entertained. *Bastard!*

She stopped, aware that her heart was racing and she put a hand to her neck, knowing that, even at her age, her skin would be blotchy with nerves.

James picked up his cup and, holding it close to his face, asked Elizabeth if she was on holiday.

"Well, not really. I wanted a few days off. I've been working hard…"

"Ah, we all need a break, don't we? This business can take a toll on all of us."

Bland words yet Elizabeth flinched. "Things have been, well they've been frantic at my company." She stopped, uncomfortable with the way James was looking at her.

He drained his cup and, putting it down, sat forward. "Do you have a business card?"

He wanted to leave. Elizabeth knew that and didn't know how to stop him. "Yes, I think I do." She pulled one from her bag and handed it over. "I'll be back at the office on Monday. Maybe we could talk a bit more then?"

James glanced at the card before slipping it into an inside pocket. "Yeah, I'm sure we can." He stood and, not knowing what else she could do, Elizabeth also stood.

They shook hands once more and Elizabeth resisted the impulse to grab his sleeve, to ask him to stay, to let her start all over again. She watched as he strode across the foyer and out of the hotel. *Christ, I buggered that up.*

She sat down, winded by the experience.

It had never happened before. She'd always been in control, assured, confident. She knew her business inside out. Why, why had she behaved like that? Frantic, desperate to get business from someone young enough to be her son? What had she been trying to prove?

Ah. She knew the answer. Because James had assumed she was younger, she'd seen that and had tried too hard to overcome his initial reaction at meeting her. Either that or, Elizabeth closed her eyes. Her daughters were right, she couldn't hack it. She was past it.

No, no I'm not having that. I'm bloody well not having that.

She sat for a moment, oblivious to the hotel and its staff and she made herself go over what had just happened. What had she done? She'd over-reacted, that's all. A young man, expecting a younger woman and, seeing the expression on his face, she'd gone into overdrive.

What am I? Why did I do that? Is that what Charlotte's done? Put me on the back foot? I'm not old! I'm not past it. No, I'm not.

She lifted her head and glanced at her watch. It was barely 11.20. The rest of the day threatened to stretch out forever. Just then her phone rang, it was Charlotte and Elizabeth faltered, not wanting, not ready to talk to her. Not after what had just happened. She sighed and answered.

"Hello?"

"Mum, I wanted to tell you…"

Now what?

"What is it, Charlotte?"

"I thought I should tell you, warn you, that Gareth's on his way down to see you."

"Why? How does he even know where I am?"

"He came here and, well I blurted it out where you were. He's in a bit of a state."

"Oh, for Christ's sake, Charlotte."

"I know, I know and I'm sorry. It just slipped out."

"Thanks for that."

"I'm sorry, Mum. I just wanted to let you know."

Without another word, Elizabeth put the phone down. It was a double whammy. She'd made a prat of herself in front of James and now Gareth was on his way down to see her. She felt as if she was being attacked on all sides.

CHAPTER 18

Jon was at the sink, the girls all over me, yanking at my sleeves, Sophie telling me about Henry Vlll. "Mummy, did you know he chopped his wife's head off?"

"He didn't do it himself, he got someone else to do it." I said, hugging them both, my eyes on the back of Jon's head. He hadn't moved.

His voice was low, "Girls, go and make a start on your homework."

That was a first, it was normally me who did the bad cop routine.

"Aawwhh," the girls whined in unison but, picking up on Jon's tone, I shooed them gently out of the kitchen. Jon was leaning on the sink, staring at the garden.

"Jon, what is it? Are you ok?" He was spooking me.

"Gareth's been here, looking for you."

"He's just sent me a text. I told him to fuck off. Why did he come here? He knows I'm in work."

"He wants to know where your Mum is."

I touched his arm and he flinched.

"Jon? Please, turn, look at me. Let's talk about this properly. I can't talk to the back of your head."

He lowered his head before turning. "I had to ask him to leave. He was scaring the girls."

"What? Oh, God. *No!* Was he…?" Drugs, *shit*. That was the first thing I thought and, even without knowing what was going on, I wanted to punch my brother. My head was full of *stuff* from the day and coming home, finding Gareth had upset my kids…Christ, I wanted to kill him.

Jon shook his head, "I don't think it's drugs, not as far as I could tell. He was just…" he sighed and rubbed his face. "Charlie, all this…" he dropped his hands and looked at me. "This is all getting out of hand. Gareth was in a terrible state, looked as if he'd been sleeping in a ditch. I asked if he needed money but he said he didn't, just kept asking where your mother was. Did *I* know and what time were you coming home? Why wasn't your Mum answering her phone, on and on with the same questions. The girls were frightened. He looked like a wild man."

"Where is he now? Did he say where he was staying?" I didn't care, not really. All I wanted was to keep him away from my family.

"No, he didn't but then I didn't ask. He does want to talk to your Mum though."

I tugged at Jon's arm. "Sit down, let's have a glass of wine. Please, Jon, sit with me."

Jon's the same age as me but he sat down like an old man, gingerly and with effort. Even his breathing sounded laboured. *Oh God, what am I doing?*

I touched his hand, "Don't move. I'll get the wine."

I kept my eyes on him as I opened the bottle. He was slumped as if exhausted.

"Here." I put the glasses on the table. He remained silent.

"Jon, please, let's talk about this. Please."

When he lifted his head, I saw the anguish on his face. He held my gaze for a second before speaking. "Charlie, do you know how this *battle* you're waging is having an effect on our family?" He dropped his head, "Shit, Charlie, I'm not sure I recognise you any longer."

"*What?*" That winded me. "Listen, it's not my fault my waste of space brother turned up…"

"Don't, Charlie, that's disingenuous, don't do that." His words *whooshed* out in a rush. "I've had enough, I'm working hard too. I'm looking after the girls and doing the best I can. But, and I need to tell you this, right now it feels as if I'm the only one keeping this family afloat."

"Don't, oh don't say that." I put my hand out, wanting to touch him, to let him know…what, that he was wrong? But he wasn't. I'd used him, not consciously, not maliciously but I'd always known, *understood*, that it was Jon who held it all together. We never talked about it, but without Jon, I couldn't do what I do.

My hand rested on his arm, Jon's eyes were closed as if the effort of saying those things had drained him. They'd drained me, hearing them.

I leant in closer, "Jon, first of all I'm sorry, *really, really* sorry. You're right, of course you're right. I've not been doing enough for you and the girls. I do know that." I took a deep breath, "This *thing*, this issue with Mum and the company, it's taken over my life and I shouldn't have let that happen. I was wrong, very wrong."

He hadn't moved, not even a tiny shift but I sensed he was listening, not softening, I knew him too well for that, but I felt I could continue. "Please, Jon, listen to me."

Now what? I don't know what to say to him, how to let him know that I appreciate everything he does, that I'm sorry for being such a shit when it comes to looking after our family when all I can focus on, all I can see right now, is the company and my role in it. I just need Jon to keep doing what he's doing for a bit longer. So how do I say that though?

I smiled, "Sweetheart, this will come to an end." Jon's eyes were on mine and I wasn't sure I could read his expression. "Today in work was all the proof I needed that everyone in the company is right behind me." I waited, wondering whether Jon would speak but his face was expressionless and I couldn't work out whether he was listening or just waiting for me to shut the fuck up. I decided to carry on. "We, Kate and I, we've spent the entire day working with everyone, working out who does what and setting up the new project." I paused. *This* was what I wanted to tell Jon: that it was going to happen, that I'd be heading up the new workforce, that everyone was behind me. It was set up and I was *bursting* to tell Jon how excited I was, what it would mean to the company, what it meant to me. But I couldn't, just couldn't. Instead, I waffled on about long-term projects, stabilising the staff, keeping morale high. Honestly, I could hear myself as if I was in some kind of out of body experience, looking at him as I was talking, trying to gauge his expression. He knew what I was doing but he, like me, went along with it. I know what *my* reason was but I wasn't sure I knew what Jon was thinking. Were we both playing a game, keeping things ticking over because neither of us wanted to think about the alternative? By doing what we've always done: Jon in his role, me in mine, that way at least we could *pretend* everything was ok? I didn't want to think too much about that. My motives I could live with, but Jon? That bothered me. Did it mean he'd lost all respect for me, that he was biding his time before telling me he'd had enough? That he'd walk away? Was that what both of us were doing? Playing our parts?

I closed my eyes and when I opened them, I saw that Jon was looking at me.

"Fancy a top up?" It was only when I stood that I realised Jon hadn't touched his first glass of wine.

I don't know what we talked about for another ten minutes. The truth was, I did most of the talking. I jabbered on about the renewal of house insurance, did we need to buy a new carpet for the living room, just stuff. Then I called the girls downstairs, riddled with guilt about making them go to their rooms and over compensated, hugging them, insisting they told me about their day, ignoring the faces they pulled. "I'm going to have something to eat," I'm starving," I told them, not recognising my voice, high, brittle, full of forced energy.

"Can we watch tv?" Hannah asked, realising what I was doing and making the most of it.

"Won't you sit with me? I haven't seen you all day." I wanted them near me, aware of Jon moving around, putting things away. I knew what he was doing, *See I'm a good parent, I spend more time with them than you do*.

Both girls looked at me, their expressions wary. I said of course they could watch tv. "But not for too long, it's school tomorrow." As if they didn't know.

After they'd gone, I sat at the kitchen table with a plate of scrambled eggs in front of me. Jon hadn't finished his first glass of wine and I was on my third. My eyelids felt weighed down by bricks; as soon as the girls were in bed, I'd go too. Not only because I was so tired, but because I was a coward and I didn't want anymore *anything* from Jon: no recriminations, no silent martyrdom, nothing. I thought if I went to bed, today would be over and I could face tomorrow. I also wanted to go to bed to think about what had happened in the office. I'd spent hours on the phone, on emails, on discussions and planning with Jess with all of them, making lists, drawing up worksheets and estimates and I'd loved every minute of it, every bloody minute.

Jon was emptying the dishwasher – normally I do that. We have unwritten lists of who does what in the house: Jon does the manly things: taking out the bins, the recycling and he also does the weekly shop and he cooks in the week and I do it on the weekend and I do laundry and nearly all the housework, including emptying the dishwasher. But not tonight. I opened my mouth to tell him to leave it, that I'd do it, then shrugged. Let him get on with it.

The doorbell rang. Jon turned, "If that's Gareth, I don't want him frightening the girls again."

"I'll go and if it's him, I'll tell him to piss off."

It was Gareth and Jon hadn't exaggerated. He looked awful as if he hadn't showered or changed his clothes in weeks.

"What d'you want?" I held the door, not wanting to let him in.

"Where's Mum?" His voice was hoarse. "She won't answer her phone and I need to talk to her."

"What the fuck d'you expect? What the hell have you ever done for her? For Christ's sake, Gareth, what the hell is wrong with you?"

He looked at his feet, mumbling something.

"What? For God's sake, what did you say?"

"I want to talk to her, to say I'm sorry, that it wasn't me."

"What wasn't you? Aren't you the heartless shit who's been conning money out of her for years, isn't that you or did I make a mistake?"

Once again, he mumbled and I was about to slam the door when he moved, holding his hand out, as if to force his way inside.

"Don't Gareth, don't you bloody dare."

"I'm sorry, I didn't mean to…" He stepped back and he shook his head. "I want to talk to Mum, I need to speak to her."

I don't know why I didn't slam the door in his face. I wanted to, God knows I wanted to but there was something in his appearance, his voice, that made me keep the door open. He was staring at his feet again. His trainers were filthy, mud encrusted, the laces squashed and trailing on the floor. Thirty eight and he still looked like a hormonal teenager. A dirty one.

"Charlie?" It was Jon's voice and I turned.

"It's ok, Gareth is just leaving."

Jon stood next to me. "What d'you want, Gareth? I've already asked you to leave once."

Gareth shook his head. "I know and I'm sorry. I want to know where Mum is. I don't want anything from her. I just want to see her. I need to say something. I need to put things right, to tell her…" He stopped, he shook his head.

Jon and I were standing close together, looking at Gareth and I heard Jon's breathing.

I spoke first, "You're filthy. Where are you living?"

He shrugged, "Kipping on a mate's sofa. It's not ideal and the boiler packed in a few days ago."

"A few *days* ago? You look as if you haven't showered in months."

"I know, I'm sorry." He pulled a face, "I didn't mean to frighten the girls. I wouldn't do that, I wouldn't do anything…I wouldn't."

I don't know if Jon and I had the same thought but when he said, "You can shower here and I think I can find you some clean clothes," it didn't surprise me.

Gareth mumbled his thanks and I stood aside as he came into the house. He didn't smell too good and I flinched. He muttered, "Sorry, I know…"

The girls came out of the lounge and stopped when they saw him, unsure of what to do. They looked at Jon and, when he spoke, his voice was soft, kind. "Uncle Gareth is just here to have a shower. They don't have one where he's staying so Mummy and I said he could use ours."

The girls seemed to accept that and offered Gareth the use of their *Frozen* shower gel.

If Gareth has one redeeming quality, then it's being a good

uncle. He loves the girls and they love him. Kids don't waffle, they don't hide the truth and when Sophie told Gareth that he "stunk" he cheerfully agreed. The girls bossed him around, clambering up the stairs inn their eagerness to show where he could shower and I heard squeals of laughter as he teased them. Wish I could forget how he'd scared them earlier as easily as that. Now, in their eyes, he was back to just being Uncle Gareth again.

Jon muttered something about finding clothes to fit Gareth and then he too went upstairs. Before long, there were sounds of my daughters' voices and the lower pitched rumbles of their Dad and Uncle. Listening, it felt as if I'd been left off the invitation list for a great party. How stupid was that?

I wandered into the living room, making a pretence of tidying up, picking up clothes that the girls had discarded. I sniffed at the water in a vase of roses and went into the kitchen to empty it when Jon reappeared. He told me he thought that Gareth should stay for one night, "Put him back on his feet."

"*What?* Are you mad? You know what he's like. I don't want him staying here. A shower and clean clothes, ok, I can do that but as for him under this roof where the girls are sleeping – no, Jon, I'm not having it."

"Charlie, he's homeless. He has no money, no job, he's got nothing."

"So what?" I glared at Jon. "This is the same man who, according to you, scared the girls earlier today. Now you're suggesting he sleeps under our roof, no doubt the moment he thinks we're all fast asleep, he'll go through our stuff, nick everything he can and bugger off as he always does."

"So you're telling me that you'd rather your brother slept on a bench or in a shop doorway?"

"Yeah, you got that right."

"*One* night, Charlie. One night. That's all. If needs be, I'll sleep downstairs if it makes you feel better."

"Jon, for Christ's sake. He's useless. He's a waste of space, a total dickhead. He's used Mum, borrowed money with no intention of ever paying it back. He's given her endless promises that he'll try, that he'll earn a living, that he'll be independent – and now look at him! What's the phrase, he hasn't got a pot to piss in."

Jon pushed his hands through his hair. "Don't I get a say in this? Isn't this my house too?"

"Yes, of course you do. But he's *my* brother and I don't trust him. Not one bit."

"What's he done to you?"

"*What?* Jon, this is Gareth for God's sake. He's not worth arguing about. Please, I'm knackered and I don't want to do this now."

"Ok, he's your brother and, so far, he's not amounted to much. But he's got nowhere to go, that friend of his he was staying with, told him to fuck off and everything he owns is in someone else's garage. You're right, he hasn't got a pot to piss in so I'm suggesting to you that for one night, one night, Charlie, he stays here, with us."

Christ.

All I wanted to do was crawl into bed, pull the duvet over my head and sleep.

I looked at Jon but his expression was fixed. "One night, Charlie. It won't kill you."

"It's all right, Jon, I'll leave." Gareth was standing in the doorway. I hadn't heard him and hardly recognised him from the layabout who'd rung the doorbell. His hair was damp, clean and he'd shaved and his skin looked pink, healthy.

I turned away. I didn't want to look at him. I didn't want to look at Jon either.

Jon spoke softly, "You can stay, Gareth. One night though, understood?"

"Thank you, that means a lot to me. Charlie?"

I shook my head, not wanting to talk to either of them.

"Please, Charlie, I won't…" Gareth's voice was low.

I looked at him, "You won't steal from us, is that what you're saying?"

"That's not fair!" Jon spoke loudly.

"No, Jon, it is fair." Gareth's voice was firm.

"Ha! You admit it then, you have stolen before from Mum, is that what you're saying?"

Gareth's hand rested on the back of a chair. "She thinks I did but I didn't."

"What the fuck are you talking about? Why would she think that? Although it doesn't surprise me." I sensed Jon's anger but I ignored it. "Tell me, Gareth. Why on earth would Mum think you've stolen from her? Could it be because you've done it before?"

Gareth cleared his throat, "I made a mistake. I brought two of my, well, I thought they were friends, to Mum's house. We a had a business proposal for her and she didn't want to know…"

I opened my mouth but Jon lifted his hand and shook his head.

Gareth's voice was low. "I didn't know it until later but one of them," he pulled a face, "well, he stole her jewellery."

"Oh my God! He did what? Are you seriously telling me that you brought two pieces of shit into Mum's house and one of them stole from her? Fuck, Gareth, what the hell were you thinking?"

He looked at me, then at Jon. "Charlie, I made a mistake, a huge one. One of them had a plan, it sounded feasible to me." I snorted and Gareth frowned. "I know, I know but truth is, right then, I'd have listened to anything to put things right, to make my life better, to be better."

"I don't understand, why did they steal from her?" My voice had risen and Jon gave me a warning look. *Don't frighten the girls.*

"Oh, Charlie, come on! Think about it. They saw her house, her car and they thought she was loaded. When Mum wouldn't give us any money to get us started, they were pissed off with her and when, well, when Mum told us all to leave, they took her jewellery."

"And these scumbags were your *friends*? Well done, Gareth. You've really excelled yourself this time." Ok, so he hadn't stolen the jewellery himself but the fact that he'd brought those men into Mum's house was still enough to make me want to kill him.

"As soon as I'd realised what he'd done, I made him give it back to me and I put it in an envelope and pushed it through Mum's door."

"So that's all right then. What the *fuck*, Gareth?"

I had to turn away, couldn't bear to look at him and then I thought about what Mum must have felt like knowing someone had stolen her jewellery and she'd thought that someone was Gareth. She'd come into work thinking that and then I'd...*Oh God.* I felt a peculiar shifting sensation. I'd stolen from her too. I was more of a thief than Gareth.

"Charlie?" It was Jon's voice.

"What?" I was close to tears and didn't want him to see.

"Gareth has returned the jewellery to your Mum, he knows bringing those men to her house was a mistake."

I'd had it. "So you're the best of friends now, are you? I'm going to say goodnight to the girls. I'll leave you both to it."

Gareth stepped to one side and I left the kitchen.

I don't know if it was sheer tiredness but I was close to tears again and both girls complained when I hugged them.

"Mummy! You're hurting me." Hannah wriggled free and stomped off into her bedroom.

Sophie put her head to one side. "Why are you sad? Is it because Uncle Gareth is here?"

"No, sweetheart." I buried my face in her damp hair. "I'm just tired, that's all. Think I'll go to bed at the same time as you tonight."

She laughed, "No you won't. You'll have more wine with Daddy."

After the girls had gone to bed, I stood on the landing, listening to the murmur of voices from the kitchen. *Sod it, sod it.* I went downstairs.

Jon and Gareth were at the table, two bottles of beer in front of them. Neither spoke as I entered and, again I felt a sense of dislocation, of not being invited, of not being welcome.

"Want a glass of wine?" Jon asked.

"Please, Charlie…" Gareth stopped, his eyes on mine.

"I don't want any wine, thank you." I remained standing.

The silence felt incredibly loud but I didn't feel inclined to do anything about it.

Gareth coughed, "Do you know where Mum is?"

I looked at him, registering that he was wearing one of Jon's sweatshirts, a faded logo of *David Bowie Reality Tour* on the front. Why did that bother me? We'd gone together, I'd bought the sweatshirt for him but I hadn't seen him wear it in years.

"Charlie?"

"Um, not sure."

Jon looked at me, "Do you know where she is?"

"She told me she was going to Dartmouth."

Gareth's eyes widened. "Dartmouth, why has she gone away?! I shrugged, "No idea. Something about needing a break."

"Why?"

"Just told you. I don't know."

"No, why did she need a break? It's not like her not to go to work."

Jon's chair squeaked. He moved but remained silent.

I shook my head, "It isn't important."

"I think it is." Gareth's tone had shifted.

"Shut the fuck up, Gareth! You've got no right to question me about Mum. No bloody right at all. All you've ever done is sponge off her – fuck, you've given no thought to what you've done to her over the years, have you?"

"I know what I've done, Charlie. I know only too well. What have *you* done?"

This time I looked at Jon. Had he told Gareth? I couldn't read his face at all.

"None of your business. Don't start playing the dutiful son now. It's way too late for that."

"I really do need to talk to her."

"What about? Another money-making scam? Another sob story so you can ask her for more money?"

He shook his head, "No, neither of those. I simply want to talk to her."

Jon's voice was low. "Do you really not know where she's staying, Charlie."

"No, I don't."

Gareth muttered, "She and Dad went to Dartmouth for their honeymoon."

I looked at him, how did he know that and I didn't?

He sensed my thoughts, "She told us, don't you remember?"

I shrugged, "Still don't know where she's staying."

"It'll be somewhere nice though." Gareth's voice held a hint of, not sure what it was. Pride? Mockery? Either way, it infuriated me.

"Of course it will. She's worked hard for what she's got. Why shouldn't she stay somewhere nice? *Oh God*. Everything Gareth said was getting on my nerves. It wasn't only that; I had the same reaction, the one I'd been experiencing over and over. An innate need to protect Mum, to shield her from anything hurtful or damaging to her.

We'd reached a sort of impasse. Gareth kept looking at me as if he thought that, at any second, I'd pull the hotel's name out of a hat whilst Jon looked at me as if he was waiting for me to give in, to let Gareth back into my life. Well, sod the pair of them.

"If you do go to Dartmouth, how will you get there? That car of yours is held together with Sellotape."

Gareth frowned, "It should be ok if I take it slowly."

I had a strange feeling, one that made me edgy and nervous, that feeling again of not being included. *What's the matter with me?* I looked at them both, meeting their blank gazes. "Ok, I'm done. I'll leave you to it. I'm going to have a bath and then I'm going to bed." I couldn't resist it, "Some of us have jobs to go to in the morning."

Gareth half rose, "Charlie…"

I put a hand up, "Don't, just don't." Without another word, I left the kitchen.

I didn't hear Jon get into bed. I slept for nine hours, a record for me.

In the morning, the empty beer bottles were on the draining board, the kitchen chairs in their normal places but there was no sign of Gareth. I wandered about, checking that he hadn't taken anything. Jon saw me looking at the laptop on the kitchen unit. "It's still there, Charlie."

I didn't ask if he'd given Gareth any money. I didn't ask anything. Then the girls came downstairs and another day began.

CHAPTER 19

Where am I? And then she remembered. The Dart Marina Hotel. Elizabeth looked at the decoration of her room: the blue and white striped wallpaper, the prints of ships and small boats, deep, thick blue carpet, all over the top in her view. But what was she doing here? She'd run away, bolted, left her home, her family, her company. Lying there, eyes wide open, Elizabeth thought about the meeting she'd had the day before with – what was his name? *James Williamson.* She could see him now, that artful stubble, his amused smile as he listened to her sales pitch, then he'd have gone back to his office to regale everyone with her performance, playing it for laughs, mimicking her high pitched voice, the way she'd jabbered at him in her eagerness to sell her company, herself. *Her clothing. Oh God, he must have thought I was trying to sell him a second-hand Ford.* What the hell had she been thinking?

Best to pretend yesterday hadn't happened. Erase it, wipe it from her memory, like a slate, a clean slate. She'd been so caught up with her need to prove to Charlotte and Kate that she could still bring in new business, but all she'd done was give that smooth bastard a good laugh.

Well, screw him.

She got out of bed and padded over to the window. The sight of the water, its movement and changing colours soothed her. The sun shone again and seagulls flashed their wings as they flew past her window. She smiled, listening to their raucous calls. *Wonder what they're saying to each other? Maybe they're discussing where to go for breakfast and whose turn it is to look after the kids.*

"Get a grip," she spoke firmly. "Ok, yesterday, not my finest hour but today's another day."

As she sipped at the coffee the waiter had poured, Elizabeth thought about walking to Dartmouth Castle. That would take up the morning and she could catch the ferry back. Pleased by her decision, she sat back, aware that the view continued to captivate her. The tension faded from her shoulders and Elizabeth knew that the episode with James Williamson, could be shoved to one side, hidden amongst other events in her life she'd rather forget.

Her phone *pinged*. A text from Charlotte: *Just to say sorry again.*
Elizabeth pushed the phone into her handbag and left.

She stopped to look at the houses lining the steep hill leading to the castle. A few had dates carved into cream coloured stone above their wide windows. 1978, 1892, 1852. One house had been beautifully restored, painted white with window boxes full of late flowering, dark red geraniums. A newer house was opposite, its functional straight brick walls inlaid with large areas of glass, all designed to make the most of the views. *God, that's got all the appeal of a doctor's waiting room.*

Elizabeth hung the strap of her handbag around her neck and, with the weight of the bag nudging at her ribcage, returned to climbing the hill towards the castle.

At the turning, she saw what looked like an old factory, a cobbled street in front, its stones tangled with grass and rampant buddleia. *Look at that, why has that been left?*

Walking on, Elizabeth saw the castle and she was aware of other tourists holding phones up in the air, their eyes squinting in the sunshine. She heard voices, "Doesn't look much from the outside, does it?" "I've seen better in Wales."

Elizabeth knew because she'd googled it, that parts of the castle had been built in 1388 and that it was now owned by English Heritage. She also knew that to go inside, she had to book first. For some reason, she'd decided against booking, choosing instead to drink a cup of coffee in the small area near a café where, once again, she could lose herself in the views of the estuary and the castle.

The stonework of the castle had faded over the years and now it was a washed out cream. It stood a little apart from the headland which was a good thing: negative comments couldn't reach it, it couldn't know what people thought about it. She liked the idea and felt a kinship with the castle: she too was apart from other people. She too could remain silent.

Elizabeth disentangled herself from her handbag, placed it on the table and heard a noise from her phone, *ping*.

No, not now. She placed her bag on the floor between her feet and picked up her cup.

The path to the ferry meandered through the wooded area with rustic, weather-beaten signs telling her she was on the right track. Elizabeth grinned. It all looked medieval and she wondered how many feet had scrambled down the side of the hill to the ferry.

The ferryman was taciturn and Elizabeth had to bite her lip when she heard a man talking to him, "I bet you've done this trip a few times before."

She caught the ferryman's eye and he raised an eyebrow before nodding, "Too many to count."

Elizabeth sat at the side of the small boat and felt the *thrum* of its engine. Watching the ferryman cast off, she admired the way he stood, feet apart as he edged the boat away from the tiny jetty. How old was he? His skin was leathery, reddish, the colour of bricks, fine lines criss-crossed around his eyes, she guessed from years squinting at the sun. His clothes were as battered as his boat, his jeans baggy and faded at the knees, a red and white checked shirt, sleeves rolled up to his elbows. The sinews on his arms were rope-like and, although he steered with confidence, Elizabeth sensed his thoughts were somewhere else.

She'd been engrossed watching him, his clothes, his stance and was startled to find his eyes were on hers. *Oh God.* She looked away, focusing on the harbour, the rows of houses on either side of the estuary, the pale pink walls of one house next to a warm yellow of another. One house, covered in a harsh green, caught Elizabeth's eye. *That's horrible, why wasn't that stopped?* She was affronted by the garishness of the colour, marking it out like a stain.

The ferryman brought the boat to the steps leading up to the harbour and Elizabeth waited whilst the other passengers disembarked. Then, clutching her bag to her chest, she stood to leave, the ferryman holding out his hand to support her.

With a sense of embarrassment, she muttered, "Thank you," feeling his calloused fingers on her skin. She felt a ridiculous need to apologise for staring at him. She didn't want him to think she was slotting him into the fabric of her holiday: the weathered boatman, the cream teas, the castle dating back to the 1300s. She didn't say another word but felt his eyes on her as she climbed the steps.

At the top of the steps, Elizabeth stood, looking at the crowds moving around her, unsure about what to do. There seemed to be a lot of the day left. Then she remembered a pretty bistro near the art gallery and she thought she'd look at a picture that had caught her eye and then she'd have fresh crab for her lunch. *After all, I can do whatever I want.* She knew telling herself that didn't alter the fact that she wasn't sure how to switch off, how to do nothing.

Blank-faced she walked briskly towards the gallery.

The picture in its frame was heavy and it knocked against her calves as she made her way back to the hotel. She thought she'd got a bargain. The gallery owner was keen to talk to Elizabeth once she'd told him what she did and, despite her experience with James Williamson, Elizabeth spoke with pride about her company, handing her business card over at the end. The gallery owner was a large man with a plain, white shirt straining over his stomach and he told Elizabeth about the various developments in and around Dartmouth. "Bit of an issue, to be honest. There's no doubt the place needs tidying up, new business, new trade but some of the older residents aren't keen."

Elizabeth listened to his words, shaking her head when she thought it was expected and making soothing noises when the owner told her of his own struggle. They haggled in a genteel fashion over the painting and, when the owner pressed his business card into Elizabeth's hands, she knew she'd won the battle. The owner's hands were moist and fleshy and Elizabeth thought of the harsh skin on the ferryman's hands.

Next door at the bistro, she asked for a fresh crab salad and a glass of wine. She sighed, content to sit at the back. Her table held a green pottery jug with sprigs of mint which made her think of her garden. Sitting there she listened to the rise and fall of conversation from locals and tourists, discussions about which café served the best chips, whether it was worth a trip to Totnes, a conversation between the waitress and a man sitting on his own, his hands holding the lead of a frail greyhound. "Don't know what to do for the best," the man said, looking at the sad eyes of the dog. "He won't leave my side." The waitress murmured something Elizabeth didn't catch and then, putting a hand on the man's shoulder, the waitress went back to the kitchen.

After her lunch she walked slowly back to the hotel, thinking over what she'd seen and heard and knew she was walking towards the harbour steps. Was it because of the ferryman? But he wasn't there, just a short queue of people waiting in line to buy an ice-cream.

Disappointed and not understanding why she felt that way, Elizabeth looked out across the water and saw boats in various sizes and shapes moving across from Kingswear to Dartmouth. She liked seeing the movement of the boats, boats like that of the ferryman crossed the water all the time. Then, swapping hands to relieve the pressure on her fingers, she made her way to the hotel.

She saw Gareth's legs before the receptionist told her he'd arrived. He was sitting near a large castor oil plant, its glossy leaves hiding most of him, only the sprawl of his legs visible. She saw his trainers, the backs of them crushed, just like he'd done as a child, the laces, grey and fraying snaked around his feet. Elizabeth wanted to snap at him, "For God's sake, do your laces up, you'll trip if you don't."

She thought about leaving, pretending she hadn't seen him, but then he heard the receptionist call her name and Elizabeth saw Gareth's feet move before she heard him,

"Hello, Mum."

"How did you find me?"

He shrugged, "It wasn't difficult. My car broke down and I had to walk down the hill and this was the first hotel I saw."

"Where is your car now?"

Gareth pointed in the direction of the door. "Out there. I pushed it off the road."

Looking at him, Elizabeth struggled to control her irritation."

"Gareth, why are you here?"

"Could we go somewhere, have a cup of tea or something?"

Oh, Christ. No. Elizabeth didn't want him in the hotel and then she felt ashamed, ashamed because he looked so awful, his eyes red-rimmed, hair shaggy and unkempt his jeans too short. She was ashamed to be seen with her own son – what did that say about her?

"Let me get rid of this," she gestured to the bag she was carrying, "and then we can find somewhere to sit."

Not wanting to see the expression on his face, she went to her room.

Once there, she sat on the edge of her bed, trying to work out what Gareth's visit meant. She didn't think either of the girls would have sanctioned a visit from him – neither Kate nor Charlotte would have trusted Gareth to smooth their mother's feathers. Besides, she hadn't spoken to him since her jewellery had been stolen. It had been returned, but that didn't change the fact that someone had stolen from her. Anyway, it wasn't just that, it was more about not wanting anyone with her. That meant no-one, especially not her family. *What the hell is he doing here?*

Elizabeth stood, took a deep breath and left the room to rejoin Gareth.

She had a peculiar sense of wanting to protect the views she'd grown to love, so when Gareth commented on the number of boats on the water, she barked at him, "Most of them are working boats."

She ignored his look of confusion, choosing instead to point to a small park where a café served afternoon tea.

They crossed the road in silence and found a table set apart from the others. Gareth picked up the menu. "I'm starving, do you think I could have a sandwich?"

"Are you asking me?" She couldn't control her anger.

"S'ok, I'll check with the waitress."

Elizabeth asked for a pot of tea, turning her head as Gareth asked for sandwiches and a plate of cakes. She thought about walking away, sitting on a bench, looking at the view, anywhere on her own. Whatever this was about, she didn't want to listen to him.

"This is nice, Mum."

"What is?"

"Here, Dartmouth, it's lovely."

Elizabeth looked at him, "Why are you here?"

He pulled at the skin on his fingers, "I wanted to say sorry."

"What for? Stealing from me? For bringing those awful men into my home? For letting me down time and time again? Just what are you apologising for, Gareth?"

She knew her voice had risen, she saw Gareth look around and then the waitress brought their order. Elizabeth sat silently whilst the cups, jug, plates of food were placed on the table. She saw the way the waitress looked first at Gareth and then at her. Elizabeth's smile was brief, "Thank you." With obvious relief, the waitress left them.

Gareth picked up a sandwich and, to Elizabeth's fury, took out the slices of tomato, putting them on the side of his plate. "Do you have to do that?"

He looked up, "I don't like tomato, you know that."

She *did* know but everything he did was annoying her. "Gareth, tell me why you've driven all the way here. What d'you hope to achieve?"

His mouth full, he mumbled, "I told you, I want to apologise."

She leant forward, hissing at him, "What the hell for? I haven't got all day and it's going to take longer than that to apologise for all the grief you've given me over the years."

He stopped chewing and she heard the harsh gulp as he swallowed. "Mum, please, listen, just listen. I've thought about this."

Elizabeth picked up her cup of tea. She didn't want or need

Gareth's apologies. She wasn't sure what she was feeling. It was a sort of *weariness*. She didn't, couldn't even formulate what she was thinking – all she knew was that she didn't want to hear him, to look at him and oh, God, she most definitely didn't want to be with him, not now. The tea tasted metallic and she put the cup down.

"What are you going to do about your car? You can't just leave it."

"What?" Gareth shook his head, "Mum, I don't want to talk about my car. I want to tell you… I want to tell you how sorry I am for everything I've done. Please, please, listen to me."

"What have you done with your things?"

"What *things?* I don't know what you mean." His tone was tetchy.

"Your things, your clothes. You can't have come down here with just the things you're wearing. They don't fit, the sleeves on that sweatshirt…they aren't your clothes, are they?"

Gareth shook his head, "No, they're Jon's. I stayed with them last night and Jon gave me these…" He looked at his lap, "I'm taller than Jon."

"So, let me get this straight. You turned up at Jon and Charlotte's house, stayed there overnight, borrowed his clothes and then you came here and your car broke down. Did I miss anything out?"

"It wasn't like that!" His voice was low, "God, Mum, you're making this so hard."

"No, I'm not. I'm just stating the facts." Elizabeth took a breath. "I don't want to listen to anything you've got to say. I've heard it all before. You're going to change, you're going to find a job, you're going to pay me back and oh, yes, you're going to save the planet in the process." She stood, "Finish your sandwiches. I'm going to sit where I can look at the view."

"Mum…"

"Christ, you haven't got any money, have you? Here…" Elizabeth grabbed her purse and threw two ten pound notes on the table. Then she walked away.

A man was sitting on a bench as Elizabeth crossed the road. He looked at Elizabeth and stood, "Here, I was just about to leave."

"Thank you," she wondered if he heard the tears in her voice.

Then she sat, shoulders sagging and she closed her eyes.

When she opened them, seagulls were pecking hopefully around her feet. She watched them, seeing the way their heads jerked forward, their beadlike eyes. *I wouldn't mind being a seagull. I could bugger off right now.* She shifted, trying to dislodge whatever it was that was making her uncomfortable. She lifted her head, wanting to feel the sun's rays on her face.

"Mum? Mum, are you ok?"

She felt a tugging on her sleeve and thought about keeping her eyes shut, blocking him out entirely. "What?"

"You worried me, are you ok?"

She moved her arm, "I'm fine. What time is it?"

"It's almost five."

Elizabeth blinked. "Where are you staying?" She asked the question, knowing what the answer would be and also knew she'd have to do something about it.

"Um…"

"I'll see if there's a room at the hotel, if not, you'll have to find a B&B somewhere."

"I'm sorry, Mum. I really want to talk to you, to tell you how sorry I am."

Idly Elizabeth wondered what it must have been like for Elizabethan women who wore voluminous skirts, heavy and ornate, how the weight of them must have dragged them down.

It felt like that, listening to Gareth, hearing for the millionth time how he was going to change, be a better person, do something with his life. It felt as if she was wearing heavy clothes and she longed to step out of them.

Standing, she spoke quickly. "I'm going back to the hotel. I need a gin and tonic. I'll see if they have a room for you."

"Shall I come with you?" Gareth's voice was low.

"I suppose you should."

And with that, Elizabeth walked off, listening to the slop, slop sound of his trainers as Gareth walked alongside her.

There was a room available and Elizabeth handed over her credit card. She turned to look at Gareth. "I take it you don't have a change of clothes or any toiletries?"

He shook his head.

Why is it my business? "You'll have to make do with what you've got." Elizabeth turned, " I need a drink."

The whole *performance* soothed her. The white coated waiter, bowing slightly as he took their order, his practised smile, the way the bowl of crisps was placed on the table, the satisfying sound of ice in her drink. Elizabeth felt that she was regaining ground. She felt better, no, that wasn't the right word, but at least she was less irritated by Gareth, more in control.

Sitting back, feeling the cold glass in her hand, Elizabeth looked at her son. "Start again, tell me why you thought coming here was a good idea."

He sat forward, "Mum, I know you'll say you've heard this before and you have, there's no doubt of that. But this time, I want to tell you first of all how sorry I am for…" he stopped and took a sip of his beer, "for being useless. I am, I know I am." He glanced at Elizabeth as if waiting for her to step in but Elizabeth remained silent. "I've used you. I've taken from you and never given anything back."

He's reading from a script. It sounds as if he's been testing words, phrases, wondering which ones would placate me, make me forgive him. She had an image of that reptilian Myles, "Myles with a y," standing close to Gareth, urging him on, telling him what to say, telling him his mother would melt under the barrage of sentiment. Elizabeth looked at the eagerness on Gareth's face, the way his skin tone darkened as he leant towards her, his voice rising and falling with earnestness, his *need* to make her understand.

He'd been her *late* baby. That's what people said after his birth. She hadn't wanted any more children, she had her girls and her business was building slowly but steadily. Things were ok, ticking over, she was just waiting for the girls to grow older, to start school. Then she came home one evening to find Chris sitting in the kitchen, waiting for her.

He'd frightened her. He told her he didn't like the way they'd been living – her driving all over the place, the girls either with childminders or a nursery waiting to be picked up by whoever came home first. "This is not how family life is supposed to be."

They sat there, Charlotte and Kate fast asleep upstairs. Elizabeth listening as Chris told her of his unhappiness, his dislike of the way she worked, the hours she spent away from home. Finally, his voice broke, "Even when you're here, you're thinking of somewhere else."

He was right. She knew that. Whenever she arrived home, her first thought was always of the girls. were they safe, were they ok and, once those questions were answered, Elizabeth's thoughts drifted back to what she'd seen that day, where she could place the chair or the bookcase once she'd restored it. She could never tell Chris, not in a million years but often, when driving home, she would give herself a shake, like a dog shaking off water, removing one part of her life before she could face another. Did she feel guilty? God, yes. Guilt battered her all the time, knowing that, when she dropped the girls off, often early in the morning, the first thing she felt was relief. Now she was on her own, now she could do what she loved without the hindrance of small children. When she came home, knowing the girls were safe, they'd come to no harm, guilt attacked her again for feeling the way she did.

Chris had stored up his distress, his anger at the way Elizabeth was shaping their lives. He told her it wasn't just because more often than not, he was the one who collected the girls, he was the one who gave them their tea, listened to their tales, comforted them. He told her how his heart broke when Elizabeth came home and the girls rushed to her, smothering her, demanding her attention. "It's as if they can't get enough of you."

Elizabeth listened to everything he said. She owed him that.

And then he asked the question he'd been leading up to the whole time. He thought it was the solution. "How do you feel about having another baby?"

She recoiled, *no, not another one*. Chris had leant forward, he caught her arm as if tethering her.

"Please, please for me. I know we said the girls were enough but," he'd shrugged, "maybe this will bring us back."

"Back from where? I didn't know we'd gone away."

Chris's smile was rueful. "I haven't, you have."

No, no, dear God, no.

Eventually he'd worn her down. Holding on to her arm, Chris talked about how another child would benefit them all, how much the girls would love a baby in the house. Elizabeth kept quiet, her heartbeat accelerating with each of his statements and then his tone softened, almost teasing. "Maybe this time we'll have a boy." And with that, she knew she'd have to do what he wanted. She felt it was a sort of *penance* she had to pay. As if by having daughters, as if by working the way she did, she owed him.

She made calculations: *nine months pregnancy. I could work through those months. I can go back to work after the baby is born.* When finally, she'd agreed to have one more child, she did so knowing, if she kept her part of the bargain, Chris would have to live with her side of it. *I'm not giving up work.*

Besides, she might not even be able to have a baby. She was older, not far off her thirty-sixth birthday and these things weren't so easy but those hopes disappeared when, a month after Chris's plea, she knew she was pregnant. The pregnancy smothered her. Only out on the road did she feel herself. At home, she operated in a robotic way, doing what needed to be done, getting through the domesticity as quickly as possible.

When Gareth was born, Chris was ecstatic. The way he uttered the words, "my son," making it sound biblical. Elizabeth knew that Chris thought Gareth was his reward, that now, with three children, Elizabeth would surrender. And for a time, she did remain at home, nursing the baby, looking after Charlotte and Kate, spending every day being the mother Chris wanted her to be. When Gareth was almost three, Elizabeth quietly told Chris she was going back to work. "I've done what you asked me and now I need to do something for me." Chris had opened his mouth to argue but Elizabeth didn't waiver. The girls were in school and she'd found a nursery for Gareth. She went back to driving around the country, feeling a sense of liberation, of utter contentment.

Elizabeth had defended Gareth when he showed no aptitude for sports or for any outdoor activity. Gareth refused to go to football matches with Chris, telling his Dad that he'd rather be with his sisters, playing with their tea-sets, doing crayoning with them. He didn't want to climb trees and he didn't want to race around the park on his blue bike either.

When Chris asked, a frown on his face, "What's the *matter* with

216

him? He's not like other boys." Elizabeth told Chris he mustn't expect Gareth to be what he wanted him to be.

"I don't, I just want him to be a normal boy." Chris never stopped trying to make Gareth into the boy he thought he should be...the son he wanted.

By the time Gareth was in school, labouring at the bottom of the class, Chris bowed to the inevitable. True, Charlotte had not had an easy time ride at university and Kate worked extremely hard to keep up, but both girls graduated with decent degrees. Gareth flatly refused to go to university.

"What's the point? You didn't go, you did all right."

Instead, Elizabeth had seen the hurt and confusion in Chris's eyes when his son drifted aimlessly from one dead end job to another, seemingly without the fierce work ethic both his sisters had inherited. "What did we do wrong?" Chris asked, over and over, looking for a reason, something he could address, something he could do to turn Gareth into the son he'd wanted.

"Nothing," Elizabeth always spoke quietly, refusing to hear the unspoken words, knowing that Chris had resented the way she'd gone back to work, refusing to allow him even to consider that, by putting their son into a nursery, somehow that had irrevocably damaged him and it was *her* fault that Gareth was a failure. She'd always known that Chris, right up until his death, believed Gareth would turn his life around, would become the son he'd always longed for, the child he'd really wanted.

Snapping back to the present, Gareth was still speaking, "...and I genuinely believe that it's about time."

"What's about time?"

"I said it's about time I sorted myself out, not relied on you, on other people."

Elizabeth bit her lip. She thought she knew what Gareth's speech would have been about: how he was going to knuckle down, find a decent job, pay his way, look after the people who meant the most to him. Same old, same old. "You need to grow up, it's as simple as that."

"That's what I've been saying. It's time I did just that."

"Why now?"

"I knew you weren't listening. I told you how awful I felt when Myles and Sean came. I didn't ask them to, not really."

"So, they told you all about that half-baked scheme of theirs, asked you if you knew anyone who might be remotely interested in backing them and you thought, "Oh yeah, good old Mum, she'll do it. You wanted them to think you could help, didn't you? You wanted them to think you had connections."

Gareth looked at his hands, Elizabeth saw that his glass of beer was almost empty and she realised that the ice in her glass had melted.

"I'm not proud of that. But at least I walked away from them when I saw what Myles had done."

"*Done?* That bastard stole my jewellery."

"I didn't know he'd done that, I swear I didn't know."

Looking at his stricken face, Elizabeth believed him. "You still let them into my house, you must have known what sort of people they were."

Gareth nodded, "Ok, I… don't know, I thought, I don't know what I thought. Maybe I was so desperate to do something, to find something…I'm so sorry."

Sitting back, sipping at her tepid drink, Elizabeth kept her eyes on Gareth's face. "So, now what?"

He shrugged, "Not sure, I wanted to do this first," he lifted a hand in her direction, "to talk to you, to apologise, to somehow make up for all the crap I've given you. That's all I could think about."

He looked at her, wanting her to tell him it was going to be all right. She also understood that he'd fail again, that without guidance, support, money, Gareth would always drift. She cleared her throat, "Gareth, you have an enormous debt hanging over you, what have you done about that, have you done *anything?*"

He looked at her, holding her gaze for a moment then, shook his head. "But I will, Mum. I will."

Elizabeth tugged at her rings, needing a moment. Lifting her head, she suggested dinner. Eating here, in the hotel would give her breathing space. It was more than that, sitting in an hotel, away from her home, that would help her in dealing with Gareth. She wondered why she felt that way. It saddened her.

Before standing, she reached into her handbag. She'd heard her phone ring, the *ping* of texts arriving and when she lifted the phone up, she saw James Williamson's name. He'd tried to call and then she read his text: *Would you call me tomorrow? I might have something of interest to us both.*

"Don't think so," she muttered before looking at messages from Kate and Charlotte. Both girls' messages were almost the same: Charlotte had written, *Are you all right? Has Gareth found you? And from Kate: Hope you're ok, let me know if you need anything.*

Walking into the restaurant, Elizabeth felt pressure on her elbow as Gareth steered her towards the table by the window. "I guess you'd prefer a table with a view?" She had a strong sense of her children's presence, realising that each of them, in their own way, was keeping an eye on her. She paused, thinking about how she felt about that.

"Mum? Is this ok for you?" Gareth gestured towards a chair, waiting for his mother.

Elizabeth nodded, "It's fine."

CHAPTER 20

Once in the car, I drive fast, impatient to get to the office, wanting to see the look on the faces of the staff, knowing that they're looking to me for guidance. I like that, knowing I'm the one keeping them in work, managing them, propelling the company forward. I can't help myself. I thump the steering wheel with excitement.

I'm so pumped up I have to practise my breathing in the car park.

Inside I see the smiles and hear, "Hi, Charlotte," as I walk towards my office. Kate is already there and she waves and gestures to the phone in her hand.

Can't put my finger on it but there's something different about Kate. She hasn't changed the way she looks, always opting for sensible rather than trendy, but something has shifted as she's more focussed, more intent. I mean, she's always done her job well, stayed on top of things but this new Kate is definitely keener, sharper somehow. Jess pops her head around the door and we go through some of the ideas we had yesterday, about diversifying, how we go about this, how to enhance our reputation. I listened as their voices tumbled over, trying to tell me their thoughts and ideas. Their enthusiasm – it was just like mine! And then I thought about Mum, her rigid approach, not wanting to change, scared. Maybe I was scared too but in a good way.

"Thank you, I hope we can meet up soon," Kate was beaming

as she talked to whoever was on the phone. "I look forward to that."

She put the phone down and brought her chair over to where I was sitting.

"Well, someone else has heard the news," she said, grinning at me. "Hope you had a good night's sleep. We've got a lot to get through."

I don't know why, but something about her tone bothered me. Jon often referred to Kate and her husband, Dan as Pinky and Perky. Well today, Kate was decidedly Perky. That made me smile and I thought about telling Jon, knowing he'd laugh. But couldn't tell him – not now at least.

Anyway, we spent pretty much all day sifting through ideas and making notes on the discussions we'd had with the staff. I had a clear idea of who would be good at what and, for the most part, Jess and Kate agreed with me. Kate wavered a few times, holding a pen at the side of her mouth as she questioned our choices," Do you really think Neil can handle this?"

We got through a lot and, by the end of our session, I had a clear idea of where to begin with our new venture and who to use on each team. I'd been so engrossed I hadn't realised what the time was. Outside I'd heard phones ringing, voices chattering but for that period, I had a sense of being cocooned, somehow apart from the others.

At some point in the day, Kate offered to get sandwiches and when she disappeared, Jess looked at me, "Kate's very keen, isn't she?"

I shrugged, "I guess so. She's keen to be on board."

"Mm, " Jess pulled a face, "She's not like you or your mother."

I laughed, "Surely that's a good thing?"

Jess gave me a strange look, "No, it's not."

But before I had time to think about it, Kate returned, her arms full of packets of sandwiches and a bag of apples. Anyhow, we hammered out our plan, chopped and changed, arguing about where to start first, which was the best way to approach this and what we should be putting in our proposals. At six we decided to call it a day and we gave each other a high five. "We did it," I beamed at Jess and Kate. "We bloody did it!"

I didn't want to go home. I didn't want the euphoria to leave me, the bubbles of excitement to *pop* because I knew, as soon as I put my key into the front door, that everything would go flat again. I suggested to Kate and Jess that maybe we should have a drink, "to celebrate, to say well done to us." My voice was high, unnatural and I saw the way Kate looked at me and then I saw the way she looked at Jess. When she spoke Kate's voice was firm. "No, I must go home. It's Dan's night for his evening class."

Jess touched my arm, "Sorry, Charlie, can't tonight. Promised I'd be home on time."

I understood, of course I did. They both wanted to go home. I didn't.

I made a pretence of tidying my desk, fussing about, saying I needed to put spreadsheets in some order. I smiled and said, "goodnight," to them both and then I sat for a while, thinking about what we'd done, wanting to tell Jon. Knowing I had no other excuse to linger, I searched for my phone. Nothing from Jon, not even a *don't forget to get milk on the way home.* There was a text from Mum: *Will you call me when you can? Your brother is here.*

Your brother? Why didn't she say Gareth? Oh, God, now what.

I sat down, glad of a reason to delay going home. Before I called Mum, I sent a text to Jon purely to appease him and to keep my conscience clear. *Mum wants to talk to me. Will be a bit late coming home.* There, he'll approve of that.

I held my phone, looking at the screen, trying to work out what

Mum wanted. The screen was as blank as I felt. All the euphoria had leaked away. I pressed her number and listened to the ringing tone.

"Hello? Charlotte?"

"Hi, are you ok?"

"Yeah, it's been nice. I'd forgotten how beautiful Dartmouth is."

"Good, I'm glad to hear it." I closed my eyes, she sounded normal, friendly, warm. We could have been discussing a long-planned holiday rather than my mother running away from a situation fraught with bitterness and recriminations.

She was quiet and I thought I heard laughter. "Where are you?"

"At the Dart Marina Hotel." She paused, "Gareth's here with me."

"He's staying at the hotel too?"

Her voice became brisk, "Well, it seemed the best thing to do." *Who for, you or him?*

I tried to match her tone, "D'you know when you'll be coming back?"

"Not for a few more days." Her voice sounded muffled as if she'd turned her head away and I wondered if Gareth was sitting next to her.

"Mum?"

"Yes, sorry." She paused, "Something has come up, Charlotte, something I want to explore, think about. I'm not ready to talk about what it is just yet."

"Mum? Are you all right? You sound a bit, I don't know, a bit off."

"*Off?* Hardly surprising in view of what has happened, what you..."

"No! No, I didn't meant that. *Oh God, I take one step forward and two back.* "No, Mum, I'm sorry. All I meant was, all I wanted to say was..."

"I'm thinking of moving here, to Dartmouth. Selling my house and buying something here."

She didn't say that. I didn't hear it properly. Stupidly I looked at the phone, why the hell did I do that?

"What did you say? You want to move to Dartmouth?"

"That's exactly what I said. I think it would be a good thing for me."

"You can't! You can't mean it. What about us, what about Kate and me, the girls, they'll miss you."

"Will they? And what about you?" Her voice was soft, "Will you miss me, Charlotte?"

Christ. My eyes were filling up and I shook my head, trying to dislodge the tears. "Oh, Mum, please don't, please don't ask me that. Don't do anything just yet. Please, this is far too big a conversation to be having over the phone. Can't you come back so we can talk about this? Please, come back."

I heard her sigh, "As I said, there are things I'd like to explore here. Things I need to think through and I'd rather be here when I make those decisions."

Shit, that's telling me.

"Is Gareth helping you with those decisions?" The question made me sound petty, jealous, but I didn't like the thought of him sitting there whilst Mum made all these important decisions. Gareth, for God's sake!

"I'm quite capable of making decisions for myself."

"Of course you are. When, when will you…?"

"When will I make my mind up? Is that what you're asking me?"

"Mum, I…"

"I'll let you know when I have." She sounded amused.

"Oh, right." The thought of Mum moving, living in Devon, miles from the rest of us, shook me. I couldn't think beyond that.

I didn't know what else to say. "Mum, are you…?"

"I'm perfectly ok, Charlotte. I've had some lovely meals, decent glasses of wine and I've explored Dartmouth, revisiting places I'd almost forgotten."

I don't want to hear that, don't want to hear any of it.

"Good, that's good to hear."

What did she mean, "something has come up?" What was the something? Had she seen a house she liked? Was that what it was? Although it didn't sound like that. Oh, Christ, my mind was running all over the place. *Are you thinking of moving because of me? Because I destroyed everything we had, destroyed your trust in me?*

At first I didn't catch what Mum said, "Sorry?"

"I said this is not about you, Charlotte, this is about me." It was almost as if she knew what I'd been thinking. "I'll let you know what I've decided and when I'm coming back. I just thought you should know my thoughts and well, that I'm ok."

"Thank you." More than anything, I wanted to touch her, to let her know how sorry I was, how I couldn't *bear* the thought of her moving away.

"Ok, I'll let you get on. Are you at home?"

"No, not yet. I'm still at the office." The moment I'd spoken, I knew I shouldn't have said that.

"Oh? Well don't be late home. The girls need to see you."

"I'm leaving now."

We said goodbye and I sat there, holding the phone, reliving the conversation, resisting the impulse to call her back, beg her to tell me what was going on. And oh, God, I hated the thought that Gareth was there with her. I *hated* that thought.

But she was right: I had to go home. *Shit.* I'd told Jon that I was ringing Mum. He'd ask and I'd have to tell him that she wanted to move, to buy a house in Dartmouth. And then I'd have to look at the expression on his face. *Fuck, fuck.*

Going home, I drove slowly, taking my time at traffic lights, waiting at junctions. It seemed to be no time at all before I turned into the drive, parking behind Jon's car.

"Mummy! Mummy!" The girls ran towards me, elbowing each other, trying to get to me first. I grabbed them both, holding them close, listening to their voices, shrill with excitement. "Lucy in school is having a party and she's invited the *whole* class! Daddy said I could choose the colour when he paints my bedroom!"

If I stayed there, kneeling on the floor, listening as the girls told me everything they'd done, I could handle that. Staying in the children's world meant I didn't need to face the adult world, face Jon.

I heard him in the kitchen, did the saucepans need to be bashed together like that? What was he doing? I stood and, holding the girls' hands, walked into the kitchen.

Jon wore a blue and white striped apron, one the girls and I had given him for Christmas the year before. He nodded at me, "You ok?" His tone was soft.

"I'm fine." I felt odd as if the floor was moving so I gripped the girls' hands, wanting to feel stable.

"Here, take a seat." He pulled out a chair, gesturing for me to sit down.

The girls dropped my hands and, giggling, pushed me forward.

"I've made a fish pie and we left some for you." Jon's words were easy, warm and I wondered if this, this *play-acting*, was for the girls' benefit. I went along with it.

"Thank you, it smells delicious."

Jon winked at the girls and they fussed around, giving me a glass of water, making sure I had a clean napkin and Jon ladled out a hefty dollop of fish pie and put the plate in front of me.

They sat with me as I ate, the girls chatting, laughing and Jon telling me all about a teacher at his school who wants to change the curriculum. "She's got no chance, but she's determined, I'll give her that."

Does that mean something? Is he talking in a code? If that's the case, I don't understand it.

Afterwards we got the girls ready for bed, cleared up the bathroom after getting them out of the bath, doing it together as we'd always done, as a team. As I sat on Hannah's bed, reading her a story, I heard Jon's voice as he read to Sophie in the next room. For once there'd been no argument about both girls going to bed at the same time.

We closed the girls' doors and I followed Jon downstairs, my mouth was dry.

We sat in the living room, Jon switched on the lamps, the room looked as it should: comfortable, welcoming. I was *uncomfortable*, uneasy and I shook my head when Jon asked if I wanted a glass of wine. I didn't want alcohol blurring any edges.

He sat, crossing his legs and looked at me, "How's your mother?"

"She's fine, she's…" I looked straight at him. "She's thinking of moving to Dartmouth, buying a house there."

My words seemed to linger, I could almost see a bubble around them, like something out of a kid's comic.

Jon shifted and shook his head, "What, selling her house here and moving there?"

"That's what she said."

"Did she say why? I mean, that's a big thing for her, moving at her age."

"All she said was that she needed time to think things through, but she was seriously thinking of moving to Dartmouth."

"Christ." He put his head to one side, "How does that make you feel?"

"The truth? As if I've been punched. I can't get my head around it."

Jon was silent, his fingers steepled.

"Jon? What are you thinking? " I didn't want to know, yet needed to hear what he had to say.

"I just, I mean, you, the girls, Kate, all of us meeting up, that meant the world to her."

I nodded. Did he know he was speaking in the past tense?

"I feel…" I stopped, not ready to admit how I felt. The sense of guilt was enormous, it made me feel raw.

"Go on, " he nodded, "tell me, Charlie."

I looked at him, at his expression and amazingly there was no anger, it was just Jon waiting to hear what I had to say.

I shuddered. "Guilty, that's how I feel, guilty as hell." My voice was breaking, "I don't want her to move, I don't want to lose her."

Jon knelt in front of me and took my hands. "Listen, listen to me. You won't lose her, that won't happen. You might misplace her for a while, but you'll find her again. That much I know."

My face was wet and I wiped my eyes with my hand. "I can't bear the thought of her moving, how will that make her feel? She loves her house, her garden."

"Hey, this isn't about her garden." He tugged at my hands, "Your mother is one of the strongest people I know and, if this is what she wants to do, I'm sure she's given it a lot of thought. Your Mum doesn't make hasty decisions, she thinks about things, she will have considered all of her options and, if she's considering moving to Dartmouth, then it'll be for a good reason. It won't be to spite you or make you miserable, but because it's something she wants to do.

I sniffed. "Are you telling me that to make me feel better? I've taken her company, Jon! Don't pretend you're not unhappy with that, because you've made your feelings perfectly clear. Is that it? Is Mum punishing me?"

"Oh, Charlie, this isn't about your decision. It's *her* decision and whilst your actions no doubt played a part, your Mum will have weighed up all her options. She always does. "He looked at me, "Somehow, I can't imagine your Mum retiring to Devon and eating cream teas for the rest of her life."

I pulled a face, "She did say there was something she wanted to think about, something had come up." I shook my head, "I don't think she was talking about the house move. It was something else."

"There you go! Knowing your Mum, she probably wants to rebuild the harbour." Jon mock punched me, "This isn't about you – you need to think about what your Mum wants. Give her time and she'll tell you when she's ready."

My voice was breaking, "I didn't mean this to happen."

Jon pulled me close, "Listen, you need to support your Mum, you owe her that." I heard his words rumbling in his chest. "Besides, think of the cheap holidays we can have."

I laughed because he wanted me to. Jon wanted me to feel better, but I didn't I couldn't.

In bed, I looked at the phone; no, nothing from Mum. I wondered if she was in bed, lying awake thinking of God knows what. I wondered if she'd fallen in love with a house she'd seen. I wondered what this "something" was. Was it my useless brother? Bloody Gareth. I bet he'll have given Mum his two-pennyworth. Another stab, this time not of guilt but of envy. If she was making big decisions, I wanted to be there, to listen, to be with her.

I stretched out, inching my toes to the foot of the bed. Closing my eyes, I thought about what Jess, Kate and I had done today. I felt a bubble of excitement over the new project, the new contracts we'd make. I'd told Jon about my day and he'd listened, his eyes widening when I told him how *perky* Kate had been. "Hmm, wonder what that's all about? Don't underestimate her, Charlie. This whole thing will have implications for her too. Just watch her." I promised I would but the person I wanted to tell, was Mum. Against all the odds, I wanted to see the look on her face, to see her pride in me.

I checked my phone again, touched Mum's number. *Oh, Mum, are you ok?*

CHAPTER 21

The decision had been easy and, having made it, Elizabeth wondered if it had been too easy. Everything dovetailed into place, James Williamson's offer, asking her to work with them on the deserted factory she'd seen near the castle. "It's a niche development," he said, "apartments for retired people and we're marketing them for Dartmouth people too, giving them a home near the estuary."

Niche. Elizabeth smiled. She could be niche too.

She'd gone to see him at his office on the top floor of a compact building where Charles Haywood and Partners ran their company. The exterior walls of the building were covered in dark grey slate, a feature Elizabeth admired. Before meeting James, Elizabeth dithered about what to wear; knowing this time she had to get it right. There was no time to buy anything new so she wore her red leather jacket, the one she'd bought in Italy two years earlier. She saw his eyes widen as she approached.

There was no mention of their previous meeting and she sat on the wooden chair in front of his desk and listened intently as he told her about the new development. "We've had our eye on the factory for a while and we think it'll be good for the community and for...um..." His voice dropped, "Er, for older people who want to retire here, to enjoy the views. Our research has flagged up that, for a lot of older people, whilst they would like to downsize, they're not ready yet for full-blown retirement living."

His eyes flickered across her face and Elizabeth, sensing his unspoken thoughts, touched the lapel of her jacket. Fleetingly she thought of David Armstrong and his retirement village.

After that, they discussed completion dates, budgets, colour schemes and, when James, ("Please call me, Jamie, everyone else does,") asked whether she was interested in his proposition, Elizabeth nodded.

"Very much so," she sat forward. "Why me? There must be people around here, people you've used before, local people."

Jamie smiled, "You come highly recommended." He put his elbows on the desk. "I looked you up before our chat the other day." He paused and Elizabeth flinched, thinking of her manic behaviour. "And then I spoke to a number of your clients and, well, it was all good, very good." He looked at her. "My one concern is that, living where you do, will you be able to work with us? It's quite a commute for you isn't it?"

"Not a problem," Elizabeth smiled, her words glib. "I've got that in hand."

They chatted for a while, Jamie boasting about earlier developments and the company's focus on providing affordable housing and then, when it became obvious that the meeting was at an end, Elizabeth stood, hearing the creak of the leather in her jacket.

"Thank you, it's been a pleasure," she smiled brightly as Jamie walked her to the office entrance.

"We'll be in touch," he smiled and Elizabeth knew he was already thinking about something else.

After leaving Jamie's office, Elizabeth walked back towards the castle, wanting to see the disused factory again, to get a feel for the building.

She had no idea where Gareth was, he'd muttered something about his car, about trying to get it started, to put it into the hotel car park. She was glad to be on her own, with time to sift through all the implications. Her thoughts bashed around in her head, one thought hurling itself against another.

At the foot of the hill, Elizabeth saw the art gallery, the shop selling fudge, the cluttered window of an antique shop with its pots of waving bamboo on either side of the doorway. She didn't move. *There it was.* She'd move, sell her house and buy one here. She could find people to work with her, Dartmouth was a town full of people. *God, it was easy, that simple.*

Was it? Could it be that simple?

She crossed the road, looking again at the view and then she spoke out loud, talking to the view, "Yes, it could be. Why not?"

She smiled, feeling her heart rate quicken. The view still entranced her and now, with her decision made, she felt an almost proprietorial buzz as she looked at it. She watched the boats glide across the harbour, sails flapping in the wind. She saw the tree-line on either side of the estuary and she knew, knew with a fierce intensity that wherever she bought her new house, it would have to have a view like the one she was looking at now.

Standing outside the factory building, looking at the dark green paint on the ugly metal framed windows, Elizabeth thought about Charlotte, about what she'd say when she knew of her mother's plans. She thought too about some of her staff, thinking of those who had an instinctive understanding of what colours and fabrics should be used to show off any interior. *Maybe I could…no, this is mine. I can do this.* Looking at the factory and feeling its air of abandonment, Elizabeth frowned. She'd done it once, she could do it again. Wasn't she the one who'd driven around the streets of the UK in a battered van, a rusting hole in its floor? Yeah, that was her. Ok, she'd been younger then but what the hell. She was still the same woman, the one who'd dreamt of her own design company and then achieved that. That was her. Her company would function without her, it had a new trajectory under Charlotte's guidance. It was branching out but she was the one who'd put down its roots. Delighted with her analogy, Elizabeth looked again at the dilapidated factory. The buddleia caught her eye, its roots were tenacious and it would became unmanageable if left untended.

Elizabeth walked back down the hill, lost in thought. She'd have a coffee and then she'd look at the estate agents' windows, there might be something, who knows? It was a big thing, buying a house, moving to a new area but she was keen to start the ball rolling. Whose opinion did she have to ask? No-one. If she saw something that appealed to her, she was the only one who had to like it. Knowing that both pleased and frightened her. Elizabeth walked towards the first estate agents' window.

On her way towards the hotel, Elizabeth saw two men standing near a car in the car park. Its bonnet was up and, getting closer, she saw Gareth was one of the men. *Christ, now what?*

Not wanting to get involved, yet unable to stop herself, Elizabeth moved closer to the car.

Gareth saw her and smiled, "Hi, Mum. This is Clive, he's helped me with the car."

Clive was dressed in a blue overall. "Hi," he looked at Elizabeth. "Just telling your son here that the engine's seized, it's..."

"Doesn't surprise me," Elizabeth said. "How did it get here?"

Gareth appeared to be in a buoyant mood, "Clive was passing, Mum. He has a garage." He pointed and, turning, Elizabeth saw a pick-up truck nearby. Her excitement leaked away.

"How much do we owe you?" Her tone was flat.

Clive shook his head, "No, nothing. I was coming here

anyway."

Elizabeth opened her bag, "Please, let me give you something, have a drink at least…"

Beside her, Gareth shifted and, taking the twenty pound note from Elizabeth's hand, Clive spoke quickly, "I've explained to your son that, in my opinion, this isn't worth repairing but, of course, it's up to him."

No, it's not.

Elizabeth spoke briskly, "I would be grateful if your garage could arrange to take this to a breaker's yard. I'm assuming that would be the best course of action." She heard Gareth's squeak of protest and ignored it.

Clive appeared embarrassed, his tone was subdued, "Well, yes, of course we could do that for you."

"Thank you. My son and I are staying here for a few days, anytime to suit you would be fine. Please let me know what we owe you." She held her hand out to shake Clive's hand and he wiped his hand across the seat of his trousers before shaking her hand.

Elizabeth turned to walk away, then heard Gareth mutter, "Thanks, mate. I'm grateful and I'm sorry for…"

Was he apologising for her behaviour or for his rubbish car? Elizabeth didn't care.

Once inside the hotel, Elizabeth asked for a window seat in the restaurant and took out her notebook. Charlotte always teased her about her unwillingness to put things into her phone but Elizabeth liked the physicality of writing notes, jotting down random thoughts and ideas into the leather-backed notebook she carried everywhere. She wrote quickly, thinking of the site she'd visited, of the discussion she'd had with Jamie. *Distressed brickwork, industrial lighting, stripped flooring, Kitchen? Colour of units?* She didn't see Gareth until she heard a chair move and, looking up, she saw him sitting opposite.

A waiter appeared and handed over two menus before moving away. Elizabeth didn't want to talk to Gareth, to hear more apologies, more vague promises or, even worse, how he thought his car would somehow repair itself. She put her notebook away, not wanting her son to see what she'd written, to know where she'd been that morning.

"Mum?"

Here it comes.

"When are we going back?"

"We?"

"Yeah, I didn't think you'd want me to stay here, it's expensive."

Elizabeth glared at him. He still wore Jon's sweatshirt, Jon's jeans, so short they left his ankles exposed and seeing his white skin made Elizabeth cringe. The sweatshirt he wore had a streak of oil across the front.

Elizabeth felt a tide of rage and her voice was harsh. "Gareth, what are you going to do?"

"What d'you mean?"

Elizabeth resisted the urge to lean across the table and grab the neck of the sweatshirt, *Jon's bloody sweatshirt* and shout at him: *For Christ's sake, you're an adult, you should know what you're going to do next!*

To give herself time, Elizabeth sipped at a glass of water. She spoke calmly, hoping her voice was low, "My plans are to stay here a while longer, there are a few things I want to do and…"

"What things?" Gareth frowned. "I thought you were here for a short break."

"I am, that's still the case but something has come up and I want to give it some thought."

"God, Mum, you do talk crap sometimes."

"I talk crap! This from the half-wit who wanted to buy homes in Italy for one euro?" Elizabeth slumped back. "Christ, Gareth, you're…"

"I'm sorry, I didn't mean…I only meant that, sometimes, it's difficult to know what's going on in your head."

She looked at him, *because you wouldn't know a business plan if it bit you on the arse.* "If you must know, a project has come up and it's interested me and I need to think about it, what its implications are."

That satisfied him, she knew it would and, leaning back, he picked up the menu. "Oh, ok, that sounds good. What d'you fancy to eat, Mum? I'm starving."

In her room, laptop in front of her on the dressing table, Elizabeth peered at the screen. The estate agent had sent over details of houses for sale and, as she sat on the edge of the bed, she looked at various interiors, *Oh, that needs a new kitchen. God, who'd have orange walls in the bathroom?*

She'd already spoken to an estate agent she knew near her home and had asked for a valuation on her present house. She'd told him that she'd be home at the weekend and, looking at the Dartmouth houses, Elizabeth felt a sense of quiet acceptance. Even if the project with Jamie didn't work out and it might not, but even if it didn't happen, she was going to move. *That* would happen.

Closing the laptop, Elizabeth settled back against the pillows, shutting her eyes for second. The sound of knocking startled her and she blinked, *what?*

"Mum? Mum? Are you all right? Can I come in?" Gareth's voice was high.

Swinging her legs to the side, Elizabeth sat up, realising that, spending time with Gareth had exhausted her. She'd always had energy for her work, with her company but this Gareth energy depleted her, she was constantly propping him up. Not only was she paying his bills, she was feeling his presence all the time. *God, what sort of a mother does that make me?*

"Yes, come in."

He bounded in looking, Elizabeth felt as if the energy she'd lost, had transplanted its way into him.

"You ok?" Without waiting for an answer, he wrapped his arms across his chest in an attempt to control his excitement. "Clive has offered me a job, a good job!"

For a second Elizabeth didn't know who he was talking about. "Clive?"

"Yeah, yeah, Clive, the bloke from the garage. It turns out he's been looking for someone to help him and…"

"Gareth, Clive has a garage, what d'you know about cars?"

Shaking his head, Gareth spoke rapidly, "No, not cars. He's got a caravan park near Brixham, well his Dad has and now his Dad wants to retire and Clive can't cope with the garage and looking after the caravans…" He stopped talking, he took a breath, "Mum, best of all, Clive says I can stay at the park, there's a static caravan I can use. He wants me to keep an eye on things, make sure that the toilets and the shower blocks are kept clean, bit of gardening. I can live there, Mum."

She can see the excitement in his eyes, excitement mixed with relief. She felt it too – the relief that is, not the excitement. He thought he'd found the answer, he'd redeemed himself in her eyes. With one chance meeting, he was sorted. *If only.* Looking at him, Elizabeth thought about Charlotte and Kate, how they worked, how they brought up their families, just like she'd done. Gareth couldn't get his words out fast enough. "When Clive came to pick the car up, I went with him and we got talking and he showed me the caravan park and he said I can move in straight away."

"Oh, that's good." She didn't know what else to say.

"So, I won't be going back with you and, if it's ok with you, Mum, I thought I'd move in today, get a feel for things. I told Clive I'd give the park a quick recce and see what needs to be done. He said his Dad had let things slide."

Elizabeth watched as another thought struck him. "It'll be good for you too, Mum. Living in Brixham means that, if you work here, I won't be far away." He beamed and she thought how little he'd changed over the years. *Most of us learn, adapt, mature but my son is constantly looking for a rainbow.* The years of worry and guilt felt like a vast, grey wall, one she didn't have the energy to knock her way through.

She smiled at him, "It sounds promising. Did you say you're going to see the caravans now?"

Gareth nodded, "Yeah, you don't mind, do you? I mean, you'll be on your own…"

"No, I don't mind."

He lurched towards her, wrapped his arms around her and muttered, "Thanks, Mum." He seemed reluctant to let go and Elizabeth tensed. Easing herself away from him, "You need money, don't you?"

"Just to tide me over, please. I'll pay you back when I get paid." Elizabeth heard no trace of guilt in his voice.

She picked up her purse and took out another £20 note. "This is all I've got."

Gareth looked at it, he hesitated before taking it. "Thanks, Mum." His smile was brief. "I won't be using the room here now, won't cost you so much."

Elizabeth wondered if he thought he was doing her a favour. He left the room and Elizabeth breathed out. Brixham. Not far but it didn't mean a thing, not for Gareth.

She found her phone and sent a text to Charlotte, asking for a chat. Then, sitting on the edge of the bed, Elizabeth picked up her notebook and wrote down everything she wanted to do.

"Will the gentleman be joining you, madam?"

Gentleman? Who? He means Gareth. "No," Elizabeth shook her head. "No, I'm dining alone this evening.

It never failed to amuse her but, whenever she'd been on holiday or away for a few days on a work-related trip, how soon a pattern established itself. Tonight was no exception, the waiter showed her to a table overlooking the water, one she'd used throughout her stay. It felt as if she'd been at the Dart Marina Hotel for weeks and it had only been a few days.

She asked for a glass of wine and sat looking at the view. She'd found her new home, she knew she had. The estate agent had called and told her something had just come on the market. "It's exactly what you're looking for." Elizabeth doubted that but agreed to view it.

He'd been right. It was perfect. Set back from the road with panoramic views of the estuary, the house had been renovated to a high standard and with a garden Elizabeth knew she could easily manage. She'd wandered through each room, mentally working out where her furniture would go, what she'd need, what she'd discard. There were four bedrooms, plenty of room for the family should they visit her. And, best of all, there was a huge attic space; the owners had worked from home and set it all up as an office. Elizabeth tried to control her rising excitement. She could run her company from here. *I could live here and who knows, I might even buy a rocking chair to put near the window. I can look at that view every day.* Walking away from the house, Elizabeth knew she'd offer the asking price.

Sitting there, thinking about the house, Elizabeth smiled and picked up her glass of wine and, telling the waiter she'd be outside for a moment, she wandered, glass in hand, out onto the patio area outside the hotel. Lights twinkled on the water and she felt a chill but had no wish to go back inside. She sipped at the wine and thought about Chris, wanting to reach over and touch his hand, wanting to say, "We made it, you always said one day we'd stay here."

She'd let him down. Her work, her passion for what she did had devoured her. Elizabeth knew she'd always thought of her job as her reward, a payment for giving Chris what he'd wanted: a wife and family. She'd paid lip service, played the required part. She'd wander with the children, taking them out for the day; a beach, a park, her mind darting all over the place, *look at the colour of that door! What is that called*? She talked to the children, she'd point out the swans on the lake, the kites high above their heads. She soothed them when they fell, she was the overseer of their battles. She never neglected them - quite the opposite – she saw now that her attention to their safety, their health, was excessive, making her over-zealous, her way of counteracting the guilt she felt each day she spent working. She simply wanted to be on her own, striving to find the perfect colour, the exact contrast or match.

Once, Chris had accused her of being in another world, "one where we can't find you." She'd argued, telling him again and again, that she'd never neglected the children or him. "There are different forms of neglect." She remembered his exact words, had carried them inside her for years.

Elizabeth heard the soft *chugging* as the last ferry made its way across the water. She thought about her company, she thought about the contracts she'd worked on, the people she knew. She waited for a pang of loss, of regret, but if there was one, it was faint. It was time for her to move on. She knew that Charlotte was more like her than either Kate or Gareth. She'd seen the determination in Charlotte and, as supportive as Jon was, Charlotte was following in her mother's footsteps. *God knows what will happen to Gareth. Kate, I know she's biding her time. Charlotte must be aware of that.* After she'd spoken to Charlotte, Elizabeth had heard the distress in her daughter's voice when Elizabeth had told her of her decision. There might once have been a time when she'd have changed her mind, altered her plans. But that time had gone.

Elizabeth lifted her glass in a silent toast. She was starting all over again and this time, she wouldn't have to answer to anybody. This time there'd be no guilt, no need to rush back home for anything, no need to attend to whatever was required of her. What would Chris have said? She hoped he'd like the fact that, after all this time, she'd returned to Dartmouth where they'd begun their marriage. In some ways, it felt as if she'd repaid him.

She was about to turn, to go back into the hotel when she heard the ferry and saw that it had reached the jetty. She watched as the crew, two men in matching blue dungarees, leapt off the boat, she saw them fastening the ropes, keeping the ferry secure, ready for the next day.

She heard one of them call to the other, "G'night, mate. See you tomorrow."

Elizabeth went back into the hotel.

Also published by Watermark Press

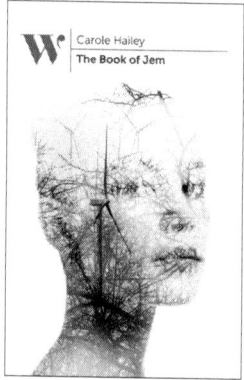

Carole Hailey
The Book of Jem

In the aftermath of catastrophic religious wars, God has been banned.

As snow begins to fall, a young woman – Jem – arrives in Underhill. The isolated community offers her shelter, unwittingly unleashing events that threaten their very existence.

Jem announces that she has been sent to Underhill by God to prepare the villagers to fulfil a devastating purpose. Some believe she is a prophet and defy the law to join her God's Threads religion. Others are certain she is lying.

With their fragile community beginning to fracture, Eileen, the first and most devoted of the believers, decides to record the birth of this new religion in her own Book of Jem.

As God's Threads gather for the apocalypse, the words Eileen has written will determine the fate of Underhill and, ultimately, of Jem herself. But can Eileen be trusted to tell the truth? And how can anyone know what to believe?

'Bold storytelling, with the satirical force of Naomi Alderman's *The Power* but its own claustrophobic sense of place.'
Francis Spufford, author of *Golden Hill*

Alan Bilton
The End of the Yellow House

Central Russia, the black earth forest, near Voronezh, 1919. As the civil war rages, White forces, accompanied by feared Cossack divisions, advance ever closer to Moscow. In the chaos, the Yellow House, a sanatorium at Bezumiye, becomes cut off, the superintendent found murdered, a strange black box atop his head.

As the distinction between doctors and 'guests' frays, the murder sets in motion a nightmarish series of events involving mysterious experiments, the secret police, the Tsar's double, prophetic dreams, giant corpses, possessed cats, sorcery, and the overwhelming madness of war. Into this dangerously combustible mix, a ragged and eccentric police officer arrives, calling himself Inspector Tutyshkin and claiming he has travelled to the house to investigate the superintendent's suspicious demise.

But in this strange game of madness, doubles and disguises, are any of the players truly who they seem?

'A bold and confident novel that throws us into the deep end of post-revolutionary Russian life with fervour and wit. There are knowing nods to Gogol and Bulgakov but the voice is entirely original, with a gem of a phrase on every page.'
Mark Blayney

'A brutal, but often witty and tender tale, *The End of the Yellow House* is a twistedly brilliant emotional rollercoaster.'
David Towsey

Carolyn Lewis
Some Sort of Twilight

These twelve stories are of people unsure of their place in the world – Cassie who discovers she can fly and has no-one to tell, Christine who's been in her friend's shadow for a long time, Bernard who loses his job through no fault of his own and Hannah who knows her father is waiting for her to sort his life out.

These stories combine pathos, humour and wisdom to explore how the ordinary can be strange, heartbreaking or comic, illuminating the inner lives of people who feel in some way they're on the edge of their own lives.

'Carolyn's stories are a joy to read. Her characters are so perfectly formed that we feel we have always known them. Of course people collect coat hangers! Who doesn't one day find they can fly? Her empathy for them all shines through and we feel in very safe hands.'

SALLY BRAMLEY, WINNER 2021 CALEDONIA NOVEL PRIZE.

Edward Matthews
Border Memories

Why live one life, when you could live a thousand?

Sol works for a start-up that traffics in the underground memory trade – harvesting memories from donors in Mexico and implanting them in Americans.

Sol's newest client is Mr. Bray – old, rich, well-connected, blind. Mr. Bray hears rumours of a graveyard where miracles occur and has tracked down a young librarian, Nora, who remembers it.

Sol's task is simple – find Nora, extract her memory.

But when Sol befriends Nora, he begins to understand who Mr. Bray is and what he is capable of doing…

'As genuine art should, *Border Memories* explores important and ongoing problems and confidently reimagines them for a new audience.'
MARGARITA PINTADO, AUTHOR OF *UNA MUCHACHA QUE SE PARECE A MÍ*

'*Border Memories* sires a dusk-fallen near future of abandoned lots and rusted chain-link. Written with elegant restraint and a raptor's eye for the small details, Matthews is less interested in whether memories make us who we are, than who we become once memories are ours to give away.'
GLEN JAMES BROWN, AUTHOR OF *IRONOPOLIS*

Alan Bilton
At Dawn, Two Nightingales

At Dawn, Two Nightingales is rumoured to be the most dangerous poem in the world, its haunted verses said to be invested with mysterious, supernatural powers. The impoverished Count Mitrovsky believes that within the enchanted stanzas lies the key to his beautiful neighbour Mařenka's heart, but other parties are searching for the poem too – sinister censors, dangerous criminals, bandits and brigands of all stripes.

A comic opera in novel form – part quest, part pantomime, part unexpected ghost story – *At Dawn Two Nightingales* is both playful and heartbreaking, an uproarious adventure that upends the conventions of the historical novel at every turn.

'A richly comic and darkly disturbing story of unrequited love, fantastical adventure and the quest for a mysterious poem, masterfully delivered in gloriously luscious prose.'
CAROLE HAILEY

'Bilton's work is a Bohemian romp, an amuse-bouche which keeps on giving.'
JULIAN STANNARD